THE ALTERNATOR

B.H. NEWTON

CONTENTS

For Amanda
My candle in the wind
You loved this stuff

JOY TO THE WORLD

He traced the river delta cut into his mind, seeing the branches in the aged cracks of the powder-blue Formica table. He pressed down hard on those fingers with the really bitten-down nails, feeling sharp pain in the quicks as he traveled back up the Mississippi, along the Rogue river, the Snake, the all-defining Rio Grande, how the Tennessee flowed north up into Kentucky Lake. He didn't even need to reference the Rand McNally any more, it was all stacked upstairs, a library of maps imprinted on his psyche, more a part of him than anything a stranger could gather from his scant words or actions. He was fused to the nervous system of America, its blacktop veins, neurons firing imaginary station wagons and motor homes through the Gateway Arch to the Black Hills and Mount Rush-more onward on orderly numbered byways to all points west where Lewis and Clark and novice gold prospectors traveled blind, solely dependent on scouts and stars. As he grew up under the white buzzing lights, there were usually a few of the cockier truckers who could be goaded by the regulars to yell over at him from their spinning countertop stools, asking which roads would get them to Bakersfield from Salt Lake or how many tolls would they pay rolling into the chaos of Boston. He'd slowly take off his fuzzy orange headphones as if gathering up the data flowers in his poppy-field mind and suddenly explode in a way that could make them jump a bit and get a jingle of the crowded keyrings they all wore clipped to the belt loop of their stale stiff jeans… reciting a route that sounded straight out of an ancient Latin Bible of lost scripture, a monotone chant that was exact and chilling. The caffeined-up interlopers would laugh nervously into their chipped mugs and sip the last of their bitter black coffee, until they left a meager tip and crawled back up into their cabs and took a gander at the pages themselves. His sermon was always true and, if they were humble, they would learn a thing or two and cut their run by half a day.

Most days you could find him in the very last booth by the bathrooms facing the door, next to a dull window he rarely gazed through. There might be a piece of half-eaten toast smeared with orange marmalade sitting next to a scabby elbow and half a glass of thick whole milk that the kid guzzled religiously. He still had the trusty maps, his atlas, with him every day, held together with paper clips and duct tape, even if he no longer needed it. There he would be, pushed into the corner of split vinyl and concrete wall, whether it was a sunny humid soup or a cold wet winter day under low-hanging clouds just a few feet away on the other side, flipping from state to state, each page its own story, its own equation of green state parks holding the lines against human encroachment or secret government testing grounds. One page turn would transport you from Utah to Vermont. He could reach to the back and take a swim through the sparse two-laners of territorial Northern Canada or the dense chaos of Mexico. If his companion wasn't splayed out on the table with tired pages begging a final release from the rusty staples of the once glossy cover in a crooked stack, it was rolled up with a fat rubber band on the bench next to him waiting ever-patiently for their next adventure.

His dear old dad stole a glance every now and then, in between flipping a mat of hash browns or a row of fatty grey sawdust-infused patties. He was proud in a curious, itchy way that he never could communicate. He never could find the map that bridged the gap into his son's world. Even when he was showing him off to the customers, "Ask my boy over there, he knows every road on this continent, by God," he felt to be no more than a carnival barker and was left only hoping if his son's exploits would produce more loose change scattered on top of the check. Still, it was sure good having him around and he loved him dearly from afar. Slaving eight days a week cooking breakfast and lunch in a no-name interstate truck stop didn't leave much time for father-son bonding activities, so a man took what he could get through osmosis, 20 feet away, breathing the same food-ridden air. Felt like he had a permanent ticket to a show sometimes, seeing his offspring grow up sitting in a booth as if on a stage, the only one noticing the nuance in his son's performance, barely ever a glimmer of emotion exposed to the crowd but it was there if you knew the tells, the slight tics, a tiny cough before he reached for the milk glass. Second-guessing always hung heavy on his thick shoulders. Was it the right thing years ago when he first started leading the boy over to the diner before daylight? Got him out of his mother's hair as she was overrun by those days already with a host of demons. He didn't protest, just put on his little overalls and took his daddy's calloused hand and out the door they went into the still-sleeping world. It was just a bit more than a stone's throw from their mobile (not any more) home to the diner, walking around potholes filled with fetid water, cheap beer cans, abandoned truck tires and oil-slicked mud but he never needed to be carried, walked true like a little soldier. The very first day he grabbed that atlas – it was about as big as he was then – out of the wobbly spinning metal rack and climbed up into the booth and stared right through the thing with big eyes like he had been waiting to do it since he came into this world. Never had a day of schooling, he would brag to anyone, and no one ever did come around to check in as to why. Somehow, through the maps, he learned to read, meeting his fingers together time after time after time along the mileage tables he learned his math. His classroom was the whole US of A, the father reckoned – he would study the Everglades down to the Keys in the morning and be floating along the Colorado by lunch. Sometimes in those early days, his dad would walk over during that lull between breakfast and lunch, sit across from him and push across a fresh glass of milk, point to that glossy oversized book and ask the tiny kiddo if he wanted him to show where the two of them were in all that. Intensely green doe eyes, the green of a jungle as seen from a plane after a hard rain, would look up from maybe the top-heavy mess that was Delaware and there would be no connection. Dad would try to explain that it was a map of the country, their country, and they lived in it along with millions of others. Everybody was in there. It was real if you looked out the window. Nothing seemed to land. His mouth would open a bit and some jam might get reclaimed from the corner of his mouth with a flick of the tongue. He would understand one of these days, Dad would figure, it was a lot to bite into. One day he just flipped the upside-down pages to Alabama, the very first map in the book, as it so happened, and left a greasy fingerprint from the morning orders a hair off I-65 right near nowhere.

"Here," was all he said.

Like a true scholar from a forgotten time working by a candelabra or a whale-oil lamp, the boy carefully earmarked the top corner of the now sacred page, a text that was beyond him now but would be understood with divine providence at a later date and went back to the Great Lakes. Dad slid out of the booth, mussed up his son's stiff unruly hair and went back to scrape the griddle. He had an ignorant faith. The kid would turn out just fine.

2

LOOK AWAY

It was a mist that gathered thick on the windshield as soon as the wiper blades swung past. The clouds were heavy and low over the scarred blacktop, too tired to make real rain. Everything looked lost, the brick buildings with faded signs in a row waiting in a breadline that never moved, retired school buses dead and rusting, a mossy cop car strategically parked to catch speeders with no one inside. Ghosts policing ghosts. Even the stoplights were dim, the reds and greens switching on their own time, washed out from neglect as an invisible dog barked for ever. He knew America in 1989, the forgotten heart that was a slow, faint corroded beat at best. It was expected when you took the business spur away from 75 with its strip malls and bulk stores but the used-up whore some still called the industry district didn't bring down his nervous joy. He was heading to a lot somewhere deep in the rust of Dayton, Ohio, to pick up his very first load. The smell of burnt plastic off his freshly laminated CDL could still be picked up if he took a big enough sniff. He had been eating away miles on the interstate as soon as they handed it over to what was now his truck, a seasoned Mack, big, black and waxed to a sweaty sheen. The silver grill grinned at the bugs it devoured, the fresh tires humming a happy tune from the thick tread-slapping pavement. All was primed for a run to Dallas, the perfect distance to bust his cherry. Even if he had already seen the country laid out in his mind a thousand times over, he could barely contain his excitement at doing it for real, run after run, city after city, long stretches of nothingness, sunrises and sunsets to chase down. Escape had been achieved, unmentionable horrors trapped in the rearview and now the only thing keeping him between the lines of experience was the low salted metal guardrails stretching down the coastlines. He was going to bounce back and forth and eat it all up like a starved Pac-Man. An untethered life lived along the mileage signs, rest stops, runaway truck lanes at the bottom of mountain descents. He couldn't wait to tear down one of those as the airbrakes screamed. Nothing could taint his destiny. At an empty intersection, he reached over to flick the nondescript gold hoop earring hanging behind the rearview mirror. This memento was a trophy of sorts, a talisman that kept the steamer trunk locked and in the back of the attic. He turned up the top 40 countdown and yelled in his best Highlander voice to no one and everyone: "There can be only one!"

"Doing the Lord's work, yes sir," Derrick Gold thought with a toothy smile in holier-than-thou satisfaction. The gospel would soon be all across this great land, with his message alerting all of Jesus' flock to the dangers of the devil infiltrating the vulnerable minds of our youth, ages 13 to 18. It was his job to minister to those who had been entrusted in his stewardship, yep, and the good Lord saw fit to deliver him even further along the path, beyond a simple biblical tale of warning or uplifting badminton game to spread the good word on the moving billboards of the USA, tractor-trailers! Derrick was tagging every trailer in the lot with his homemade message, bumper stickers with red letters on a black background: "Satan is in Dayton!" There was as much stealth in his movements as substance in the words as he speed-walked tall between the containers with legs too close together as if on a desperate yet discreet trip to the toilet. Wearing a pink button-down under a plaid vest and pleated blue khakis did little to conceal his mission. He was perhaps overly enthusiastic as he had just picked up the box of stickers from the eye-rolling printer and had recently "cased the joint" after visiting the adult superstore a block away last Tuesday evening in an attempt to see what ole Beelzebub was up to on the front lines of the war for souls. He tried to avoid the sinners while nonchalantly perusing the countless rows of VHS tapes stacked tightly on the shelves like library books, hiding the screenshots of their nasty secrets. The wrap-around sunglasses he wore below a do-rag made it even harder to make out the content on the boxes he did pull so, in an increasingly feverish panic, he had wound up with a random array of food torture porn, summer-camp boys in trouble and a rather faithful hardcore parody of The Mary Tyler Moore Show. The demons of perversion were apparently well versed in the struggles of the seventies working woman, even if the actor who portrayed Ed Asner was stiff in his delivery. The producers were probably in league with Planned Parenthood and their far-reaching schemes to kill the innocent unborn and promoting feminism, hell-bent on destroying the Christian family unit. There was not a line in the bible about a woman having to file a W-2. His wife had wanted to work, talked him into part-time, next thing he knew she was taking a flesh deposit in her little vault at the bank after hours from a loan officer named Brent, or so her letter he found stuck on the fridge alluded to in too much detail to be at all tasteful. Alas, she was now lost in the vast carnal desert of delights but the righteous would prevail. The worldly may have their pornographic videos and the Dolly Parton workforce and his wife's letter may have been photocopied and shared at the church's Easter potluck dinner but Derrick Gold held his flaming sword pointed squarely at the dark lord, sharing the good word affixed to one ground shipment at a time.

With a passing lack of interest The Driver had seen the pear-shaped female-looking man reaching into a fanny pack and slapping on a sticker as soon as he pulled into the lot. In fact, he took him for a husky lesbian trucker looking to leave a future message for the next time a minivan full of Cheeto-dust-covered ragamuffins with pissed-in short pants happened to be trapped behind a big rig on a two-lane road and were forced to read her sentiments. It was the utter disregard for placing them on straight that first rubbed him up the wrong way. He watched for a bit before he walked the cinder-block steps up to the prefab trailer on blocks that was the office. If you were going to go to all that trouble to be out here defacing property, wouldn't you want to strive for symmetry? People were the worst.

Inside was what one would expect. A low ceiling, obscured by menthol cigarette smoke and a pungent waft of invisible cat shit. Since small talk was akin to death for him, he signed what was needed to be signed, dropped the pen attached to a string that itself was attached to nothing next to a Styrofoam cup half full of paperclips, pennies, lint and a few used mints, tipped his cap to the fat summer-teeth clerk and about jogged back out of the door, inhaling deep the damp chemical smell of outside Dayton as if he had just been rescued from a mine-shaft accident. Now that it was all official, his veins were thick with adrenaline-fueled blood and his wide, tall frame was a quivering bull in the chute. The buzzing edge his physicality involuntarily exhibited both frightened and aroused him. While the encounter inside was brief and uneventful, annoyance at the mere presence of someone who could wallow in filth like that fired off images of the string pen piercing ink through that fat skull, forced suffocation in an overflowing litter box. The dark matter inside his psyche had become that dangerous friend he always had memorable fun with, albeit always with an inherent risk that it could at any time manifest and damage others without any discernible restraint. He had to keep true to the code and hold any professional interactions that were necessary to a minimum for everyone's well-being and to guarantee his lifelong calling had the bright future he deserved. Calmness must continue to prevail inside despite the stormiest of seas. Hug the coast. Retreat to the rivers and roads. Rivers and roads. The beautiful paths of glory.

He got the trailer all hooked up and secure toot sweet, no wasted motions, a one-man pit crew. He had gone over the checklist a hundred times in the last couple of days, closing the distance to his maiden voyage. Lying on his back diagonally in the cab at night, his pantomime motions created shadows from the rest stop lights on to the roof of the cab as he gnawed on hunks of peppered jerky. The maps and motions had already surrendered to him every possible angle; to the inch they were absorbed into his reflexes. Thus he was able to back right up on the first try, just using his mirrors. The clerk watched judgmentally through his tiny window in between bent blinds, expecting a greenhorn's back and forth but the kid was as good as any old salty pro. So far, everything fit like a supple leather glove. Lady destiny had prophesized a prodigy of cartography who was to transform into the Casey Jones of long-haul. He was checking the running, turn and brake lights so very bright in the grayness of the day before pulling out toward all points southwest when that clerk lumbered out of the door of the office, carrying high a sawed-off shotgun and a shortness of breath. He was drawing a bead on a pink bulbous mass weaving through the metal sentinels patiently waiting their turn to be pulled out of the wasteland. The passenger door swung open, bringing in the wet afternoon and with it, a panicked Derrick Gold holding tight his limp fanny pack of stickers.

"Take me!"

The Driver motioned a noncommittal question with his long hands. He was far from being invested in saving someone who didn't respect leveling. Were all the pictures hanging in this guy's house crooked? Madness.

"Away from that shotgun? Please?"

He shifted into gear with Derrick still clinging on to the doorframe, trying to keep purchase on the slick running board as the truck lurched out into the street. One foot slid off and it looked like Derrick's getaway would be aborted before it began. Instead of bothering to look over at his stowaway's predicament The Driver kept his hands at ten and two and focused on the stoplight he was quickly approaching. If it stayed green, this situation would settle itself as he would speed through a left turn and let physics take its course. The light changed yellow right as he was about to push in the clutch and accelerate. He slowed down and downshifted to a stop, noticing the clerk tiny in the rearview mirror head back inside his stink. The new co-pilot climbed in and used both hands to close the door.

"Thank you, Jesus!" Derrick let out a nervous laugh and used his shirttail to pat the moisture off the exposed stickers. More like thanks to the Dayton Public Works for timing that light. The truck soon leaned forward again, Derrick really afraid to talk to this strange huge man behind the wheel of a huge truck. and The Driver, well, he locked the doors. He had his own set of fears, too. A doofus hijacking the thrill of his maiden voyage was not on the manifest. Heavy clouds began to gather behind his eyes.

They were an hour past the south side of Cincinnati on I-71 when Derrick realized he needed to assess the situation. There was getting away from a gun-toting mouth-breathing maniac but there was also heading 80 miles an hour nonstop away from your studio apartment with a youth fellowship the following evening at the shuffleboard court you were scheduled to lead. He did love him some shuffleboard, he couldn't believe senior citizens didn't just go at it all day. The nondescript landscape flying by offered no homesick heart tugs. Maybe it'd be nice to leave it all behind, a new beginning someplace where the sun was warm the whole year and the women were not succubus cuckolding deviants. A few loops down on the ole bible belt might do the trick, where women knew their place in open-floor plan plantation-style kitchens with copper pans hanging from hooks and men drove American-made lawn mowers all day sipping on sweet tea from the cup holder and daydreaming of the next monster truck extravaganza. Missionary-style sex was on the menu every Thursday night and you watched the kids play horrific soccer games on the weekend. He sneaked his eyes over at this behemoth that now was barreling him through Kentucky. The sun was finally breaking through the seams of the rainy-day blanket, an approaching sunset roaring through the windshield gathered up and ladled by angles over a thick head of golden hair. He was in the presence of an almost seven-foot monster in vigorous youth, Derrick wondered if he was even 20 years of age, if there was still growing to do, feet breaking straight through the floorboards to propel them Fred Flintstone style at bullet-train speed straight into the Gulf of Mexico. A whole lot of bright blue denim made up the XXXL overalls that looked brand new, with fresh initials on the tag inside. The stone-carved face was just short of as expressive as a goodwill-store mannequin, blank and chills-inducing cold, yet he could sense calculations being performed incessantly behind the curtain. His country-mile jawline was a constant clenching of rippling muscle, yet hairless below green eyes that reflected the sky as a rain forest canopy would. Not quite traditionally hand-some, something beyond that, striking. Someone who if you saw them before a wedding, you wouldn't know what side of the aisle they were going to sit on but you hoped it was the other side. Behind them he peeked to make out the sleeper cabin, holding a single thin mattress, with white sheets made up tight, military style. It perched seemingly uncomfortably on top of a row of gunmetal-black square lockers running from window to window, each with its own padlock. None of the usual personal items were to be seen, no picture of a sweetheart or spaghetti-sauce-smeared toddler faces next to the speedometer and no bouncing Jesus glued to the dash, unfortunately. In fact, the only things up front was in between them, a dull gold hoop encircling the base of the mirror and an old rolled-up road atlas that had definitely seen better days on the bench seat.

"Listen umm, sir, I didn't get your name, I'm Derrick Gold. Humble servant of the Lord our savior Jesus Christ."

After a too-long, too-tense silence, "No. You didn't." Not even a glance over.

"Right. So I appreciate your help back there – my mission went a bit sideways, as you witnessed. Figure it's best I be getting to heading back in the other direction, though, so if you could just drop me off at the next exit, I can call for a ride from the church shuttle or maybe even risk hitchhiking. I don't mind. Give me a chance to testify."

"Not stopping till Little Rock. Left with a full tank." The Driver took his eyes off the road for a split second to gaze down at the fuel gauge, first time he had looked at anything other than asphalt since the run began.

Panic pitched up Derrick's voice. "Well I just can't do that. I can't ask Brother Phil to send someone there and back, nope. Any more than a few hours is just really inconveniencing someone and most of our older alderman can't really see well at night. So I mean, it's just a couple minutes out of your way to pull off the interstate and let me off. There, see? Next exit is a mile away, I really need to get on home, if you could help me out. The man upstairs would appreciate the solid you did for one of the flock."

"I already helped you out. I don't make unscheduled stops on a run."

Derrick felt another jolt of panic low in his gut. This giant evil driving robot was serious.

"Little Rock is hundreds of miles away! How do you pee? Do you eat? Don't you need to stretch those tree-trunk legs?"

"Don't drink, don't pee. Eat jerky. Don't need to stretch. I'll stretch in Little Rock."

Silence reclaimed the cab, just the droning of the engine and Derrick's labored whistle-nosed breathing. He was trapped in a mobile prison that moved further from his couch by the second. It wasn't a very comfortable couch, came with the place and was itchy as all get out, the past tenant must have had cats, but still. The glorious slide of shuffleboard discs seemed infinitely beyond him.

"This is like a kidnapping! This isn't legal."

"You can get out whenever you want." The Driver reached down and unlocked the doors. A semi-truck having automatic locks and windows momentarily mesmerized Derrick. He had never really thought about that. Figured they would be more primitive, bare-boned. Of course these people, lowly truckers, they lived in these things so it made sense. He looked out the window at the blur of ground and considered jumping out. They were doing at least 70 miles an hour. He didn't know if it would kill him but it would sure hurt, then there he would be paralyzed in a ditch in the middle of nowhere to be picked at by raccoons and coyotes until, well he probably would never be found. He could wait for a traffic jam but who could count on that, especially when you actually needed one? He began a loop of prayer for brake lights ahead.

"What about those weigh stations? Don't you have to stop at those?"

"Go around them. I know where every weigh station is. Only pass by when they are closed. Weigh stations are for drivers that aren't in a hurry. I'm in a hurry. Shut up till we hit Little Rock." He turned to deliver a granite stare for emphasis. Derrick physically shrank under it, hugged his pack tight to his chest, wondering how he seemed to always make life harder without trying. Back to the road ahead, The Driver gripped the wheel tighter. It was just what he needed, a negative nancy looking to divert perfection on his first-ever run. Well, if life gives you lemons, you have to forget the little lemon is there. Or he could squeeze it dry. No. No time for such indulgence. He so badly wanted to take a gander at the face of the guy who sees him pulling into the lot in Dallas early tomorrow morning. A face filled to the brim with a man-to-man admiration that he did the run non-stop like a true road warrior. Non-stop. Leading up to his calling, he had made Black Betty his own, made sure to get a second 150-gallon gas tank installed on her thick sexy body. He had lied to placate the party crasher; he wasn't stopping in Little Rock. Hell to the no.

The path to this moment started at the trailhead known as Petty who took that seminal chance on him, immediately recognized the promise, the drive, the pinpoint focus the kid had. Somehow it was all revealed through those vicious emerald eyes when he first pulled him bleeding and broken out of the rubble, away from his dead...

Whoa, much too early to get into all that. Not on the very first run.

...and far away from the incubated existence he had known. It hadn't been much of a life. Still wasn't in relation to a popstar rolling around in a pile of lavender-scented bodies in Malibu, an airline pilot who saves every single life on a plane and no one ever knows, the separation of conjoined twins by an alcoholic surgeon who still has steady hands. No need to stoke the great fire into hyperdrive right then, though – that quiet, steady little voice that preached patience still ruled the day. He concentrated on the simple fact that today was the first day of the rest of his life. Today was the first day. The first day. He chanted the mantra engulfed in a rare sustained internal peace all the way to Bowling Green.

The night had deepened as they found themselves on I-40, that dull stretch between Nashville and Memphis full of straight sad miles of sandy pines and dead farmland trapped between wide muddy rivers. That pass through is rewarded with a too-brief relatively exciting trip under a queer accumulation of grey girders over the Mississippi with a fleeting glimpse of the Pyramid, rising from reclaimed southern mud, by distance and flair a far cry from the majesty of Giza. One would wish for a thousand pyramids once crossing the threshold into a sick purgatory known as Eastern Arkansas. Nondescript ugly and flat, like the miserable mousy little man staring at his restless hands on the metro bus, a stimuli wasteland with only the potholes to provide a diversion or give the need to touch the steering wheel, the perfect situation to drive fast and loose under a new moon. One of the first crumbled craters the rig surrendered to jostled Derrick awake. He had drifted off soon after The Driver's strong rebuke more as a coping mechanism than from exhaustion. After his treacherous wife changed the locks to their modest home, he slept in his Saturn right in the driveway for three straight days, not knowing what else to do in terms of next moves. Only the combination of prayer and the arrival of a tow truck shocked his system into action.

"Oh man, I have to pee so bad. Where are we?"

"Trucker buddy." The Driver pointed down under the seat without taking eyes off the road.

Derrick undid the seat belt he didn't remember putting on and reached under the bench.

"I don't feel anything."

A shrug was the only help offered. Derrick slid off the seat and got down on the floorboard on his hands and knees. It was an awkward position that exacerbated the pain in his full bladder. He looked up with red teary eyes.

"I just want to pee, man." The sympathy he wasn't expecting didn't come. He somehow slithered down lower on to his belly and reached as far back as he could, his shoulder stretched. His probing wiggling fingers felt what seemed like a garden hose, or maybe a snake. He let out an elementary school girl shriek but pulled it out anyway. It was rubber and attached to a cup on one end, a jug on the other.

"Trucker buddy."

"You seriously want me to use this?" Met with another shrug. Choices were limited to two, it appeared and the pain in his urethra was slashing the choice to one in a hurry. He thought of asking for The Driver to look the other way but the beast had not cared to look Derrick's way since he had first climbed in. First time for everything, he decided, and unzipped his trousers. He worked himself out of the hole in his tighty-whities and placed the cup over the tip. Nothing. He couldn't pull the trigger. Like when he had to poop in the woods during the youth camp-out last fall, he could not relax whatever muscles it required to evacuate with the crisp air kissing his buttocks. That trip left him constipated for a week, despite a box of prunes and he feared this trauma might rupture his bladder with pressure and leave him in sepsis. An unorthodox prayer called upon Him most high to help a lowly mortal start a stream. Part the seas of reticence, slay Goliath with a yellow rope of relief. Jesus could walk on water, please oh please help this tortured soul make water! Amen.

A single drip, then a sharp short squirt prologue led to the deluge, the dam broke. Hallelujah! Thank you, Jesus! He almost cried with gratitude. It roared into the jug, competing with the top 40 countdown that seemed still to be continuing since the lot in Dayton. The math was beyond him. The Driver, as if heeding his own higher calling, tuned into a frequency beyond the urine splashing and cookie-cutter hit-factory song and let go of the wheel. The rig held true, hugging the white line for what could be eternity. If it remained smooth and true through this evacuation of waste next to him, if not a drop escaped the contraption, he would stop in Little Rock and send the freak on his way. He was right after all; a few minutes wouldn't hurt in the big scheme of things. Hell, maybe he would get himself a hot coffee with cream, maybe a bear claw. Celebrate what remained of this voyage, the first of many, alone as intended. He saw it coming in the high beams though. A pothole. A big, nasty son of a bitch. Must have been a lot of rain lately or they were just too lazy and cheap in Arkansas to fix a simple road hazard. They hit it going 78 miles per hour. Derrick, still out of his seat belt, flew four feet up off the seat. His piss, not completed by any means, continued mid-stream unencumbered on to the dash, the passenger door window, the windshield. Fate had picked its dance partner. The driver seized control of the rig before it jackknifed with one hand while pushing a recessed button on the arm of his door. The passenger door flew open. The rush of wind overwhelmed the sounds of Derrick screaming in helpless terror. He turned his soaked head to The Driver for some sort of answer or the open door or to simply apologize for his inability to quell the fleshy fire hose in his hand. His face was met with a size 15 cowboy boot carrying a mighty force that jettisoned Derrick Gold of Dayton, Ohio out of the cab and into the absolute darkness. The Driver settled back into his seat calmly as the door closed and switched his right foot back to its rightful spot on the gas pedal. In his right hand he held the trucker buddy, examining the level in the jug. Half full. He was an optimist unclipping the clasps of his overalls. Might as well be comfortable. Lots of road left to Dallas.

3

HOLD ON

E arly morning and it was just about time to leave Cheyenne. He watched the breath puff out of his nose like a Pamplona bull through the predawn light. A few antelope stared at him from the edge of barbed wire across the street then calmly went back to their breakfast. Humans outside of their metal monsters were considered non-threatening to their wild ways. He climbed into the warmed-up all-toasty cab and tried again to find something other than country on the dial. He would hit something faint around the 98 FM range but not quite strong enough to make it out, just ghosts of a drum machine and maybe a keyboard, the distant cry of a girl in pink pleather and feather earrings pleading for reassurance? It would be lean listening between here and Flagstaff, not exactly the hotbed of pop music but he would be diligent, homing in on whatever sounded the least bit promising. He needed his big hits, the one-hit wonders or the newest single from a superstar who dripped greatness off their golden tongue like he needed recycled oxygen, jerky and the wheel humming gentle under his fingers. This explosion of classic rock stations the last couple of years disgusted him. Music was like milk, it had an expiration date, if it didn't, why did people keep making new songs? He didn't need to hear the past and he had more reason than most. She loved the old songs, held on to them while blindfolded from her present hells. Screw that, everything moves forward, he was excited for the next new catchy song with the hook that repeats, repeats, repeats in your head as you try to silence your mind and go to sleep at night and is right there back again when you wake up in the morning, your very own radio show that is constantly rolling out new episodes. No room for the reruns upstairs. Songs tied to memories had become the late-night cable movie he wasn't allowed to watch. He had no one to hide the remote from him. He was the parent and child. A delicate dance. What he watched now was a shy pink sky appear above the high prairie as Cheyenne was to become yet another memory he filed high and tight in a vessel behind his eyes, a damp room that was filled with them inside a vast storehouse with a series of locks with not a single key.

Things picked up as he approached Denver, in both the volume of traffic and volume of the local top 40 station he blared. Fingertips danced akimbo along the hard leather of the wheel. The sun had come into its own and lit up the cab with a glowing mustard seed of yellow deliciousness. He felt wetness in his armpits and a deep whiff from a raised arm gave reason to file the need for a truck-stop shower in the near future. Looking up from his pit off to the western right he saw the Rockies in the distance, peaks still dusted white, defiant of the coming summer days. What a tease to live in this flat, gridded city when the allure of elevated chaos towered just on the horizon. Either be in it neck deep or keep it out of sight, he sighed with a wave to no one. He would wake up each morning engulfed in pure misery living here among the low-hanging chimney-smoke pollution and hordes of humanity lacking any definitive style or character. The mountain overlords stole the spirit of the neutered mindless, their sacrifice to indifferent gods. When you could see your escape just outside your grimy office window, it was a life sentence in a prison where you can see over the wall. Blue balls of the bridled spirit. Had to break a man eventually. Denver omelets were the claim to fame? A filling of drones sitting in a lukewarm bubbleless egg bath of timid stupidity. No thanks. He felt the sudden urge to turn the rig right, dive in, cutting through the aspen woods to the colors and rock reaching up to tickle the heavens. Seeing more than this humdrum expanse of interstate till the city skyline revealed itself, mile markers the only measure of accomplishment. He went inside himself to the easy access folders and lifted maps to the forefront of thought. Colorado. Cutting over and down into Arizona, there was a way. He would chop it due west on to highway 50 just north of Pueblo, slide down on 550 from there and venture through Durango and pop west again on 160 to enter Arizona via the Four Corners. A nexus of imaginary lines sounded good for the soul. The plan brought a smile and a fresh piece of jerky to his lips. This day was the embodiment of his lifestyle, a fruition of pure desire and playing to your strengths. He pulled the air horn in salute to his best friend Casey Kasem recounting a brief rendezvous between Cyndi Lauper and a one-armed fishmonger at a bowling alley in Modesto that was even inspiring to those who could pick up a ball with either hand. We were only on number 36 and The Driver was racing nothing but sweet sunshine, the first to that western horizon was the big winner.

Standing statue-still in the Four Corners, feeling the pull of the different states, maidens vying for his attention and a path to possible doom. It was a little early in the year for the sticky-finger kids running rampant, parents hating life as they corralled them back into the van and on to the Grand Canyon. Just a couple of bored old couples and a well-to-do slight Frenchman in a white linen suit aiming a prime lens in his direction, boldly taking his picture. He felt that familiar pull either to model for the man as the quintessential American steel cowboy or take the camera strap and twist, squeeze his protruding Adam's apple till he heard those satisfying pops and gurgles. He looked down; his feet were in Colorado and New Mexico, respectively. If he killed this little foreigner right here, of which state would he be wanted for murder in? The extradition process would take decades. He closed his eyes and fought the battle inside. Lady Chance was his divining rod and hadn't steered him wrong since he had succumbed to her will. He raised his arms and spun in a circle, eyes locked on the blurred horizon. He made for a strange image for the photographer who giggled and rattled off shots in his outdoor studio. An unwritten rule presented itself as he spun. If he wound up standing in one state, he would smile and head back to the truck, onward and upward. If he wound up in two or more, his prey would die today. He halted the spin and lifted his eyes up to the powder-blue sky, still hearing the camera clicking. The Frenchman was right in front of him looking through the lens of his Leica rangefinder.

"You make quite the subject, Mr America! Big strong man straddling the states like a modern-day Colossus of Rhodes!" His accent was apparent but his English smooth and confident. Looking down, both feet were now squarely in Arizona. He should have figured as much when he felt the sun warm on his neck. The other neck too would feel the warmth of this day. Chance had spoken and with that he turned to walk back to the rig. The Frenchman, not knowing his good fortune, followed behind, not wanting his muse to escape just yet – he was attracted to this behemoth American and all that he stood for.

"Where may I ask are you off to, Monsieur?"

"Flagstaff."

"Ah, quaint little city. Pretty. A trap for the tourist but gateway to the great canyon, yes. May I suggest a detour? There is a vision that not many get to experience and you are so very close. A sacred place for those that have an open heart and a vast mind." Since this pushy feminine fella wasn't marked for death, a bit of civility now ruled the day.

"Ship Rock, right?"

The Frenchman smiled ear to ear. "Yes, my friend! You know of it? Glorious!"

"I know of everywhere."

"So you have seen it?"

"No."

"Well, let's go! This day is perfection! It will be sheer majesty against this Bleu de France sky! My name is Gaspard and I am at your service. If you will allow me to take your picture in front of the Ship Rock I would be for ever in your debt. What an opportunity! It is as if I have met the Marlboro man and we are off to the horse corral to saddle fine steeds! My John Wayne in the desert! Yes!"

He looked over this pushy little runt making plans. Focused on his oily hair and a jagged Kentucky-shaped brown mole on his neck, that neck, one hand would fit around it snug. If he only knew. Maybe Chance would again want to roll the dice. Nevada was indeed close. But he would like to see the rock. He had seen it on a coffee-stained postcard he had found once when he was small, left behind by mistake at the diner, addressed to a Judy Barton in Newark who would never receive it. Even in four by six inches, it was a stark vision that stirred his tiny heart. It was revered as a religious epicenter for the Navajo, a monolith of myth. Gaspard the tiny bastard was right, it was less than an hour away. It would just mean some backtracking on highway 64. Worth the couple of hours to witness geological beauty. The rock was worth the tick-tock. Take the extra clock to see Ship Rock. They should put something like that on a bumper sticker. Bumper stickers. Why did that stir up something? He nodded his assent. Gaspard jumped for joy. More of a vertical than one would surmise – must have played soccer in his younger days.

"Let's take my jeep, my friend, I know the way!"

"No."

Gaspard was momentarily stunned by the refusal but followed along, half-jogging, behind the long strides of the stranger heading in the opposite direction. He would have to ask about the curious denim pantsuit this man wore. Was his profession shoveling coal on a train? It never crossed his mind that he would be in any sort of danger. He had strong intuition and this man was the strong and silent type of cinema, the protagonist in the Western left to save the town single-handedly, the selfless soldier saving his wounded buddy during trench warfare. He was in this country for adventure, to immerse his Euro soul in the rough-and-tumble romance of the USA and steal its essence on to rectangles of 35mm film. This session was to be his masterpiece, a tribute to the great Cartier-Bresson! They came up to the big rig and Gaspard let out a tittering giggle.

"Well, of course, my friend! The perfect vehicle for a romp into the American frontier! You must let me take some shots of this vessel, yes?" He had to scale the side to shimmy in but was quick with his movements. Soon they were pulling out and back on to the baked highway.

"Hi Ho Silver! Yes?" Gaspard was the toddler in a booster seat excited about his jar of cinnamon apples. After a few minutes of listening to the number five hit of the week, Gaspard realized he did not know the name of this man who was driving him out into the high desert.

"I have not asked you your name, mon ami." His fun manner was rewarded with a long silence, just the radio a bit loud and obnoxious for his taste, the faint thud of a few grasshoppers slamming into the windshield. A second guess of taking on this jaunt flickered through his mind and was quickly dismissed. The point of no return left him steadfast in his judgment.

"Ah, the man with no name! The Clint Eastwood of the gunslingers. I would have brought my cigarillos if I had known I was in the presence of such a legend."

"No smoking in here."

"But of course. Just a reference to the Sergio Leone films.

They were popular in my youth. I remember actually running to the theater in Saint-Michel for a marathon of all three, one summer evening. Trying not to spill my homemade popcorn I was carrying in an old water bucket and failing miserably. Ducks following behind gobbling up my jetsam as if I was the Pied Piper, ha!"

"The castle? Mont Saint-Michel?"

"Oh yes, the very one. The old girl is majestic. A wonder of the world, I would argue. Many days we would play hide and seek among the narrow streets, the odd corners and dark spaces. Ghosts ran with us, I can assure you; I felt the cold rush up my spine more than once. Fear and wild abandon mixed in an endless glee, racing home to beat the tide. I cherish such a treasure given to me at birth. Have you been?"

"No but I know it. The coast of Normandy is dense with the settled dust of conquered land, roads upon roads layered in age and forgotten uses like the rings of a tree."

Gaspard was taken aback by the eloquence of this poster child for masculinity. "Profound, man with no name. You surprise me with such a poignant observation."

"I like maps."

"Indeed. I should consult one to get us to the Ship Rock, yes?"

"No need." The Driver pointed across toward the passenger window too close to Gaspard's head, the meaty hand with its long piano-player fingers Gaspard noted was larger than his entire face. He followed the direction and spotted the rock in the distance, sitting alien on the horizon as if a forgetful god had left a bauble there by mistake. There was nothing but flatness around for what seemed like for ever. They could be a day away for what he had to use for any relation to actual distance. Soon enough, they left the pavement and created a sandstorm in their wake as they headed on to Indian service roads to the protected site. Reckless men of decades past had died trying to climb it and the Navajo had shifted their mythology of the volcanic outcropping from a deliverance of their people to a cursed place where the carrion birds feast on foolish souls. The truck approached from the north and the rock gradually grew in their view to exceed all awe it inspired to any beings that were drawn to it. For eons a magnet of imagination aloft in a land bereft of it. The contrast was so striking, akin to a cornfield in Manhattan or an honest man seated in the Senate. The sparse spring wildflowers worshipped at their temple and the gliding wide vultures above gravitated to its sheer face but kept a respectful distance, swirling down its sides and enjoying the anomaly mother nature had blessed them with. Gaspard jumped out of the door before the dust had settled, misjudging the distance to the ground and rolling his ankle over. An unrecognizable French expletive escaped chapped lips as he hopped around but he accepted it as excitement mixed in with the pain and continued to run/limp to the base. He looked straight up as he approached, tripping through fallen rock and pointing childlike to the top.

"Amazing yes? What a treasure of this New Mexico. Come, come, let me photograph you here. The light is approaching the hour of magic."

The Driver shut down the diesel and stepped out on to the running board. A warm wind greeted him, one fragrant and yet teased with a touch of wild death. This indeed was a dark place, even in its beauty. Maybe that was why it was beautiful. Gaspard was cleaning his lens and examining the crags up high for the perfect composition. The Driver jumped down and sauntered over the sharp threshold into the swathe of shadow the low-hanging sun married to the monadnock provided. The change in temperature and atmosphere was striking. A slow-moving eclipse that denied the light and its favors.

She craved the shadows. Blankets over every window, as if brightness would expose the boils of insanity that festered unchecked. The threat was just another reason to live in the diner all day. Eat whatever his father had too much stock of that week. Hot dogs six days in a row or catfish for breakfast. Now inside like a stiff worn glove, he again imagined himself on the dark side of some moon separated from human experience as he did when trapped with Her on long afternoons. To be among a different breed of creatures, more bloodthirsty, ruthless, real and true. Unfathomable beasts with no names, devouring without discretion. The comfort in an existence fraught with pain.

"Please sir, come back to the light. The exposure I must have. It is golden, a rich pudding to relish in, yes? Just over here. Sunsets are fleeting!" Gaspard pointed to a flat tabletop boulder that was being gently showered with the late rays. "You stand up there, I will get low on the belly. The true hero shot. The giant modern cowboy and his volcanic talisman. Reminiscent of Life magazine cover, yes?" The Driver stared at Gaspard from the shadow, a standoff of wills. He finally decided to step back into the light, humor the man who was tormented over losing precious seconds to the coming dusk. He climbed on to the boulder and looked down into the lens Gaspard held an inch off the desert floor. After a few clicks and numerous exaggerated "ouis" from the photographer, he heard a rattle come from underneath his boots. He looked down and met eyes with the snake, sheer shiny doom that seemed to have been stolen from the shadowland. He had disturbed this creature's last respite from the coming cold of night. He felt no fear, rather a kinship. The snake itself calmed its tail. They were bonded for a fleeting moment, cold-blooded predators intertwined in the cosmic soup that led them to this rock, at this time, kindred spirits sharing the remnants of the day. As soon as it was recognized, it ended with a boot kicking the snake off the pedestal right on to Gaspard who may have seen the incoming coil through his 50mm lens. The snake was surely enraged as it landed on the Frenchman's head and neck, still level with the cooling ground. Gaspard screaming and grabbing blindly for the party crasher did not help its mood. The rattler sank huge fangs into the Adam's apple, a tragic distortion of Eden. The Driver reflexively licked his lips. Lucky bastard, his tubular friend. Gaspard struggled to his knees gasping, the snake hanging from his neck.

"Nice tie." The Driver couldn't resist. He jumped down and moseyed over, picked up the camera and took a couple of high shutter shots of the stricken man.

"You are going to love these." He threw the camera strap over his shoulder and grabbed the snake, pulling it from the man's engorged neck and throwing it back toward the dying light. Gaspard vomited red over the red sand and some low, vibrant bush sage.

"Good to get that out now. Before your throat…" The Driver made a closing fist gesture with his hand and Gaspard's eyes grew in panic. The daylight was pushing out its last breaths now, much like his companion. The throat was swelling to the size of a cantaloupe, releasing nothing more than a labored faint wheeze. He grasped his ward by the pointy shoulders and lifted Gaspard up to eye level, a broken ventriloquist's doll at best now, limp and frothing at the mouth staring through The Driver at a slideshow of his life waiting at the curb to be picked up for his fast-approaching date with death.

"If I hear an animal cry here in the twilight, I'll suck out the venom. Which of the nocturnal brethren will save this soul? The burrowing owl on a mission for darting rodents, the playful whinny of a wild mustang? If the chilling air remains silent, this forsaken man too will add to that peaceful stillness, become one with the ghosts of rock." The Driver waited, examining the bite mark, not really thrilled to extract, hoping for quiet. He was about to drop the sack of flesh as a coyote howl erupted from the distance, bouncing off the staggered faces of Ship Rock, creating what seemed to be a chorus of guttural growling instincts. An invisible pack closing in on the injured, a feast of the feeble. Without a second thought the driver locked his mouth over the bite and sucked. A metallic bitterness assaulted his tongue. He spat out what he could and returned to the wound. He repeated the ritual, closing off his own swallowing reflex from the mouthful of fluids. That snake had dropped quite a load. Gaspard's breathing remained labored but steady. Eventually, what he drew into his mouth tasted more of blood than poison. The sensation of draining a pulsing life force was pleasing and erotic, embodying within it an understanding of the fascination with vampires as he sucked harder on the wound. He closed his eyes and relished the thick flavors, missing the bouncing head-lights in the distance speeding their way. Hearing a door slam, he dropped Gaspard to the ground and could faintly make out a Navajo Tribal Police pickup truck pulled up next to his rig as he wiped evidence from his mouth. A stout female officer emerged and walked over to what resembled an interruption of the biblical sacrifice of Isaac.

"Never seen a damn semi-truck out here before. Definitely not allowed. You broken down or something?"

"No, Ma'am Officer. Just wanted to see the rock. My friend got a rattlesnake bite." It felt like he still had blood on his chin but he fought the urge to wipe it off.

The officer shone her flashlight down on Gaspard. He tried to say "help me" but it was nothing more than a slow-leaking balloon.

"How long ago did this happen?"

"Five minutes give or take. Sucked out the venom."

The flashlight met his eyes. Held for long seconds as he savored the blood still lingering on his tongue. It went back down to Gaspard.

"Well, he needs medical attention." She pulled him up and threw him over her shoulder, sack-of-flour style. "I'm taking him to the hospital in town if you want to follow."

"OK," was all he said as she turned and struggled away under the weight of a gasping duffel bag.

Gaspard was placed with a grunt not so gently in the bed of the truck. Then it was bright blue lights and kicked up rocks hurrying him the 10 miles to town and the Navajo hospital. Just like that, The Driver was left there in the absolute night, temperature dropping to match the blood in his veins. He licked his lips, searching for one more fleeting taste of iron and, being denied, let out a deep sigh. Stars in their multitudes had all come out to see him tonight, his audience flickering silent approval at his adherence to the code. Below them a simple white man trespassing but a transgression allowed by the spirits as he was a hero this day, a lifesaver. Felt good to know that he had that inside him too, to wrestle with the squalls of evil that blew through his soul. The coyote howled again, joined by others in a wholly different choir of affirmation that he did right by them and his mistress of serendipity. He shivered and started carefully hiking blindly back to the rig, only then realizing he still had the fancy Leica hanging off his shoulder.

4

(EVERYTHING I DO) I DO IT FOR YOU

He focused on making some semblance of a bowel movement since he had gone to the trouble of coming into the truck stop bathroom to sit bare assed in the filthy stall. He needed a shower and this was a necessary part of his routine, especially since he got a free one for filling up his rig with their pricey diesel. He was about to start a run from Morgantown to Charleston and he had recently succumbed to the ritual of a shit, shower and shave before each run. Nourished whatever humanity he still clung to. Entering his third year hauling, he was beginning to get a reputation for ridiculously fast and efficient runs that were adding up to a six-figure-a-year income. He was working on topping off the second of the row of lock boxes in the back of his cab with cash. Only need he had for banks and their greedy tentacles was to cash out a check for work well done. Those mini steel safes he'd had welded in, so unless someone was able to steal the whole kit and caboodle without him in it, that money was as safe as the FDIC. One day, he'd have to spend all that cheddar on something, if he ever felt the need to stop. Just wasn't much a man needed when he drove 365 a year. He pretty much lived off jerky and maybe a jug of whole milk for old time's sake. Roadside diner food was wasted on him long ago. It was nothing more than a good way to waste time and get fat while trying to pinch a little waitress ass. He remembered as a boy watching the truck drivers come in for breakfast and still be sitting on the same stool ordering lunch hours later. He supposed most of the shipping clerks and other three-toed sloths that passed for drivers he overtook in the left lane just gossiped on the radio that the mystery man was hopped up on speed or had some police-grade radar detector or just never stopped his rig, had some autopilot mechanism he had devised to keep him on the long white line while he snoozed. The sewing circle had it all wrong except the speed but it was no more than naturally occurring adrenaline pushing to the finish line with unrelenting focus, never dependent on much if any sleep, food or even water. He was a machine built to drive and the only time he could rest his eyes and the knots in his shoulders was when the trailer left his hitch. He was looking at the various phone numbers of ex-wives and cheating whore girlfriends who were sure to provide a good time and who all seemed to enjoy getting it in the back door when a crushed-up ball of toilet paper was pushed out of a hole in the wall separating him from whatever was happening in the next one over.

"Hey. You need a little release, cowboy?" It was a woman's voice, he was pretty sure, but throaty and harsh, vainly trying to sweeten it up with a plantation-debutante twang. Definitely not something he would consider blindly trusting his manhood to in a men's truck stop bathroom.

"No." Well, that window closed. No way he was going to be able to go now. He stood up and reached down for his overall straps.

"Wow. You're packing the whole summer sausage, aren't ya, big boy? Don't know if we could squeeze that through the hole over to my man pleaser anyway. Maybe we should meet again a little later in a more accessible situation." Black mascara layered around a stormy blue eye was sizing him up through the jagged circle. Throwing a wrench into his entire pre-game plan was unacceptable. He thought of sticking something else through, a rusty ice pick would work nicely. "I'll check you later, tater. Trust me, it'll be the cat's pajamas." The other stall door opened and the click of high heels on the urine-stained tile faded from earshot. Should he try again or just go take a shower? She better hope she doesn't find me. Rituals must be followed or blood flows over the altar, either way the gods are to be appeased.

That swamp moon-yellow hair was still wet and clinging to his neck as he walked through the gasoline air of the parking lot full of idling road leviathans. It could make you feel faint if you worked the rows turning tricks, an inopportune match blowing metal into the night before the flame reached your off-brand cig. It was that time of the evening where most traffic had given up for the day, the wife and kids having coaxed dad to pull off on to whatever exit had the shiniest lights. The dedicated day drivers were sitting at their kitchen tables crushing their fifth beer, wishing they had bought another six-pack, reluctant to think about doing the exact same route tomorrow. Construction was usually called off till morning and the late-shift state troopers were settling in to their hidden-by-trees naps in the widest median they could find. All in all, a perfect time to start a run. His good mood was just returning to a full tank when he saw a long and lean woman up on the running board, checking out her makeup in the dim light reflection of his side mirror.

"Hey, there's my tall dark stranger." She didn't even look his way as she applied another layer of obscenely red lipstick. Of course, from the voice he instantly knew his bathroom companion had made good on her vow. He stepped up right behind her, caught a whiff of strawberries, unlocked the door and swung it open. She had to jump down before the heavy metal took her out. She was left sitting hard on the wet pavement, leather skirt ridden up to reveal a lack of underwear and a broken heel on her pump. If he had any sympathy or even a libido it would have kicked in, her there exposed and inviting anything and everything with a dirty-leg attractiveness, looking up with a sultry whimper and puppy-dog eyes. Instead, he turned the engine over and got himself situated.

"You know the least you could do would be to help me up and give me a ride on outta here. I need some new scenery and you could have some fun, to boot. This damn glory hole is slower than a short bus on the first day of school." He reached into his pocket and found a left-over shower token, flipped it to her. She snatched it out of the air in defiance.

"Don't you have any urge to be with a woman?" she shouted, questioning his manhood.

"I grew up with one. So, no." He slammed shut the door, threw the truck in gear and pulled out. She threw the token at the truck with all she had. It careened off the trailer with a ping, the sound mostly drowned out by her scream of: "Cocksucker!"

Rolling down 79, The Driver wished he had just run her over but she had caught the token. Another service to the code. He wondered if she would have been so coordinated there sprawled out on the wet pavement showing off her wares if she knew her pathetic life depended on it. Probably not. Most people were not wired to perform in a life-or-death situation. He had seen war movies, always on mute as not to disturb the perpetual storm brewing in the back bedroom of the trailer, and what Hollywood defined as heroism, running into the jaws of live fire, shooting down the enemy without missing a shot or jumping on a grenade to save the platoon. He knew it all was as realistic as Bigfoot jumping rope double-dutch. War was pure hell and fear of death ruled the day. Those boys that had just fought on the other side of the world in the swirling sand where chaos ruled, they just wanted to be back in the States eating a whopper and watching The Fresh Prince while they tried to listen to their pregnant high-school sweetheart talk about the new store at the mall, they weren't looking to kill the enemy or save others in exchange for an early grave. What would the ultimate sacrifice be for? So gas would be cheaper? It took nothing more than insanity to put someone else's life before your own or to die for country and the preservation of "freedom". People only wanted to live, to see another day. The few true heroes who came home not in a box were missing a leg or mentally scarred, crying at nothing but a warm breeze or a larger-than-life cartoon rabbit on a billboard. Knowing that they narrowly escaped dying for nothing and not being able to say why. Lady Chance was the only arbitrator of our lives and it was a random dance no one knew the steps to. It was better that the truth was lost under desperate beliefs in faith and science. People would be lying in puddles of despair if they knew the reason. Only the strong, those that saw the patterns in the roads, the bridges, the arteries of a nation could ride the wave. The rest were fodder to be flung in the air, clay pigeons for his double-barrel shotgun, their lives dependent on what was or wasn't in the chamber.

It was right before Weston when the obnoxious flashing lights in the rearview shook wet humility on his omnipotent thoughts. His heart rate jumped up a couple of beats but it wasn't the first time he was pulled over, wouldn't be the last. He had all his paperwork at the ready and everything was up to snuff. He downshifted and leaned the rig on to the shoulder of the interstate. Good way for an officer to get clipped by a passing car, prancing around on the side of a road at night. Would be a shame. These bastards always took for ever. That was what irked him the most. Give me the ticket, let me move on, hijacking time was a vicious affront to a trucker on a schedule. Basically stealing money. At least that Navajo chick last year was no nonsense. Of course, it was a matter of life and death but he appreciated her brevity. These self-important palefaces patrolling his canvas were drunk with petty power. Finally, he caught a wide silhouette step out, put on a wide brim hat. For what? To shield the moonlight? And waddle on up to his window.

"I'm gonna need you to step out of the vehicle." After the blindness from a high beam flashlight subsided, The Driver took in a gap-toothed young bear with a touch of adult acne raging on his forehead. Seemed mighty satisfied with himself, unaware that his breath smelled like a tuna fish sandwich wrapped in a dirty diaper. The white-capped constellation of baby boils must have been the reason for the big-ass hat. Vanity ran strong in this profession, he had gathered. A symptom of pride, that deadly sin amounted to just another annoyance to add to the long list of reasons to not be a fan of traffic cops. Regardless, the game was afoot, so The Driver opened the door slowly and dropped down to the road a good eight inches taller than his foe.

"You got any weapons on ya?" He was visibly angry that this lowly trucker was bigger, taller, more handsome in a haunting way. A pang of regret that he didn't call for back-up tugged at his pinched-up balls. Damn pants were too tight. Did he bite off more than he could chew?

"No."

"OK. Let's go, big man. Back to the patrol car." The Driver wanted to ask what the hell was the problem. He was speeding, sure, but not egregiously. As they walked back, it dawned on him that his radar detector, a not-exactly-street-legal Cobra hadn't sounded off, so this wasn't a moving violation. Racked his brain for reasons, found plenty but nothing this khaki beach ball with legs would be privy to. Then he got a look through the windshield. The blue and red lights were dancing across the face of the truckstop prostitute sitting with a smile in the passenger seat, chomping on a tired piece of gum. She winked at him. He projected death along their locked gaze. Her smile faded.

"Stay here." The Driver read "Rhodes" on the reflective gold nameplate over the trooper's man-boobs pocket. The irony was not lost on him. Rhodes cop-walked his way over to the passenger side, smug hands hanging on his utility belt and a handgun that would be fumbled and dropped in a panic. If his license plate hadn't been called in, The Driver reckoned he could've just walked up behind and crush the soft skull of this oxygen thief between his hands like a water balloon, snap this snitch witch's neck and be on his merry way. Instead, he had to let this charade play out and figure out which pegs to pull. The two talked, shoulders were shrugged. Rhodes became frustrated. He grabbed her arm and pulled her roughly out of the car. Soon enough, all three were standing in a huddle before the moth-strewn headlight beams. The Driver felt the occasional hot wind from the other trucks as they blew by, failing to care enough to merge into the left lane. So much for solidarity among the long-haulers.

"Now take a real good look, Honey. Is this the guy?" Rhodes shone that damn flashlight back into The Driver's eyes. A short fantasy played out behind the pain of closed eyelids. Of grabbing that torch and shoving it right up this guy's ass. See what really made this tubby ghoul tick. A shell consisting of a pile of rancid apple fritters, NASCAR tank tops and an overly friendly older sister. Leaving the door cracked during bathtime. Making him sit on the pink shag carpet toilet seat cover, crying with his sleeve rolled up to the shoulder hunting through the bubbles for his favorite Hot Wheels Smokey and the Bandit T-top Firebird she dropped in the water. The flashlight spun away, over to her face. The Driver opened his eyes back up. She was still attractive, even in the harsh light. He figured 10 years and a myriad bad decisions past her prime. He could see how she had survived in the dark parking lots and lonely bathrooms of America's byways. She had learned the hard way where the buttons and switches were.

"I don't know. Maybe. Maybe not. Actually, nah, don't think so. This guy, he's too damn large. Shit heel that tried raping me, he was more, like, your size." She looked down at Rhodes's fly, which was wide open and stained with that whore red lipstick, the same she had reapplied in abundance. Rhodes took a beat, let the complex calculations tally up. Carried the one, dotted the T's, crossed the I's. She took a baby step toward The Driver, as if they had been reunited after insurmountable odds. The Driver had to admire her moxie, blackmailing a state trooper on the side of the interstate in the middle of the night, cozying up to a man who would just as well see her shot full of holes than offer to corroborate her story. She was rolling the big fuzzy dice and needed a hard eight. First things first, Rhodes zipped up his fly and licked his thumb to see if he could remove the scarlet letter around his junk. No luck. Without further ado, unable to counteract the trickery of this crafty hooker, he took his memory of a decent but too-toothy blowjob and shrank into the cruiser, turned off his flashers and rolled back on to the interstate without another word.

Just like that, they were alone in a staring contest, faintly illuminated by the dim amber running lights from the trailer. Only the hum of the idling diesel engine and the sharp rhythm of crickets accompanied them in battle. Here was a rare second chance, he thought, to be rid of this scheming succubus. A dead prostitute pulled 100 yards or so into the woods from some random mile interstate mile marker in West Virginia might never be found and, if so, he knew one member of law enforcement who would be a prime suspect in her senseless murder. He got tickled at imagining the coyotes or even a brazen wolf pulling apart her limbs to feed hungry pups. The majesty of an industrious great horned owl pulling out a bloody lock of dyed hair to reinforce a nest high up in a giant hemlock tree. There would be no haggard mom and pop on the local amateur-hour Morgantown news affiliate pleading for prayer and justice for a dear lost daughter who was so kind, would give you the shirt off her back and was always ready with a smile. It would just be a thin file folder deep in the cabinet and a plastic baggie of unclaimed ash. A forgotten soul fallen through the cracks of the machine to land and exist as nothing more than a sticky penny under the couch cushion of humanity. If they remained in this low humming silence for another 10 seconds, no high beam headlights slashing by, he would close the last chapter in an abused paperback book filled with a life of missing pages and spelling errors. He began a countdown, flexing and releasing a pinky toe as he moved across the first foot. She stood there, hands on hips, not grasping her existence was a fickle flame and the breeze was picking up.

"What are we doing? Let's go daddy, I need to kick the heels off these barking dogs, get some night-nights." She threw out a smile that was more hard than genuine. Six, five, four, three, two…

Before he could even register the angry overbearing sound or where it was coming from, out of nowhere, one of those Japanese superbikes buzzed by, traveling defiant on the far side of 100mph. Just as soon as it flashed, it was gone, a faint echo disappearing into oblivion. Damn. Did that count? Yes, the silent gods answered. So close. This chick should be posted up on a casino floor in Vegas, hitting a 16 with a cosmo splashing on to the felt.

"Whew! Crazy son of a bitch right there! If that butt plug hits a deer it's gonna be nothing but assholes and antlers across both lanes! C'mon let's see if he's at least wrapped around a tree up there!" She strode up to him and grabbed his crotch. "Speaking of trees… wink wink." She poked her tongue against her cheek and raised her eyebrows. She had a one-track mind. So did he. They were different tracks.

The show-me-where-he-touched-you Chatty Cathy had divulged most of her life story by the time they jumped on 77 South. The clichés danced about the cab as he tried hard to concentrate on the radio pumping out the latest pop diva professing her undying love in the face of an indifferent beau. You know when that pig called her Honey? Well that wasn't him throwing out some misogynistic too-familiar affection, that was her actual name. *Fade in*: A gangly girl raised by an indifferent grandmother as her mom preferred the needle, gang raped in the back seat of a Mercury Cougar after a homecoming dance and too much strawberry wine. May or may not have involved a German shepherd and a jar of crunchy peanut butter. Depended on who recounted the tale as the glee club claimed to have photographic evidence but it never made the yearbook. Her free spirit obsessed with The Rolling Stones' Wild Horses, attempts to fill the hole in her soul with a series of horny, awkward future coalminers who used her as nothing more than a crash-test dummy, the eventual botched abortion before her junior year that left her barren and bedridden, too far behind and dejected to contemplate going back and getting a diploma. Instead, she surrendered herself to mastering the art of seduction to make ends meet but that white knight who could have rescued her from the sandpaper that eventually ground down her looks and shallow pool of optimism never crossed her path. She had had her chances, some rube on the road selling imitation-ivory hairbrushes away from his fat, abusive wife, a real hayseed who seemed to fall in love with her in those fleeting early days, never quite winning the stuffed animal at the fixed carnival game but continuing to try again and again and again even after the barker begged him to stop. Now she accepted her lot plying her faded wares day by day or rather night by night where the shadows were kinder to her rough edges, floating along the currents on a boat with a broken sail, no hope of ever reaching shore. As they careened on into Virginia, she painted pity with a heavy brush, not realizing she was relying on a strategy that would fall on deaf ears. Part of her repertoire was the sensation of the female touch, usually a powerful tool that awoke a spark in most men who were resistant to her audible charms. She would run a hand up a thigh or press-on nails down the back of the neck but tonight it was like touching a marble statue. The dude was a museum piece, hard and cold, non-responsive. Maybe this side of beef played for the other team. Just her luck.

"You're a tough nut to bust, mister man. What's your story, anyway? They make you in a lab or something?" She reached for his chin, to steal his eyes, one of her signature moves. "Somebody must have really hurt you, sugar bear." Sugar bear. A lightning flash, real or imagined tore through his center. From his periphery and the pools of sodium lights that washed by, she resembled Her back then, *sugar bear*, a lyric she always hit hard from one of her favorite songs, one he unfortunately remembered all too well. Singing along at the top of her lungs on repeat as thunder rattled the thin prefab walls. He turned up the radio even louder to drown out the memory, this irritating woman vying for his attention, the ghosts of pain.

Honey yelled over the music ignoring his obvious attempt to silence the one-sided conversation. "OK, let's try an easier question. Where we headin'?"

"Charleston." Her eyes got big at the answer, partly because he had spoken to her, partly because she couldn't believe the coincidence.

"You gotta be shittin' me. Dip my tits in sweet milk and put me in a kitchen full of kittens. That's exactly where I been meaning to get to. I got family down there. Probably the only family I got left. My sorry-ass mom's sister. My mom is deader than a judge's dick but my aunt, she met this freaky dude Artie at a Jimmy Buffet concert she had hitched to in Myrtle Beach. They got along pretty good and he drug her back to Charleston guess it's been about 15 years or so ago. That ass hat tried throwing a space heater in their above-ground pool one day when a cold front had moved in. He did a cannonball into that bad boy and it about killed him. He don't talk so good anymore, of course my Aunt Samoa – you know, like them girl scout cookies? She would tell ya he never really did. Guess he fried his brain pretty good back in the day eating acid like they was gummy bears down in Key West for a solid year. Anyway, the only other symptom is he will only eat with his feet now. Has to pick up his food with a couple of toes and lay on his back and drop it down into his gullet. It's a helluva mess on spaghetti night, as you might imagine. Samoa sent me a postcard ages ago from Charleston. I still got it in my bag and I bet you can still make out the address. You know where Wadmalaw Island is? They live out on the edge of some old plantation. Sounds creepy as hell but ain't like I haven't seen about all the wacky shit there is to see. Hell, figure I could help her out, reinvent myself. I ain't a Korean but I like to do nails. Maybe I could do that. You think? You gotta go to school for that? You gotta know Korean? You know Korean? That why you don't talk much? English your second language?"

He had to shut her up or there would be steaming viscera all over his immaculate cab. The lion was roaring under the skin, rage and hunger. They were crossing the state line into North Carolina any second now. If she saw the sign and mentioned it, it would be the last state she ever saw. Third time's a charm, right? She can't roll sevens for ever. His insistence on ignoring her had for the moment left her sputtered out, looking at her nails with a little flashlight she had produced on a key ring clogged up with doodads, basically anything you could slip on to one except an actual key. Wouldn't it just be his luck that the first time she shuts her trap and gets distracted is when North Carolina is begging to welcome her to the Tar Heel state. Sure enough, they crested a tiny hill and there was the sign. Cheating the game for the sake of his sanity, he cleared his throat. She looked up expectant when yes, she saw that sign reflecting in the strong headlights, blind white eyes delivering up the secrets to a sleeping world.

"Lift your feet! You gotta lift 'em when you go across to a new state or it's bad luck. She raised her feet up, spun around and placed them in his lap.

"Welcome to North Carolina, sugar bear."

"You too. Honey bear." She giggled at that one. Now they were cooking with grease, she thought. She was well on her way to something better and this sexy moose was her golden ticket. Feeling damn generous due to her good fortune, if he played his cards right, as in if he just kept driving and let her do the voodoo she do so well, he was gonna get a serving of the house special… on the house.

They made it through North Carolina fast and not so furious as they had settled into a coexistence that left them on a tightrope of pretty good terms. He had tamed the beast inside

41

for the time being, meditating on the empty pavement and pulse of white stripes relenting to the left wheel. She had even dozed off just north of Charlotte after a lengthy tale chronicling her recent expulsion from night school to prepare her for the GED test. Apparently, the teacher did not like to be "rubbed up on" and was not amused by the rash of crabs that left half the class frantically scratching the crotch of their MC Hammer pants. Honey admitted she was the Typhoid Mary but they were the ones who kept on inviting her back to study group. As the teacher gave barely a glance to her deep cleavage or Basic Instinct leg crosses, she thought he was just some stuck-up asexual taxidermist freak show or some such. Then came the weekend before the big test when she jumped out of a happy customer's rig and happened upon ole Teach and his "girlfriend", a sex doll he had dutifully dressed up in her Sunday best, having a delightful picnic at a rest stop near the state park outside Fairmont. She did have to admit they looked truly in love, even though it was creepy as hell hearing their conversation, the teacher handling both sides with an inconsistent pitch in his voice. When Honey snuck up behind and interrupted their bliss by twisting the head off the plastic torso while laughing a cruel yet dejected laugh at the poor bastard, that was the end of her tour of duty and the test was never taken.

The Driver pondered how some succumbed to using sex as their tool, their weapon of choice to bushwhack their way through the world. Unless you possessed some real talent or at the least a shot of charisma to couple with the sex appeal, your success officed out of a windowless basement with low ceilings. It was the lowest common denominator, that primal urge to procreate driving down the hammer of instinctual behavior. The base impulse was less than an afterthought to a higher mind like his. A faint blip on the sonar, a submarine well out of range. He was playing bridge without a partner while this softly snoring meat next to him was losing at go fish. The desolate straight-as-an-arrow stretch of sandy pine south of Columbia on 26 would be the place to take the final trick.

An ambulance streaking through the deep night jarred Honey awake. She resumed chewing the gum that had hibernated in some lost crevice of her mouth.

"Oh looky, the exit for the University of South Carolina. You know they are the Gamecocks? Could you imagine being a cock for the rest of your life? So stupid. What is that? A rooster or something? Who made that decision? Not so smart for a place of learnin', that's for damn sure. We getting close huh? Guess we're in South Carolina now." She looked down trying to figure out why there was no handle or button or really anything on the passenger door other than cold, hard black vinyl. "How do you roll down the window? I want to see if I can smell the ocean yet."

"You don't."

"Well what kind of bullshit is that? Is this a rollin' prison or something? What if I gotta throw out my gum?" She senselessly felt around the door, as if there were a trick to it.

"Two hours to Charleston. Nothing to smell but Gamecocks."

"Two hours huh?" She slid across the bench seat. He nodded. The lights of Columbia were quickly receding into more of the thousands of miles he had tallied in the last few years. Honey slid that money-maker hand up his thigh again, hoping for some reciprocation, some hint that she was still the Midas of members. This time he responded. The throb tickled her spine. She never had a Christmas morning with surprises wrapped under a dead tree but the anticipation must have been something akin to this. He unsnapped his overall buttons and started pulling the heavy denim down. She pulled his mitt away and shucked his torso.

"I gotcha. Lift that ass up." He did and she pulled, revealing what she suspected.

"Disco." She took out the exhausted gum and pressed it on the dash. He stared at this affront and the rage he thought was all but extinguished sparked back up and consumed the firebox.

Before she bent over into his lap, he motioned back behind them to the back of the cab and the line of lockboxes.

"Reach into the third one from the left." She did as ordered and pulled out a gas mask, military grade. He motioned for her to hand it over, which she did with quizzical raised eyebrows.

"Ain't you a kinky son of a bitch." He slipped it over his head and secured it snug without taking his eyes off the road. The smell was a touch musty but sterile and empty, a welcome respite from Honey's perfume masking road-born body odor and dried, rancid sweat. A handful of her crinkly lacey top pulled her back into position. Before she got to it she giggled, that ignorant, lack of respect for other's property, trying to get him arrested, throwing her nether parts out for all to see in a filthy oil-streaked parking lot, giggle that enraged every cell of his being. He thought he would feel more but the walls built to keep any and all physical sensations away were high and thick. He looked down and noticed dandruff clinging loosely to her bobbing scalp. With his right hand he roughly forced her head down, gagging her. With his left he flipped a small orange switch low on the dash. Carbon monoxide started filling the cab, redirected from the exhaust to accept an invitation to be an invisible participant in a threesome of death. It took a few labored breaths through Honey's nose but when the gas took up residence in her lungs, panic replaced joy. Her body struggled against the weight of his meat hook arm pressed down on her back, his hand controlling her with a final ass grab, the flesh that controlled her past destiny used one last time as no more than an anchor point. Soon enough Honey's half-hearted muffled groans were drowned out by the infinite countdown, Casey K was somewhere in the low twenties, not even halfway. He wondered if they would hit number one by the time they made it to Wadmalaw Island. He waited till the current song was over and checked her pulse during commercial. It was a faint beat, he likened it to a song played on another floor of a building with thin walls you cannot make out. He stayed in position, gripping her buttocks with his weight across her back till the beat ended. Then he casually rolled down his window, picked off that offensive gum and flicked it into the black cauldron of wind. He must have looked horrific to the wife who happened to open her eyes at that second, face roughly caressed by a pillow pressed against the passenger window of a minivan that was passing in the left lane. If she had only known what he had settled still in his lap it would have only added to the stuff of reoccurring nightmares she would come to dread in the coming years. That truck driver with the mask, staring at her blankly through the circles. If he had known Karen, who would eventually leave her family entirely and spend a good deal of her trust fund on therapy, would he apologize for her witnessing such an image in the hours before sunrise on a long drive home from Gettysburg and the tedious fulfillment of her husband's Civil War field-surgery obsession?

No.

As soon as he located Auntie Samoa's tattered postcard in Honey's "bag of transient survival" and made out the address, he had the route mapped. It would steer him over an hour from the drop but a necessary detour, just the same. He glanced down at her glassed-over eyes still wide from panic from across the floorboard. Much prettier this way, silenced and looking not for her next trick but into the great beyond. He wondered if anyone ever told her that, that she was her most alluring while pondering, her oversexed personality in neutral. All in all, she had made it far, farther than most that crossed his path and ran afoul of the randomness of his judgment. She deserved to be delivered back to her blood instead of tossed in a gas station dumpster. He was not without honor but it was just as fickle as a tropical storm teasing the Nicaraguan coast. For now, he was committed to providing closure. The sunlight was just burning the black off the blue sky when he bounced south on to 526 and down to Honey's extended brood.

He knew when he got to the last turn he would have to

continue on foot, a dirt road too narrow for his rig to turn around and too long and wiggly for even him to have to navigate in reverse. He found a sandy turn out with a sign that welcomed Boy Scouts to a wilderness camp and killed the engine. Without having to look, he reached back and pulled out a tightly folded canvas bag from one of his trusty lock boxes. It pained him to realize he was suddenly starving, his stomach betraying him when it damn well knew this deed must get done before dawn got too far up the ladder. A huge piece of peppered jerky shoved in his cheek was all he allowed himself as he unzipped the bag and shoved her in. The floorboard was sticky with her expiring fluids, he made a note to clean off the rubber mats when he returned to the cab.

It was a good 300 yards of rutted road to the address on the card. He carried the bag easily, strap slung over the shoulder as if he was a hockey goalie in his street clothes heading briskly to the rink to get dressed out before the puck dropped. A leaning mailbox advertised the house number via black spray paint, 10 yards before a dead end and a swathe of thick foliage almost completely concealing a wide field of tea plants. Must be the plantation Honey mentioned. He turned right and strode up the trash-strewn driveway, a big-wheel missing its big wheel, rusty empty cans of cheap beer riddled with bird shot, a cracked laundry hamper that may have one time worked as middleman to a clothesline that was now defeated snaked across weeds, still tied to a fallen post. Not a shock this led to a house that could have passed for slave quarters a couple hundred years ago. Not much more than a shack, squat and square with Kudzu vine on the offensive over much of the peeling east side. Frantic barking stopped him in his tracks. Where there was a dog, there should be people and where there was a barking dog there would be awake people. He made ready to drop the bag where he was and take off back to the rig posthaste. The barking continued but he could detect no other movement. Either these people were deaf or dead or long gone. He made for the house again, picking his way around to the back to find what he expected, an above-ground pool that was no more now than a 24-foot-wide Petri dish. The fact that it could still hold water in such a neglected condition was astonishing. It truly was built to last. A thorny raspberry bush had taken over the filter system and a set of homemade steps up to the top were long ago eaten and shat out by termites. He didn't really want to look into the tepid green water, afraid of what he might find. He sat down the bag down leaning up against the pool. Seeing Honey there reminded him of a movie he had seen about 10 years ago, right before the end of things as they were. Of dead Aunt Edna, wrapped in a blanket and discarded on the front porch of her son because the family had a vacation to get to. It made perfect sense then and made sense now. He unzipped the bag and lifted Honey up, placing her gently into the pool. He gave her a push, somewhere between a toy sailboat in Central Park and a Viking funeral pyre. A perfunctory glance of the floating-away corpse banging up against the opposite wall of this tiny sea and the deed was settled inside him. After a cleansing blink he looked away and let curiosity lead him to the source of the barking that had not abated. He scooped up the bag in his arms, folding it as he walked over to the back of the house across a cracked patch of cement and around a tipped-over barrel barbecue grill, its mouth agape in some forgotten agony. Cupped hands offered a foggy view into sheer chaos, the dog leaped up from the other side of the ill-fitted patio door but did not garner a flinch from him. Behind, anything and everything that could be destroyed was, many times over. The dog dropped a piece of an electrical cord to bark with more insistence. The cord had once been attached to a toaster that was pushed up against a corner of what once served as a kitchen. They must have left in a hurry, as there was too much disarray for a house that had been packed up. The doorknob did not give way to his grip as he expected. Without hesitation he picked up the barrel grill and threw it discus style through the glass of the door. The dog jumped back around the corner of the short hallway as the shattered glass settled into chewed-up carpet and ripped-up linoleum. No telling what this fella has had to eat to keep alive, he thought. If Samoa and Artie had left this dog behind locked up to die, they deserved to be tied to cinder blocks and thrown into the green abyss behind him. People were the absolute worst. Brown round eyes met his from around the corner of a gnawed wall. Hopefully the pup understood his salvation had been delivered. A half-hearted bark, a high-pitched whine was all the aggression he offered. He took a step back and motioned for the dog to come out from the hell he had endured. Delivered! Come out to the light! The dog broke into a sprint and hurdled the busted door and the shards of glass landing with a skid at the edge of the tall grass, tail wagging hummingbird speed. The cute mutt shook dirt and dander off to reveal a white coat, a still off-white except for a black head from which emitted a bark again but this one was different. It was a sound of thanks.

"You're welcome."

Walking slowly back up the driveway, not too worried about the state of the day and being discovered now, he felt the dog following tentatively a few feet behind. When they reached the road, he turned back to the dog, who stopped in his tracks and studied this giant human, puzzled with issues of trust, renewed freedom. He pulled a piece of jerky out of an inside pocket of his overalls and got down on a knee, offering it. The dog approached, head down. No telling the last time he had seen or smelled anything actually edible. He gently took it from the outstretched hand. With the jerky firmly in mouth the two locked eyes for what seemed an eternity. The dog saw all, more than he wanted. All his instincts triggered a confused flight that yes this was his savior but was not anyway suitable for that emotional, unbreakable bond between man and beast. He scampered away with his precious snack past the end of the road, into the break of woods and the morning dew of the fields beyond.

5

END OF THE ROAD

S alt Lake City held a heavy strangeness in the heat of summer that you felt pushing in and drying out the mushy marrow of your bones. It was nothing more than this point of origin, another random point on the map, of just another run but he had never really spent much time in the too-clean, too-sterile grid of smiling white people drinking juice and strapping skis to things. So on this occasion he had splurged for a couple of days of hotel-room living before he picked up the next hook. Spent most of the time laying his heap of flesh on top of a stiff green-and-red flowered bedspread on a mattress that was too short, flipping through the Book of Mormon, reading about golden plates you didn't eat off and a vault under a mountain where every single person's name is written in a book to be saved by proxy. He'd like to have seen what they had down for him, his dad, Her. Hope they had written it in pencil, that's for sure. He would have normally stretched his legs and gone out more, breathed deep the naked soul of the city, ingested what made it tick, the unique ingredients that gave it its special flavor. Or he might even have followed for a few blocks some real piece of work in too much scarf who came out of a drugstore refusing to cover their mouth when they sneezed, fantasizing of different ways to kill them with that scarf but here he realized none of that gritty realness existed, the native blood hosed off to reveal a shiny, hollow shell. He guessed the local nightly news was just three minutes of snowfall amounts and maybe some high-school basketball highlights, as nothing sinister could be happening. No strip clubs, no bars, no biker gangs pulling long knives from their boots after a drug deal gone bad or desperate pimps smackin' their hoes a lesson on MLK Blvd. Just fanatics living on the fringes with gaggles of passively fighting wives, guarding those caves with all the world's secrets protected from the inferior races, the heathens and heretics that truly did the dirty work needed to win the West. It was all the same to him but he felt more uneasy here than on the wrong side of a late night in south Chicago. Even though he spent most of the 48 prone, sleep eluded him. Just wrestling with the gremlins of evil thoughts and surrendered to the ear worms of the latest pop songs cooing softly from the clock radio blinking with the wrong time. When the right morning finally came, there was nothing to pack, nothing to rearrange. The maid would be hard pressed to prove anyone had checked in or out. Rolling off the still-made bed. he brushed his teeth with a tiny bar of soap and an index finger then, with another in a series of endless struggles, he was able to move his stingy bowels and wipe with a few pages of the good book. A short drive on Paranoia Avenue to the lot where it seemed judgmental eyes were watching his every move from every window and taking detailed mental notes, then finally the giddy adrenaline of embarking on a fresh run, driving north on 84, on the way to Seattle and the gloomy overripe sweetness of the Pacific coast.

Leaving the urban sprawl approaching Idaho was to slide into a cartoon, expecting to see a coyote carrying TNT or the nemesis bird flicking its tongue, so damn cocky. What did the coyote eat? Why didn't he just order a pizza with all that money he sent to the Acme Company? It was a teaching tool, of course, of the struggle between the predator and prey, how devious hunger could never be sated. Embracing a blissful ignorance in dismissing those who seek to destroy you. How easy it was to escape the clutches of those who tried too hard, developed elaborate schemes only to have them blow up in their faces. He knew better. Nothing was that black and white. Sometimes a well-laid trap worked to perfection or just plain dumb luck led to your demise. The best path was to read the room, think lightly, strike decisively. It was something that could not be taught, it was an instinctive feel, the essence of a true alpha predator. The coyote didn't have it, that knowledge that his teeth were his best weapon, teeth hidden behind an indifference that would lure in the silly bird, mystified and unaware of what sharpness lay in wait.

The serpent blue guarded the vast richness of nameless majestic ranges as he crossed the bumpy dirt of southwest Idaho over into Oregon. He pictured the pioneers struggling to keep wagon wheels in the ruts, one eye peeled for Indian raiding parties, the other lost in the emptiness of a transient existence. Sure was a fine time for their only guide to be blinded by a freak fall into a patch of prickly pear last week. It was too late to turn back; the cold weather was noticeably gaining momentum as they stared at the same billion stars night after night. How would they cross the Snake? Did they turn upstream for days hoping to find shallows? Flip their last Liberty-Head coin and hope downstream held a better chance for a slow ford? Any deviation from chasing the western horizon must have crushed spirits, seeing the hardtack and bacon dwindle, doing solemn math in the back of their heads as their five children gazed at them forlorn from around the canvas. Which one would you eat first if it came to it? Would you sacrifice one to save the other four? Black thoughts under a dusty sun. We have cured much of the savagery of such circumstances, a bodega on every corner, discount food warehouses, dollar tacos. Do the victims of a cruel nature swirl around the cosmic soup before being reincarnated, ladled out into a kinder, lazier world? Was that the nirvana our spirits climbed the ladder to achieve? Does our past violence follow us? He hoped he once scalped overconfident cavalry, gutted through French Catholics aboard a merchant ship in sight of the Antilles, was a fervent attacker in a Mongol horde, clubbed brain matter splattered on his glistening yellow steed. These flights of fancy got him into Eastern Oregon but just short of Baker City. Such vivid fantasies left him physically spent, as if he had indeed seen battle. There was a faded billboard for a truck stop up ahead in the scrubby emptiness. Time to reload the jerky supply.

Wasn't it the worst when you thought it was going to be a quick stop right off I-84 and it winds up being two miles down a windy road? He was pot committed by the time the ramp that had delivered him on to this fool's errand had disappeared from the rear-view. False advertising was what it was. Bait and switch. He sure as hell was not going to give them any more than necessary. Too bad he had no urge to defecate as leaving a present in the upper tank would prove fitting for this deception. He passed a haphazard collection of depressing trailers that reminded him too much of his former life. There were faces hidden in plain sight as he drove through, twitching behind thin coarse curtains all linked by some low consciousness. Beyond their stalled-forever caravans, nothing but tumbleweeds, fat jackrabbits fleeing into the wastelands and the teasing of a wall of mountains far to the west that you could see only on the clearest of days. Were these descendants of failed gold rush expeditions? Those who just grew too weary and decided to cut their losses and inhabit this empty place? Circle their wagons and pray to God for survival or at the least a divine, peaceful death? This was a free land; one always had the ability to live anywhere, no matter the means. A trailer here or homeless on Venice Beach? A mansion next to a dog-food factory or a shack on the edge of Yellowstone with the Tetons outside your drafty window? Or that of a noble modern-day gypsy, the long-haul trucker, where your view was determined by the pull of a slot machine handle, always varying, the good with the bad but never the same. An ocean view on Cape Cod, your sweater tied around your shoulders as you sip stem-cell tea would eventually become mundane if your eyes gorged on the foamy waves every day. Yes, this was it. Even driving down desolation row to a truck stop on the precipice of purgatory, variety was the chicken soup for the soul.

There wasn't much to expect as the establishment came into view and it held up to the low bar. Sitting slanted next to a dry creek bed, it was fronted with reclaimed barn wood that would have been better fit for a bonfire. The two gas pumps that stood for nostalgia's sake were rusted-out dead sentries that guarded a screen door patched in places with flattened soda cans. An orange cat, whether from the dust or its fur, traced its forgotten name in the air with a scabby tail. Gold eyes dismissed him as trivial as he opened the door to the sound of a bell sick with consumption. A subtle-rich smell of death that he knew all too well crept up his nose. The cooler along the far wall danced to its own tune with a flickering fluorescent beat. A few shelves were lined with a cast list from the island of misfit snacks. Root beer barrels fused together, a knock-off brand of animal crackers that displayed screaming creatures in an agony of captivity. Boxes of milk duds scattered from a tipped-over stack, a valiant attempt to reach the expired pork rinds before they were raptured to convenience-store heaven. Dated beer posters crooked with too many lost thumbtack holes, busty blondes for ever in suspended animation, never growing old. Closer to the front counter, next to a few bags of pumpkin seeds nobody would ever buy was what he would have to settle for, a large bag of teriyaki-flavored jerky. Now he hated sweet meat and always had. If the syrup from his pancakes touched the sausage links, breakfast was over. Pineapple on a pizza was a cardinal offense, rather cut your throat and use the blood instead of ketchup on a hot dog or burger but he would be goddamned if he'd leave this retail mausoleum empty-handed. The bag was dropped on the counter, but maybe there was another flavor in the back. There was the hum of a table saw whirring behind swinging doors with porthole windows that you would see in a restaurant in a Three Stooges movie. He couldn't make out anything beyond. Guess the clerk was making a birdhouse in between customer transactions.

"Hello?" He shouted. The saw slowed to a stop and some muffled murmuring could be heard. He had another urge to just walk out but who knew what was going to walk through those doors? He had to see this. Not what he expected, a clean-cut man in a short-sleeve plaid shirt tucked into jean shorts. Slip on Hush Puppies with no socks. Fit, slightly tan with thick hair. Looked like he belonged in a JC Penny catalog, playing Frisbee with his son or power-walking with his head down into a porn shop. The American male personified. Didn't add up, this live-action mannequin working in a dive in the middle of a hellhole.

"Well, hello yourself mister! What can I do ya for?" He slapped his hands down on the counter, smiling past the ears.

The Driver picked up the old jerky bag. "This the only bag you got?" The man eyed him close, determining something.

"Are you a police officer, friend?"

"Truck driver."

"Well, I had to ask. They have to say so if they are, I saw that on Murder She Wrote one time. My name is Andi, with an 'I'. Welcome to our little slice of heaven. You say you are interested in some jerky, then?"

"Yes."

"How much you need?" Andi's eyebrows hinged on a secret he was offering to let this stranger in on. A wink offered in an act of faith.

"How much you got?"

Andi smiled, relieved that this fella was willing to play ball. "Oh boy. Quite a bit. Quite. A. Bit. Yes sir-ee. You got a palate that hankers for the exotic?"

"Sure."

"Give me a sec." Andi walked backwards facing The Driver.

"You are gonna love this, I can already tell." He kicked back one of the swinging doors and disappeared. There were some old TV guides and slightly used flyswatters for sale in a sand bucket with a smiley face on it next to the register. Not really priced to move, The Driver noticed. He heard some rummaging and a loud, "Sssshhhh!" then Andi sauntered back up to the counter. He held out a thick piece of meat. The color lighter with some translucence The Driver found off-putting.

Try this dried piece of manna, my man." The Driver took it, gave it a quick sniff. Ostrich? Buffalo? "Bottoms up!" Andi threw a piece into his mouth. They chewed together, eyes locked. It was pretty good, he thought. Not too tough, savory with little greasiness on the tongue. He couldn't quite place the source but it was leagues better than that ass Teriyaki he was about to settle for.

"What do you think? Good, right?" Andi smacked as he attacked his piece, he had too many teeth. The Driver nodded. Andi gave him one more scrupulous look before again succumbing to a sheepish grin that hinted at big secrets. "Want to see how the sausage is made?" He cocked his head to the back room. The Driver shrugged. He was curious and he did really enjoy a good piece of jerky. Seeing an operation could be interesting. Inquiring minds want to know. He walked alongside Andi then around the counter.

"Right this way." They walked through the swinging doors into a macabre scene right out of an eighties low-budget slasher flick, the kind that is just raw enough to look hyper-realistic, where you wonder in that small part of your brain: "Are they really doing that?" A large square metal table dominated the center of the room. On it, a bearded young man, gagged and freshly missing his right arm. There was also a left leg missing but the stump was wrapped and the wound older. There were a few mattresses along the walls, stained with all manner of bodily fluids, shackles lying on them in wait for their next chore. Baby-puke-green-painted shelves stood out in frozen unchoreographed space with various tools of cutting, slicing, all in ill repair from no semblance of sanitation. The floor was covered with a thick layer of sawdust, soft on the feet, used to soak up whatever dripped down. The whole scene was a mix between a slaughterhouse and a barn on a cloudy day, just bright enough to do your task but too dark to read the instructions on the label on a brown bottle with some cotton stuck in the hole saturated with fumes while the pigs screamed in pain. Andi grabbed a machete and watched The Driver take it in, wary of a freak out, vomiting or an attack on his person. He seemed impressed by the lack of any sort of reaction.

"There is a story here, so don't think I'm some lunatic cannibal." He tapped the edge of the machete on the table, gathering up his lost thoughts, memories of sanity. "My wife and I were just on vacation, driving up to Canada. British Columbia, I hear it's beautiful. Were maybe going to swing over to Banff, you ever seen a postcard from there? Wowzer. So, anyhoo, as luck would have it, we blew a tire just outside of town on the interstate, the same road I'm sure you are traveling on. The car was a rental and we came to find out that there wasn't a spare. It was getting dark when this sadistic bastard you see on the table rolled up in his VW bus and offered to help, take us into town to call the rental company or at the least find a garage that could do a patch that would hold till we could reach Baker City. We pull up to this sorry excuse for a whatever the heck. My wife goes in to use the bathroom, I go to the pay phone. By the time I have found the number in the novella of paperwork they give you and dial, a rag full of chloroform is on my face. When I wake up I'm shackled right over there and my wife is already missing her arms. Isn't that right, Snatch?" Andi came down hard in the groin of Snatch with the butt end of the machete, producing a weak whimper through the gag. "What Ole Snatch here didn't know was that I'm a locksmith by trade. I was able to nab a hairpin from my wife who was thrashing around in immeasurable pain. Once Snatch processed some arm meat and closed up shop for the night, I picked the lock on the rather elementary restraints – they actually looked like something from a one-room frontier jail in the old Wild West – and went to gather up what was left of my wife but she had lost too much blood – the amateur had left her to die on the table. I don't know who taught him how to tie a tourniquet but his technique was straight bush league." Andi traced the machete down Snatch's remaining leg and sawed off his big toe. Snatch started to cry big wet tears as he couldn't scream with the thick oil rag taped around his mouth. Andi tossed the toe over his shoulder as if it was the empty shell of a peanut at a steak house. "Should I have called the cops? Probably, but I made the decision then and there to make this little imp suffer like my wife. My night was spent burying my soulmate and learning the intricacies of the human jerky trade. It is actually pretty simple. Cut strips to the preferred thickness, season to taste, hang to dry. The meat from the limbs isn't the best, Snatch has told me, the back and ass is where it's at. I'll find that out soon enough. Where was I? Snatch?" Yellow snot bubbled from Snatch's nose, making it hard for him to breathe. A panic wrapped up inside a hysterical cry is not pretty. The machete was drawn back up across his chest in the shape of a cross and blood rose up and out but flowed hesitant as if it knew that there wasn't much left to spare. "Oh wait, yeah, the next morning, the morning after I put my mutilated wife in this overly rocky, non-conducive-to-grave-digging soil, Snatch walked through the swinging doors, whistling Sugar Magnolia and carrying an iced coffee. I jumped into step right behind him and he got his own taste of sleepy time rag from the chloroform supply I had also discovered. So that about catches you up to the right now and yes, that delectable piece of jerky you sampled, that is 100 per cent pure Snatch, aged from the source 24 hours."

"Got more?" What the hell, it was pretty good.

"Let's see what's left on the rack." Andi walked about 20 feet to a large black metal cabinet set in the back corner. "This is what they call a dehydrator. This one looks homemade. Pretty decent welds, too. Well broken in. If the walls had ears… which they might, I haven't explored every nook and cranny." He pulled open a heavy door that creaked with a tiredness one hears in ancient, overused hinges. As he dove his head inside, The Driver pulled the tape and rag down out of Snatch's mouth, taking some red beard hair off in the process.

"Please, please kill me, man. Please."

"You talking to my boy?" Andi shouted across the room. "Ask him if he is hungry. This looks like a good batch of Snatch. Plenty to go around."

There was a circular saw that had seen its share of horror leaning precariously at the edge of the table. It was plugged in hot as far as he could tell. He could end it for this guy right now. Have to kill Andi, too, most likely, as the recently flipped insane don't take kindly to you stealing their revenge thunder.

"Listen man, this isn't my place, OK?" Snatch was talking fast in a moment of clarity, trying to plead his case with what little spirit he had left. "Me and my sister, we walked in a week or so ago. On our way back to U of O for fall. A couple of goons, have to be brothers, huge mofos like your size, they jumped us as soon as we walked in, locked us up in here. Then out of the blue they take off with Rose, my sister, man, said if I didn't bring some meat in to replace her they were gonna spit-roast her like those old jungle-tribe cartoons. They showed me what to do, how to process the meat, then knocked me out. I wake up I'm free. I didn't know what to do, man. I was gonna go to the cops but they would never find her, plus they are all probably related around here anyway. That's the way this backwoods shit works, you know what I'm saying?"

"Yawn, he telling you his origin story too?" Andi looked back over his shoulder. "Boo hoo hoo, I'm just a student, man. Just a kid. I'm from Rivertown, outside of Detroit. I have a twin sister, Rose. I don't even live here man. What a fibber!" He reached back into the dehydrator, transitioning from the mocking tone to whistling his own rendition of Sugar Magnolia as he loaded up a black plastic bag with handfuls of dried Snatch meat. "Who leaves Michigan to go to school in Oregon? The out of state tuition is ridiculous."

Snatch grabbed The Driver's forearm to refocus his attention, complete the confession, imploring this quiet priest to deliver him from hell. "Listen man, please, I just found this guy and his wife on the side of the road. I was driving around for hours freaking the fuck out. I had to do it, man. Who knows when those crazy ass cannibals are coming back? Fuckin' cannibals! Can you believe this shit? They'll be back, even if they did or didn't barbecue my sister. I know I'm toast, man. Kill me. This dude is going to drag this out at least till they come home, then who the hell knows what's gonna happen? Make it quick. Then get outta here, man. Tell somebody once you get to a real town. Maybe Rose will make it. I hope so. She's the smart one. Maybe she figured out a way. I should be in 19th-century feminist lit class right now, man, reading some Mary Shelley." Sounded convincing. The Driver wrestled his arm free and gripped the handle on the saw. Snatch closed his eyes in anticipation.

"Sister Rose. A Rose by any other name would smell as sweet, unless it's served rare with a baked potato or maybe a nice rice pilaf. You buying this savage's preposterous tale of woe? Look at that beard, who wears a beard these days? Cannibals and Santa, that's who." The Driver looked up to see that Andi was holding the end of the extension cord that had been recently plugged into the saw. He tossed over the plastic bag.

"That's like five pounds. Primo stuff. Takes a lot to make that, it shrinks like crazy and hey put your money away. That right there, it's on the house." Time slowed down as it tends to do at such forks in the road of life. There were a lot of variables, a lot of truths, lies. He waited in his removed judge bench up high for Lady Chance to reveal herself, offer up a sign of direction. He looked back down at Snatch who had opened his glassy eyes up to gaze upon oblivion.

A question was directed down at those receding waves of

consciousness. "That saying. Who wrote that? A rose by any other name would smell as sweet?" A correct answer, Chance had decreed, would end the suffering of what was left of the student Snatch. End all of this with a confiscated machete blade.

Andi raised his hand. "Oh, I know! I know! Pick me!" Trying to capture The Driver's attention away from the near-lifeless mess on the dull metal slab that licked cracked lips slowly with a complete absence of saliva.

"Shit, man. Bad time for a pop quiz," Snatch muttered, almost laughed. The Driver just shrugged.

"Gertrude... Stein?" he managed to get out.

"Wrong, dummy! It's frigging Bill Shakes! Romeo and Juliet! Duh! I played Mercutio in our community-theater production last summer in the park and I nailed it. 'No, 'tis not so deep as a well, nor so wide as a church-door; but 'tis enough, 'twill serve...'" Andi performed, Snatch struggled against his bindings and cried out for a death that was late to the station. Without another thought The Driver walked back out through the swinging doors carrying his jerky bag, one step closer to a world where Shakespearian dismemberment was not on the daily itinerary. He walked back into the sunshine, nodded a farewell to the still-languid cat and made it back to the rig, turning her over. Right before he slipped it into first gear, a muddy jacked-up pick-up truck with the "Don't Tread on Me" flag painted on the hood rolled up to the front of the store. Two giant, backwards-baseball-cap, flannel-shirt-and-stonewash-jeans-wearing, white-trash gentlemen slid out from either side, slammed shut the heavy Detroit-made doors and walked with foreboding purpose inside. He thought he could make out the back of a woman's head, a curly red tint, left behind in the center of the cab through the back window of the truck, framed on either side by a slew of white pride stickers affixed to the glass but he couldn't be sure. A Rose is a Rose is a Rose.

6

I WILL ALWAYS LOVE YOU

He had always wanted to go to Alaska. Seemed like a place that suited his peculiar disposition. Wide-open spaces, a spattering of people who have all run from something and want to be left well enough alone. Surviving months of near total darkness? Never would bother him – darkness emitted from his core. The cold? No problem, they made thermal underwear, fur hats, coats for that. They even had those chemical things you snapped and put in your pockets, instant heat. Then there were the summers: learning to fall asleep in the daylight, salmon so thick you could walk across their backs to the opposite bank, mosquitoes that would crack your windshield. It was a rugged land of extremes, something he had a tendency to indulge in. Maybe he could find some cabin away from all these roads one day, a place you have to reach by some other engine, plane or boat. He heard the state even paid you to live there, a yearly check that could go to booze or eight balls to share with chunky strippers or a new .45 for that bear that was getting a little too brave. You could catch arctic grayling with a pull tab off a beer can, moose stood around in your driveway begging you to fill the freezer with them. They never had it in the right place on those US cartoon placemats at roadside diners, always down in a little box next to Hawaii. No wonder the kids couldn't pick anything out on a map any more. Seeing the true scale yes, it was a jaunt up there for sure, traversing all that northwestern Canada had to offer and then some but when the offer came in that he had a hook to Anchorage if he could make it to Great Falls by Friday, he dropped it in the big hole.

Took some getting used to as he made his way north, going from sparse traffic as he crossed another territorial border to longer and longer intervals between even seeing another vehicle. Must be pure hell to make the run in the winter, with pop-up blizzards and black ice ready to jackknife you right off the side of a cliff face going 80 on a steep downhill grade. You would be there for days, trapped upside-down surviving on whatever ice you could reach as your nose and fingers slowly turned black. No, high July was the time to run, the birch trees leafed out next to all the scraggly black pine, bald eagles playing on the currents above, chasing a sun that would sit on the park bench of the horizon before jumping right back up into the sky. He had prepared for the lack of radio signal by making a few cassette tapes of the latest countdown that aired before his run. He recorded it, commercials and all, the biggest used car dealer in north central Montana was a repeat offender but that was fine, it all contributed to the flow, the anticipation of what hit was moving up with a bullet or fading gradually from the favor of American consciousness. It was a time capsule and he thought it a splendid idea to keep the tapes for posterity to listen to again in five, 10, 20 years. Would there even be radio then? Or tapes? He would have to transfer them over to CDs at some point or keep a jam box mothballed in some closet with a pack of a dozen D batteries. You had to prepare for the march of progress if you wanted to save a slice of days gone by. Speaking of slices, a piece of Snatch found his mouth as he pondered the advances of audio technology, he still had plenty in the bag as he had nursed the supply, even placing a dehydrating pouch in with the stash to keep it from going moldy. It was a super-special gourmet treat that could not be replenished, as he had zero desire to return to that neck of the woods. There was never a mention of the dominoes of torturous murders on the radio and he never felt the need to pick up a newspaper. Guess it had all worked out for the best. It had at least for him, best jerky he had ever tasted and it just seemed to get better and better. Those diabolical skinhead fellas, they were really on to something. What would an ad for that sound like after the number 12 song? Would it need a name that was mysterious and yet attractive to the masses? Taboo Turkey? I Can't Believe It's Not Beef? How many diehard survivalists on a 12-day hike would stuff it in their packs if they knew the origin? More than anyone would care to admit, he reckoned. Try anything once, even if it's a dried piece of your former locksmith's wife, who happened upon some tough luck.

By the time he crossed into the Yukon, he noticed how the balance had shifted from a brutal taming of the natural world, with rows of stoplights and concrete jungles to a balance where humans barely fought off the onslaught of the earth mother, living hard in little pockets that reminded him of the early settlers, where they could hear the wolf too close at night or watch their livestock wash away in a raging flood. In these parts, it was whole-hog wild. Rivers ran free and trees had never felt the saw-blade tooth. Animals might cross the two-lane artery daily their entire lives and never see a rolling hunk of steel. He felt outnumbered, outwitted, a foreign entity driving through green valleys speaking a language he could not understand. It was unsettling to know that still so much of the earth was still ruled by cruel mysteries, a food chain without our manipulations. He was a king among men but here, without this machine, he would flail blindly, a fawn oblivious to the predator drooling upwind, left to the scavengers to clean his bones. A challenge to be taken up, for sure – he wanted to learn the unwritten rules, to conquer as the glacier he could barely pick out in the range above, an unstoppable grinding force molding the rocks to his bidding. If he parked and started walking, he would certainly ascend, rise above all beasts, bend the primal forces to his will. He could feel the reserve of strength inside him rise, the tendons in his arms tighten electric. He gripped the wheel tighter, flipped the cassette. Top 10.

The days were running together but he was on the stretch run, leaving the fertile Matanuska Valley behind, heading south towards Anchorage and civilization was peeking back in its all-too-familiar grotesque splendor. He had already seen a convertible, top down, zoom past, soaking in the 2am twilight. A fast-food bag with its Styrofoam and greasy paper flung out the side. A discount store advertised the best mosquito repellant from Avon. A high-school parking lot was full of skateboard kids left without a curfew when the sun refused to extinguish the light. In contrast, the narrow road, the only road into the city, was squeezed between a steep range with snow still on its peaks and swampy deltas, close to the inlet where wide gray rivers full of silt seemed to multiply as they fingered their way to the salt. Why did people live here? It was not conducive to sprawl, the cheap too-close-to-the-road homes he could see were ragged, clumsy with unfinished additions, blue tarps nailed to rafters. More miles on the ATV parked on the lawn than the family car. Just barely hanging on to a semblance of normalcy in between the long winters. The fugitives pushed to the fringes. No longer willing to fight their way back to the center of the circle. It was titillating. These souls, they possessed a sad fire that had to be fed, stoked during the stretches of darkness. They had to. He could burn bright; would it sustain him as the shadows hung heavy and long over his soul?

Road construction ahead. A real doozy. Inefficient tax-funded government project at work. Up here with the midget summers, they probably lasted years. From his vantage point, this one looked properly FUBARed. They appeared to be widening the highway to four lanes but had temporarily created two new lanes that shot off in ninety-degree angles to either side of what would be the new road. So the southbound lane would immediately become a westbound lane for a few hundred yards, then turn hard left and run alongside of the construction slogging away in the middle. The northbound lane held a similar path. A multitude of signage alerted drivers of the approaching hard right, enough orange to be seen from the Hubble. He was already downshifting, preparing to cut the wheel when a red step-side pickup approached dead on from the other side, hauling balls. Someone had missed all the signs as the truck wasn't on the road at all but barreling through the construction, fishtailing in the loose gravel. It looked impossible to save as The Driver sat enthralled in the cab looking on, completely stopped in the road just before his turn. He hoped the maniac wouldn't sideswipe him or just plow into the rig head-on. It was a one-way game of chicken they were playing; he flexed his forearms, gripping the wheel tighter than ever before. There were a few cars pulled up behind him unaware of the coming threat, blasting their horns but he wasn't moving until he saw where this was going. As the pickup got closer, he could see three people in the cab and three more hanging on for dear life in the back. The situation had all the ingredients of some seriously tragic stew. Then, whether from skill or divinity, the pick-up slowed and seemed to regain control, albeit sliding sideways along a 20-foot embankment. The Driver couldn't help but smile at this, impressed with what had to be a calmness in the operator as most would have succumbed to panic, let Jesus take the wheel or just yanked to one side until the truck went airborne. Just before it came to a stop, a last bit of bad luck reared its head and the front right tire broke the bead and the rim caught hard dirt. The truck was at that point traveling at only about five miles per hour, so the events transpired in seemingly slow motion. The truck lurched over on its side like a hippo shot with a dart. The three people in the bed and what looked like an empty keg of beer dropped out. The truck then rolled over on its roof, with those who had fallen perfectly framed inside the bed, miraculously free of being crushed when it made its final quarter revolution and landed with a gentle poof of dust on its left side, not 15 yards away from the big rig. At first there was nothing, no movement, no sound, just a vacuum of shock. A few seagulls flew over as if the national anthem had just concluded. Then the passenger door opened up to the sky. The crash refugees from the back began to stand and wander in different dumbstruck directions. The cabmates appeared as if climbing out of a bomb shelter after a nuclear holocaust, not sure if the air was breathable. A skinny kid with plenty of arm ink was the first out, helping a thick-dyed blonde in a jean jacket climb to the ground. Last was a stocky jock with a mullet under an askew backwards baseball cap. He had a carefree face and golden eyes, a natural ringleader who got too close to the lions. The Driver stepped out and walked towards them, feeling a strange kinship with this fellow road warrior.

"Is everybody cool?" the mullet kid asked. A few nods, mostly blank stares. He walked slowly around surveying his wrecked truck. The roof was caved in, windshield spider-webbed. Looked totaled.

"Nice work. Almost had it." The Driver said from a close distance.

"Shoulda taken that left turn in Albuquerque right? Yeah. I was shifting down like a mo fo. Think I blew a tire or we would've been golden. We were bee-lining it to Wasilla to get this keg switched out. Only place around that sells this late. People at the party gonna be pissed."

"Lucky nobody got crushed." The skinny tatted dude wasn't as pleasant. He was rubbing his shoulder as if a genie might pop out of his ass.

"You hurt, Mitch?"

"Just my shoulder, man, you guys all landed on me."

"You saying I'm fat, sugar?" The girl had pulled out a bent joint and was trying to find a lighter. Mitch produced one.

"No way, baby. You know I like you on top."

"Hey, we gotta get out of here. You guys help me push it back over." The kid threw his weight into the roof. Nobody else was jumping to his assistance, a gaggle of stoners still dazed.

"I got it." The Driver threw his meat hooks on to the roof and pushed, got the truck rocking, soon enough he gave it one last monster shove and the truck creaked back on to its wheels.

"Damn, dude." The kid smiled and went to work on changing the flat. His truck-bed passengers climbed zombie-like right back over the tailgate, waiting for the train to leave the station. It was eerie as all three looked exactly the same, lean, sporting ginger-fros and wearing matching high-school football jerseys, the only difference being the numbers on their chests, a sequence in the low eighties. It was if they were made from the same assembly-line mold at the human factory. The Driver picked up the empty keg and placed it in with them. The triplets looked at him as if he were an apparition, a golden Golem created to set things back in order. The kid must have known his way around roadside repairs because he was tightening the lug nuts on the spare like a man possessed by a Daytona pit crew. A guy wearing horn-rim glasses and too much ponytail walked up to the scene from one of the vehicles behind the big rig as the last three piled into the cab hoping the wreck would start.

"Hey kid, you can't leave the scene of an accident. You have to wait for the cops. It's against the law. I will record your plate number and report you."

"Bullshit. Is anybody hurt?" he asked his gang. Silence. "Single-vehicle accident, pal. Nobody hurt. Now fuck off out of the way." He turned the key, the truck somehow roared to life. "Yeah, girl. Get us home now. Nice and easy, I promise." He patted the top of the dash, coaxing his fatally injured horse for one final ride back to the stable. Those in front had to duck down under the crushed roof and there were maybe a few inches of clean windshield to see through. He turned to The Driver who was still standing in the road, grinning like a fool.

"Hey man, I don't know your deal but you mind giving us a

bit of an escort back to Anchorage? It would help if I had something big to follow and well, you fit the bill."

"Sure." The Driver spun around and bumped into the ponytail narc, knocking him square on his ass.

"Ha! Pussy." The young owner of the beat-up chariot slid the
shifter softly into drive. Six matching middle fingers rose above
the tailgate to bid a fond farewell to the do-gooder scrambling to
his feet failing to catch the license plate and soon enough they
were heading home, pride wounded and shell-shocked but
mostly healthy, just lacking a full keg to keep the party alive till
breakfast.

A friendly knock woke him from a deep slumber, away from
being trapped inside howling winds, debris flying around him
as he fell from a great height through a bottomless night sky, his
father's severed head on a plate calling out orders, a ringing bell
that transformed into a crying half-wolf infant. She hovering
behind his ear screaming unintelligible threats, bouncing around
the room with the body of a crow. Her chest cavity opens with a
zipper but instead of a beating heart a ball of slithering worms,
the kind from the deep earth that burrow inside coffins. A shake
of the head relegated it to a quickly forgotten nightmare, similar
to the many that the sandman played from the dream juke that
left him sweaty but clear. Dark unconscious visions tended to
rinse out his soul as if confessing sins to the netherworld. The
demolition derby kid from earlier in the morning was pressing
his face against the glass trying to peer into his sanctum.

"Yo man, you awake?" The Driver rose from wet sheets and
leaned forward, cracked the door. He smiled and waved, a
foreign act that didn't feel forced for once.

"You want some food? We're grilling some meat, drinking
beers. Other side of the parking lot over there. C'mon with it."
Sounded like an ambitious breakfast till he saw the level of the
sun, had to be late afternoon, or night. Time was quickly losing
relevance. He threw on a relatively fresh pair of overalls and
killed a bottle of stale grape soda he had bought at some Cana-

dian wilderness general store. He opened the door and a swarm of mosquitoes was happy to greet him. He was parked on the side of the road in front of a prison-blue apartment complex, all cinder blocks and tiny windows. The building resembled a motel in some perpetually bombarded middle-eastern city somehow always escaping a direct hit. The prison vibe was reinforced by a group of young men on the far end of the parking lot wearing a universal uniform of cutoff jeans and pale torsos, with their T-shirts tucked in the back pocket, taking turns grunting on a bench press or otherwise yelling over the heavy-metal music coming from the open windows of a first-floor residence. He recognized the triplets as they mind-melded an endless game of hacky sack on the cracked pavement. There was indeed an old black barrel-style grill going, the meat smoke blowing over bottles of beer being drained and mixing in with puffs of off-brand cigarettes. Would be enough to intimidate most men of any age or stature but The Driver as usual refused to be fazed as he walked up to receive his subjects.

"There he is! Fuckin' denim Sasquatch! Get yourself a brew, ya bad mo fo!" The kid pointed to a dented-up cooler that had held anything from Kenai salmon to Homer halibut to Talkeetna moose parts during its illustrious history. He just stood there among these not-quite-yet men, doing everything in their power to overcompensate. A couple of the larger teens gave him challenging looks but there wasn't much resolve behind them.

"By the way, my name's Brick. These dipshits are the wreckin' crew, I guess. They're all tough guys, at least they think so. Nobody is gonna fuck with you, though, number one you're my boy and number two, I mean Jesus, look at you. I've always made it a mission to be best friends with the baddest dudes around. That way you can mostly avoid getting your ass kicked. Thing is no matter how good at ass-kicking you are, there is always somebody around the corner who can kick your ass. You may be the exception to that rule though, goddamn brick house." Brick laughed hard at that one, a dribble of beer fizz came out of his nose. "Ouch, son of a bitch that stings! What's up? You not a drinker? You want something else? Smoke a bowl?"

"I'm good. Hungry." Brick grabbed his arm and pulled him over to the grill. Mitch was manning, flipping steaks and burgers with precision. Flashes of his dad at the lunch-rush griddle wiped across the back of The Driver's eyes.

"Mitch here is a pro. Head line cook at the Rooster. Half these delinquents work there. Burger joint. Good food. Better pussy. Not a lot of hot chicks around here but about all of them take an apron and swim through the Rooster at some point and they are not shy. Something about having the power to pick and choose the dick you want makes girls loose as a roofied goose. What you want? Mitch will fix you up. We got moose steak, moose burgers. Fucking delicacy. Get after it. I need another beer and a bong rip before I dig in."

"Thanks." As Brick receded inside the apartment, The Driver realized he may have said that word for the first time in his life. It was a jarring revelation. Mitch fixed up a double patty with crispy parmesan cheese on a toasted brioche bun and handed it over.

"That'll make you cum." The Driver took a bite. Hands down the best burger or possibly the best thing period he had ever tasted other than his Snatch stash. He closed his eyes and focused in on the explosion going on inside his mouth.

"Good, right?" Mitch asked without looking at anything but the sizzle in front of him. The Driver nodded. "We may look like a bunch of convicts but the food is straight Michelin. At least when I'm around." Mitch was up in the bush for the right reasons. Warrants in Cali for possession of various drugs and handguns, no sick grandmother to keep him there. He made three times the money hustling the patties, dealing a little weed and blow to his coworkers than he ever did back home. He was the de facto father figure of the group, more The Driver's age if not a little his senior. Grateful and tranquil, a contrast to the old gang ink up and down his arms he no longer identified with. He could have been anything, a bank manager or on the city council but he had an appearance to both battle and still embrace. The double burger was gone and replaced by a rare steak topped with Boursin cheese and a side of German potato salad before Brick found his way back outside.

"Good shit, right? Mitch is a damn animal-flesh magician." The Driver grunted his agreement. The food was high-octane gasoline straight into his veins. He had been living on jerky and off-brand soda for a week. "You want to go for a ride? I gotta pick up a little sumpin' sumpin'. It's not far. You know what, kumquat? I've never been in a Mack truck before... you cool driving? I'd drive but my ride is pretty much out of commission. What ya say, Maverick?" The Driver had dropped his hook before crashing out, so it wasn't a big deal to toot around. He had actually begun to enjoy experiencing the light freedom that came without a load attached. No responsibility, no racing the clock. Might be fun to see a bit of this weird amalgamation of urbanization and savageness, how the rough edges of the plates ground together.

They jumped on to C Street down south on the way up into downtown. The burg of Anchorage looked much like any other, a lot of squat buildings that had lost street fights with the elements. An inordinate amount of yellow Subarus and ugly four-wheel-drive AMC Eagles with rusted-out bodies from the salt thrown on the roads. They passed a small lake with young people perched on towels on a steep hill that led down to the water, a whole bunch of bikinis and bare skin on display for it being in the low seventies. "Slow down, see if I recognize any betties out there. Pulled a lot of tuna out of that lake. The fishing in the summer is mighty good, wink wink." Brick pressed his face against the glass but nothing seemed to move the meter so they continued as a steady stream of bush planes flew low overhead to land in smooth spray on Lake Hood a few blocks to the west. Lots of lights, lots of shifting but The Driver enjoyed it, jumping on the green lights by revving through first gear into second. The truck was surprisingly quick off the blocks without a load of tonnage for the discerning consumer dragging it down. Was he showing off? Sure. He liked this Brick and wanted to be liked by him. He had never had a friend other than Petty. That eccentric coot. Taught him everything and nothing at the same time.

"This is pretty damn cool. Feel like I'm riding on a stepladder." Brick was excited, bouncing on the seat like a toddler as they tore past storage facilities and dive bars from such an elevated perspective. He turned his nose up at the local pop station The Driver had found on the dial.

"You got any Metallica?" Some stink eye from the left persuaded him to drop any further musical criticism. "So you're probably wondering why a dude who just pretty much totaled the shit out of his beautiful pickup isn't more down in the dumps. It's all good in the hood. I'm going down to college in September. University of Oregon. Gonna be a duck." The Driver perked up an eyebrow at the mention, small world indeed. "Was stressing over the logistics of driving but now I can fly. I'll sell what's left of Loretta, party for a couple of months with not a care in the world then I'm out. Been high time I sponsored the fun for a stretch. Plus, chicks love the dude who is providing the party favors. I'm about to get more trim than a barbershop. You dig it?"

"Man with a plan. College is good for certain people. Expands the view of the world. Reveals maps to the roads less traveled."

"Exactly man. It's like living in a snow globe up here. I want to hang with some dudes from Demark, Cameroon. Cameroonians?"

"Sounds right."

"Yeah, all the flavors. Baskin-Robbins of humanity. The first step of manhood is realizing you don't know shit about the world. NBC Thursday nights only gets you so far." Brick pulled out a pinch hitter and took a long drag as he tried to crack the window. He noticed the lack of buttons and turned to the driver, mouthed: "What the fuck?" The Driver laughed and lowered the glass a few inches. Brick exhaled the smoke and coughed hard and raspy.

"Don't get a lot of running buddies, I surmise?"

"Nope."

"What other tricky shit you got in here? Ejection seat? Trap door?" He looked around knocking on the dash in a few places like he was in a haunted mansion. He was about to peek around in the back when The Driver slammed the brakes, throwing Brick off his seat.

"Sorry. Yellow light. Thought I had it." Baby steps, friend-o. Bedroom door stays closed.

"It's cool. I didn't need those ribs.' Brick gave a shrug-it-off cough. Took a testing deep breath. Nothing that could hamper the quest. "You see the garage up the hill there on the other side of the intersection? That's our destination. There is a pad upstairs. Marny lives there. Her dad owns the garage, likes to keep her close. She's gonna hook us up. All the way up. To the moon!"

A foosball table right past the front door dominated the tiny apartment, the kind of cheap afterthought of a living space where there is no defining line between the kitchen and living room. Marny was still sporting Patrick Nagel art inside gold frames on the walls. Lots of glass and tall lamps fought for level purchase on a ratty blue carpet. There were a few people on a worn corduroy sectional, a girl who couldn't have been to a prom yet breastfeeding a baby, a couple of grease monkeys wearing "Lake Otis Lube" T-shirts and billowy pants laden with 10w-30 stains enjoying the nipple show with whispers and giggles. A few more of the city's finest were obscured by dank smoke around the kitchen sink.

"Brick! Yeah baby! Yeah! Get over here and hit this gravity

bong!" A tall but doughy guy in a hockey jersey held up the top half of a plastic gallon milk jug.

"You game?" Brick asked. The Driver stood still, taking up most of the doorway fighting a tide of claustrophobia.

"In or out? Don't need the Klootches knowing my business!" A woman had walked up to the other side of the foosball table from the back bedroom. Brick pulled The Driver up a step and closed the door.

"Sorry Marny. He's new blood."

"Insolent mouth breathers. You kids today." Ironically, it was easy to see that Marny was one of the youngest there. Her flawless pink skin was a blush as she wrapped a kimono too tight around her thick frame. "Brick. You come with me." Marny did an about-face and walked back through the dark hallway. Brick winked at the Driver and followed.

"Hey Conan, get over here and take his hit. It'll put you in the outer space of outer space, brother." The hockey boy motioned him over with a Cheshire cat smile. Thinking he had to do something or he would just start throwing people and furniture around the room like a crazed gorilla, The Driver tentatively made his way over to join the gravity bong session, already in progress.

"I think we're gonna need a bigger sink." A girl who looked like an extra in a Whitesnake video was destroying a piece of cinnamon gum while sitting on the limited counter space watching the show. She scooted over a few inches unconsciously at the approach of The Driver.

"We could try the bathtub." The hockey guy missed the easy reference like the empty net in the state semifinals. A gimmie that cost his team the season. A team that still held it against him in bitter silence. He was one of those who perpetually failed to connect with what the world was generous enough to afford them.

"Might want to try Cook Inlet." The girl had lost interest in the conversation before it started, attention now focused on checking for split ends among her sprayed-up bangs in the mirror of her compact. "Suck slow. Not only is that my advice, it's a life lesson." She raised her head up to meet his eyes with a flutter of eyelids that a child would consider seductive from watching cartoons. The fact that he had never taken any sort of drug of any kind was hammering away at his reasoning skills. Better to not think about it, what was the worst that could happen? He was the elephant in the room, his head would scrape the ceiling if he raised up his heels a few inches. No one would challenge him if he cried, puked, shit his pants or spoke in tongues.

"Put one hand over the top, the other grabs the handle of the jug, take a big exhale out, there ya go, now wrap your lips around the mouth, push down and inhale." He did as instructed. The smoke flowed strong down into him as if from a broken dam. The group cheered him on. He pushed until he felt the water on his face. Then he raised up and looked out the tiny kitchen window. From the perch on the hill you could see a lot of the city. He was fascinated by all the different colors of lights in the late afternoon. How they were so vibrant, despite the daylight. The red, yellow, green of the changing stoplight, the hot blue of a revolving diner sign, the fire-orange dollar of a pawn shop teasing through a reinforced window, the fuzzy white glow of the welcoming blink of a neon beer sign in a liquor store a block away. He could read the signs. He could read everything. All the colors. At once.

"Is dude gonna exhale?" the girl asked, fascinated. Usually a virgin would be hacking up a lung right now, breaking blood vessels in their eyes as they struggled to remain conscious. This freak, he hadn't even moved.

"Bro? You OK?" A hand on his shoulder felt foreign, the pressure breaking through a membrane that insulated his awareness of the cosmic soup, the oneness of things. Everyone in the apartment, other than Marny and Brick and whatever other wicked orchestra was being conducted in the back of the house, were now surrounding him, staring, watching, waiting for the smoke to come out – was he to be the new pope? He turned around, faced the crowd. He exhaled nothing but invisible carbon dioxide. The crowd cheered.

"The messiah!" The girl laughed and felt the urge to lean over and kiss him deep on the mouth. She felt that primal organic current of seismic energy pass through her, from her lips to her toe rings. The vibration stayed with her the rest of the day; her core invaded by the power of kings. The meek would inherit the earth, but not until this man was done with it. The Driver walked the few steps to the foosball table. The little men impaled on rods below him silent, still and yearning for his control was an apt metaphor for the boundless arena his mind was now playing in.

"You want a piece of Scotty P, big man?" Scotty, pulling off his hockey jersey to reveal an ill-fitting mustard-stained wife-beater, was always up for a game, writing checks his hand-eye coordination repeatedly failed to cash.

"P stands for pancakes. Look at those nipples. Pancakes. Why would you wear a tank top with those areolas, dude? Nobody wants to see that."

"Shut your hole, Amber. You've never seen my nipples – we always screw doggy style."

"You wish, fat boy!" Amber jumped off the counter aiming to take a pound of flesh and in Scotty's case, maybe a few more but pulled up quiet as a church mouse as she got to the table. The golden god had calmed her with his mind and she knew it. Embraced the danger in his immensity. She stood next to The Driver, drawing her line in the sand by claiming her champion. "Take this fool down." He peered down at the sassy girl. She fell out of her boat into his eyes, a warm expansive emerald ocean of his surface thoughts and she treaded there peacefully but there was also an ice-cold pocket down deep, it skimmed the underside of her feet giving her a chill. Her budding love was singed with fright, a marshmallow too close to the campfire. A typical teenager jaded to protect a vulnerable innocence, she realized just then he could easily bite through her hard candy shell. She thought she might have peed herself a little until she could break his gaze. Scotty dropped the ball into play prematurely to get off an unfair easy shot. He missed wide.

The game just got uglier from there. The Driver had never touched a foosball table before but his wrists snapped the wooden warriors with pinpoint ferocity. With every point, the peanut gallery unleashed a teasing of Scotty that grew more and more intense. His past failures served him well as he kept his cool, surrendering to the bad beats like some sad literary figure who long ago accepted the tragic fate his author created. Amber slid each bead across as the goals piled up, the numbers reinforcing her good judgment in picking the right side of the battle. This strange white knight was defending her honor and it elevated her self-worth beyond the rooftops. Brick reappeared among the clamor and took in the scene, feeling pride for introducing this omnipotent force upon his circle of friends.

"Scotty, raise the white flag, no one deserves a beat-down like this." He patted The Driver on the back. "You having fun, buddy?" He got a slow nod in response as the ball was again smacked deep into the opposite goal. There was to be no quarter given to Scotty Pancakes this day. They played on past the point where it was fun for the gang to ridicule their village idiot. Five games. Shut outs. Scotty looked up with a familiar sigh of defeat after the loud slap of the final nail faded.

"Good game, man. I mean not for me but good game." He reached across to shake hands. The Driver looked around for Brick who was in a deep conversation with the new mom on the couch, getting more info than he would ever need about the finer points of breast milk. Scotty was left hanging. A final insult.

"Who's got next?" He took it in his stride. Screw this guy. He hoped never to see him again, dreaded the fact that he might. Brick looked up and the big man was standing right behind the new mom. Good thing she wasn't looking as it might have rendered her dry.

"You ready to bail, my foosball prodigy?"

"Yeah."

"Cool. Let's make like hay and bail." Brick blew a kiss at the suckling baby and made for the door, completing a few intricately choreographed secret handshakes with his constituents along the way as a good mayor should. Amber was already stationed at the exit to see her new beau off to war. She slipped a glossy photo of the northern lights over the frozen Chugach into his hip pocket, her fingers lingering in his particular warmth.

"Stole it off the fridge. It's the aurora borealis. Wrote my number on the back. If you ever learn how to talk, give me a ring." He nodded and gave her a crooked smile that would sate her for years.

Back in the truck he felt a faint ping of paranoia that he might not be able to drive, might not remember. Once he heard the rough purr of the engine, he put that to rest. They merged into traffic, albeit at a snail-on-ludes' pace.

"Slow and low that is the tempo, I see. You must be really baked Alaska, bud. You need a boost. You gotta have some Metallica in here." Brick went to hunt again but there was nowhere to look. No glove box, no console. He remembered what happened last time he took a gander in the back so instead he concentrated on the speedometer and the laziness of the needle. "Hope we get home before the first snow." Now The Driver was paranoid all over again that he was driving too slow. He felt like he was sitting in a Jacuzzi of cream cheese. An obnoxious high-pitched car horn sounded behind him. He made his eyes slide over to the rearview mirror where he could just make out a tiny car tailgating him tight. Should he pull over, let it pass? Surrender to this little twerp? He had never been honked at before. The road was his mistress; he was not to be cuckolded by some foreign-built compact car. He felt insulted, his ears burned. He looked to his ally, his wingman for counsel. Brick was looking at the side mirror, laughing his ass off.

"Look at this fucking guy! Honking at you! I love it! I think he just flipped you the bird too! Glorious! Something I forgot to tell you, people up here, road rage is on a whole 'nother level. It's a point of pride with these psychos. I once got into a fistfight sitting in the parking lot of a Taco Bell because the guy in the car next to me didn't like how I rolled down my window. A lot of the really evil sadists, they drive around just looking for it. You see a fight in the streets at least once a week. Smashed-in windows, blood smeared all over the door. People just drive around the lost teeth. This dude here, he wants to rumble. He has no idea what he is getting into. Oh baby, it's gonna be epic. Wish I had a camera." The car shot into the other lane and the four-cylinder engine chugged hard enough to swerve in front of the rig. The other driver then immediately slammed on his brake. "Classic move." Brick braced his hand against the dash to brace for impact but The Driver downshifted and swerved right just enough to avoid rear-ending what appeared to be a Fiat. "This guy is a lunatic! You could have monster-trucked his toy car ass! He wants a punchin' party!" There was a frozen moment as if everyone was being painted for an over-the-fireplace renaissance portrait, the truck half in, half out of the road, the Fiat inches in front. Then Brick snapped back to life. "You need to get the jump on this pumpkin head. Be the aggressor. You also need a fast-forward, you can't kick ass in ganja funk town. Take this speed bump of yayo." After a quick reach into his jeans pocket, he dabbed a dime-sized pile of cocaine on the back of his hand and shoved it under The Driver's nose. It was snorted up without deliberation. "That's my boy! Go tear his head off!" Everything brightened. The hazy fog in his brain burned off time-lapse style. He felt the fibers of every muscle banging the battle drums. He could have easily ripped the door off the truck and thrown it into the sun. The immensity of vigor kept expanding, his tongue contorted inside his mouth like a weighted-down coil. So this was drugs, a chemical bridge to being a superhuman. An uncontained volcano of strength. A raging bull among a Pamplona horde of brittle glass statues. An atomic bomb in the New Mexico desert melting mannequins stationed by the clothesline. He truly didn't know if he could corral this essence, if he could give the code a fair shake. A dot on the horizon of rational thought declared if the Fiat drove away, he would let it go. Reward the cooler head, forgive this transgression as a near-miss initiation into a strange culture. He would just climb up a building instead, fight the biplanes buzzing by, wind up standing triumphant at the top shaking his fists at God, demand a parley. A small moan of pleasure escaped his twitchy lips when the driver side door of the Fiat opened up, for some reason the person inside was struggling to exit. The Driver decided to heed his trainer's advice and he jumped out of the truck, bypassing the sideboard and landing solid with a crackling thud on the street. He took giant steps towards the little car, wondering if he should just lift it up and crush it like a beer can. The mystery to why he was not immediately met by his opponent became evident as he approached, two comically large clown shoes were making it difficult to exit. The shoes matched a purple polka-dotted billowing one-piece jumpsuit, while green hair and yellow diamonds around the eyes framed the white grease-painted face.

"Holy shit! It's a clown! Watch out! There may be 12 more in there!" Brick yelled, laughing his ass off from the passenger-door sideboard of the truck.

"Making me late for my birthday gig, grandma! You ever heard of acceleration?" The clown had not looked up yet as he was still trying to work his shoes out of the car. "Let me get out of here so I make a balloon animal out of your ball sack, ya dipshit!"

He popped the last shoe out on to the pavement then looked up. And up. Just as he mouthed, "Oh no," a Thor's-hammer fist flew down from the vengeful heavens into his face as a red nose tumbled on to the street, emitting a sad squeak, happy to have escaped the siege. The hits kept coming, The Driver gripping the green wig with the other hand to keep the target in place as he dealt savage blow after savage blow. White and red flew together to create a pink mist in the air. Brick watched, now leaning up against the grill of the truck, eating a handful of sunflower seeds.

"Hey, Hulk, think you won. Let's make like Pee-Wee and beat it." The Driver failed to acknowledge the obvious and continued to blast into the clown's nasal cavity searching for an oil strike. Three more direct hits and Brick sprinted over in a panic, trying to pull The Driver away from the mutilated mess of flesh and bright satin. The Driver finally stilled with his new buddy hanging on his back, teeth grinding as a few beads of sweat meandered down his jawline. Brick looked down at the clown's face and had to fight retching. There wasn't much more than a melted hole now. Knuckles must have tickled the back of the skull. Now that the line had snapped and released all tension, The Driver walked back to the truck calmly as if he had just filled the tank and they drove off around the mess inside the Fiat and on up the street. For him the entire event was put away inside the Christmas decorations box on January 2. Brick stole mesmerized glances of the hand on the gear shifter, drying blood, meat and paint creating an abstract ballet as the muscles flexed the handle up or down. It was a weighty, uneasy silence inside the cab until the truck sat again idling in front of the apartment and Brick surmised they had not been followed. He turned to his new brother-in-arms, who he now knew not only to be a reserved good Samaritan with a predilection for parlor games but also a murderer of clowns. Oh well, he always hated clowns.

He turned to The Driver, who stared ahead at some billowing wheat field in his mind as the passenger door creaked open, "Moving forward, hoss, I think you should go by the credo the old wise man Johnny Cash suggested, let that cocaine be."

7

THE SIGN

"You doin' all right back there, partner? Thought I heard some stirrin' about." He opened his eyes to darkness but the sensation of movement was what eased him awake. A faint glow of a dashboard was the first thing he could make out from his position pinned back deep in the back of the sleeper cabin. He felt a hoop around his thumb, fingernail scratching at the remnants of dried blood. It helped him remember where he was and why. It always would, that relic from Her. A talisman forged from the evil fires. As he adjusted to the dimness, a pair of wizened grey eyes met his in the rearview mirror.

"You been asleep since Bama. Was hoping you wasn't gonna die back there. Internal injuries or some shit. You were in a helluva state when I got to ya. Stiff as a board, pupils bigger than frisbees. Didn't want to have to drop your John Doe ass carcass behind a Stuckey's, give the vultures a boy-buffet. Saw a lot of big nasty crows feasting on folks dodging Charlie's rounds on Hamburger Hill. Them bastards were fearless gluttons, let me tell ya. They were in the clean-up business and business was good during that God-forsaken war. It sure ain't pretty. They go after the soft stuff first. Really get after women and children. Path of least resistance, I reckon. Maybe I was a buzzard in a past life 'cause that's always been my motto. Name's Petty but you can call me Petty or asshole, been told they amount to about the same." The voice was gravel in a dull-bladed blender but gentle, one that might emit from an old cowboy with a white hat and a checkered past. A crescent moon hovered above the windshield and a sweet-smelling breeze sneaked through the cracked driver window, mixing with the rich smoke of pipe tobacco. He had never lain supine in a vehicle before, it was comforting, the motion, the slight tossing and bumping about. A second womb in which to prepare for his rebirth. What there wasn't was panic as to where he found himself, was this strange man a monster sharpening his teeth, biding his time? Indifferent Charon ferrying him to the other shore? A defense mechanism had followed some unimaginable catastrophe and torn up the pieces of his recent past and blown them to the corners and dark alleys. He couldn't remember what had happened, nor did he care to. He was at least able to realize that, whatever it was, he wasn't missing much. Surrendering to the road, he let it rock him softly. Rock a-bye baby.

"Get you some more shut-eye kid. I'll wake you up when we hit Tampa." Petty turned the radio low and puffed away to the slow country beat.

"Jump on I-10 and take 19 out of Tallahassee. Then pop over to the parkway at Crystal River. At least an hour quicker than I-75." The Kid rolled back to put his forehead on the soothing cold metal wall as Petty turned on the visor light and studied his roadmap.

"Son of a bitch," Petty said to himself, tracing the route with the lip of his pipe. The kid was dead-on balls.

A wistful smile formed from the dream painted his face in the morning light. He was parked in the very back of a truck stop bordered by tall wet pine, flanked by some busted-up pallets and an old blue church bus on blocks that had been commandeered by a gang of stray cats who had leisurely returned from their night shift of fights and mating under the stars. A lone phone booth with a drippy red spray-painted anarchy symbol anchored on to the back corner of a one-story cement restaurant beckoned him. He felt around in his pocket and pulled out a single quarter as if fate once again dictated his actions. He wasn't going to make today the day he ignored the subtle signs of the cosmos so out he climbed, holding Amber's phone number delicately, protecting it from any unseen elemental threats.

"Go ahead caller. You are on the air." Amber's voice stirred something deep and abstract inside him but she wasn't the reason for the season. "Hello? Big man? Is that you? I bet it is. I recognize that hot breathing. Damn, I've missed you. Last real man to cross my path. Where are you? Rescue me from the castle!"

"Eugene… Brick?"

"Brick? That moose dick? He's too good for ole AK nowadays. College man. I talked to him last week, he's sending us up some gnarly shrooms, trading out for the Matanuska Thunder Fuck. He said they just give fat caps away down there. Garbage bags full sitting in the corner of every kitchen, help yourself. I would be trippin' balls 24/7. Watching the econ 101 professor's head melt into a kaleidoscope of strawberry milk. Probably best I stick to the local community college. At least until you come to your senses and whisk my tight teenage ass away."

"Brick."

"Right. I don't talk to you for a year and that's all you can muster. Oh well, we have the rest of our lives to loosen that tasty tongue. You wanna know where Brick is. As far as I know Brick is at the Dead show at the football stadium. Him and some of his new enlightened circle-jerk buddies are camped out in the parking lot for the three-day ripe armpit and dirty ass extravaganza. He was bragging all about this VW camper van he has. It's blue, I believe. That's all I know."

"Thank you, Amber."

"I hope you know I love you, you giant teddy bear."

He put the receiver back in the cradle as a homeless man in a frayed velvet jumpsuit and a feather boa came around the corner looking for empty bottles then thought better of it. He heard those three little words but they didn't register, an incorrect password. They were not in his canon. He needed to reconnect with his only friend first. It had been a long while since he had experienced a bond with another. Since Petty.

By the time Petty happened by and took him under his wing, his future mentor didn't have a home. He had two. Two homes. Along with two wives and two sets of children. They were spaced strategically to enjoy a vastly different American experience. One was a sprawling single-story cabin nestled below the green mass of a mountain outside of Robbinsville, North Carolina, where money was an abstract concept to most and advertising was hand painted and invariably misspelled. The other just outside of Galveston, Texas, a pink house on stilts overlooking the brown hue of the western Gulf waiting with brave ignorance for the next hurricane. How he was able to afford supporting two families was never explained but he never seemed to be too worried about a set of braces or new tires for a jeep. Over the years they spent together, Petty took his apprentice to meet both broods. There was an unspoken agreement that The Kid would keep his secret and, given as The Kid had a natural disposition of general silence, Petty felt secure the cat would stay down at the bottom of the bag. Petty always said that The Kid reminded him in a lot of ways of his mountain wife, Lucinda. Dark and malevolent in her manner, she slowly became wise in those mystic unknowing ways that something was amiss. It was easy to see that she would be the one to put Petty six feet under if she discovered the truth. She was on a low branch of a family tree that leaved at least half Cherokee, gliding just below the wooden beams with cinnamon skin and big chocolate-drop eyes. She took kindly to the kindred spirit she found in The Kid, baking him sweet cornbread and squeezing an extra lemon slice or two in his tea because he ate one once out of his glass. Rarely did one witness any tokens of affection directed at her husband. There was a sizzling tension between her and Petty that lasted from the time he broke the threshold of the house till the time he exited back on to the highways and byways. Lucinda was working a perpetual case and was constantly on the lookout for clues, receipts, smells on the collar. If not for the late-night sounds of violent passion carrying out into the forest from their open window, one would have thought they were rivals rather than lovers. That animalistic coupling had produced two children, a teenage boy, Rocky, who was counting down the days until he could enlist by running up and down the switchbacks hauling a backpack full of river rocks and his younger sister Lilac, who was happiest while in conversation with whatever hungry wayward yard dog had followed her home and let her dress them up from her extensive dog wardrobe. She could be found having imaginary tea with a three-legged mutt in a tutu, a wiener-dog fireman or an old basset hound in scrubs, scratching absent-mindedly at the fleabites she had incurred during costume fitting.

"You hear that?" Petty asked as they sat on the porch looking up at the fireflies pulsing in front of the towering black wall of limestone that constituted the back yard. You had to look almost straight up to get to the stars hiding sheepishly behind the mountain. Petty lit his pipe and they sat listening for an encore. His rocking chair creaked as he sloshed the ice in his bourbon and you could hear the mumbled hum of the TV inside the house. Some Hollywood producer had gotten liberal with using the laugh track, a falseness that tipped it to suit better some macabre scene involving mental illness and a sharp ax.

"TV?" The Kid asked. He strained his ears to make out words. The darkness outside focused his hearing. He could make out an exasperated yet wise dad, a dim daughter, a snarky son. Silly family situations that turn out to be a teaching moment, foreign to his existence, an absurd opera he was never offered a ticket to.

"No. That manufactured shit is mind-numbing poison. I'm talking about out there." He pointed his pipe out to the mountainside. "In the ether. The bird. Singing at night." They sat again in silence. Then it softly called out another verse. A flittering tune that would normally wake you too early in the morning but make you happy as you rolled over to get a few more minutes of sleep.

"Yes, I hear it. Pretty."

"Sounds close, doesn't it? Like you could just get up and walk right up to it and it would swoop down on your outstretched finger like a trained hawk. Bet you want to know what it is, don't you? Head out there, have a conversation. Ask why its clock is off."

"Yeah."

"Never trust the night bird song."

"Why?"

"It's out of place. It doesn't belong. Goes against nature. Lucinda can tell you tales of the men who would follow the night bird, try to find the fragile creature that sang its tune under the moon, find out why. A siren drawing them into the wilderness they would never emerge from. Those things, those unnatural things, you will want to understand their existence but they will steer you right off the cliff of doom. Remember that."

He walked through the parking lot of the stadium searching for Brick's bus for hours. Amber was not off in her estimation; patchouli and body odor assaulted his nose as he wove around young trust-funders from California reinventing the hippie lifestyle in $100 tie-dye tank tops and $300 Euro-handmade sandals. Some were hallucinating as they wandered, talking to a pet rock or following a man in an Indian headdress blowing giant bubbles. Humans with no plan beyond today, somehow everything would work out, even if they found themselves in a nightmare bad trip of ants and scissors devouring their flesh while an inside-out Ginsberg recited the Torah. Normally someone of his hulking stature and uniform of coveralls and cowboy boots would stick out in a crowd, but here nothing was unusual save for a uniformed cop or a three-piece Armani suit. All were here to expand the mind and soak in the sounds of the truth that you could see out of the corner of your eye but was never fully revealed. Even when it was, as you peaked immaculate under the cotton candy sky, that moment of clarity revealed most simply, your unique yet common place in the master plan of the universe shown to you, just as quickly the map would be pulled away, rolled up and put back on God's shelf, too high for you to reach. That quest, to catch the snipe, is what drove these kids to tumble into vehicles hung together with scotch tape and clothes hangers and follow the band. Exist in the center of the sun, blinded by the light until their parents cut off their checking accounts. He came up on a large crowd waiting to buy giant balloons from a guy with a tank on the tailgate of his station wagon. Seemed weird that adults were so keen on purchasing balloons but this was a carnival of arrested development. As he waited for the crowd to shift so he could slip past, he heard Brick call out.

"Hey man! Hold up!" Brick had just bought a big yellow balloon and was holding it high to protect it from popping. He made his way to The Driver, grinning from ear to ear, basted with the dirt and sweat of others.

"Dude! My dude! I cannot believe you are here! This is fucking amazing! Here! Suck on this nipple! The mother's milk!" He put the end of the balloon up to The Driver's mouth, who took it in and inhaled deep. The nitrous stormed through the tissues of his brain, a 747 taking off over and over. As the plane ascended away clear from his internal runway, he felt giddy and light as if his head and the balloon had switched molecules.

"Fun right? That's nitrous. We used to have to buy it in little metal canisters at the porn shop back in AK or hit the whipped-cream aisle at the grocery store. Here, 20 bucks gets you this big, fat bad-boy laugh factory. I gotta take it back to home base but you get all the hits you want, brother. Follow me, let's follow the yellow brick road." He held the balloon up and pointed at it. "Get it? Yellow? Brick? I'm a goddamn genius."

They wove through the maze trying to share the balloon conservatively through eruptions of giggles, not getting any closer to their target.

"We gotta get back to base. Up periscope!" Brick jumped on the Driver's back and shimmied up to his shoulders. The Driver laughed and Brick held on rodeo style for the regulation eight seconds. He spotted the van right before losing his balance and falling back, bouncing off the packed earth.

"Can't catch my breath." He heaved as The Driver sucked another gasp of the balloon. They both started cracking up, even with lungs devoid of oxygen. "Jesus, man, that was like a 10-foot drop. Remind me to never ride that ride again." The Driver offered his hand and yanked Brick back to his feet, actually lifting him into the air before the Tevas again touched solid ground. "I found the van, though. It's about half a click, 10 o'clock vector. You like that? I just watched Platoon again. Great fucking movie. Give me that balloon, looks like a saggy tit now. They are gonna make me get another one and then I'm gonna get lost again, caught in an infinite time loop. Oh well, at least it will be a gas. Ha! Let's make like a G-string and hike up."

After another 30 minutes of dusty wrong turns, leading to propositioning, bargaining and purchasing of an array of drugs,they reached the tired, trashed little patch of gravel the van was parked on.

"Welcome home!" The side door was open revealing a squat college kid with an over-abundance of body hair lounging ancient-Greek-scholar-style on a rancid loveseat plucking at an ukulele along with the concert music one could hear when the wind blew right.

"Classic setlist today. They've been lost in Dark Star for like, eons, man."

"That's Renfro. He's a space cadet. But he's cool. We only got tix to Sunday's show. You gotta be pretty damn hardcore to hit multiple shows. That's a lot of tripping, turn your brain into cottage cheese."

"Large curd of small curd? Why don't they make a medium curd? This world is getting too extreme, man. People are brainwashed into taking sides. Ginger. Mary Ann. Black. White. Coke. Pepsi. Chevy. Ford. Where is the touch of grey, man? I want to drink a Dr Pepper, drive a Dodge, see what Lovey is cooking with, you dig?"

"Calm down Ren. Strum your tiny guitar and feel the flow. Here, hit this balloon."

"Dude." Renfro took a big suck. "You got ripped off – this thing is flatter than Earth."

"Well I had to take out my cut."

"Some cut. By the way, who's this Aryan Paul Bunyan motherfucker? I bet he gulped most of it and chased it down with a keg of Henry Weinhard's."

"This is my chum from up north. We go way back. He came to see what university life holds."

"Well there ain't no way he fits in here with you, me and Trenton. He will have to sleep on the roof."

"He can sleep in his big-ass ride. My man is a long-haul trucker." Brick looked up for confirmation, The Driver nodded. There had to be a big box store parking lot around there somewhere. Back out in the real world.

"Trucker? Paul Bunyan is a trucker now? Guess deforestation has left many a lumberjack searching for a new gig. Where's Babe the blue ox? Bet that fat bastard got 'roided up, carved up and put into every Big Mac in Minnesota. Back when they used to use beef anyway. Golden arch Styrofoam demons of the wastelands."

"Hey, you are seriously bringing us down, bud."

"The truth is a bitter pill. The sheep would rather be hand-fed the sweets that will soon be their demise." Renfro tuned the out-of-tune uke further out of tune.

"Where is Trenton? I need the Yin to your Yang."

"Ha! Oh man, that fruit loop, he blasted off about two hours ago. Got into some opium somehow. Dude has been up there sitting behind the wheel ever since. Thinks he is driving us to Marrakesh under the waning gibbous. Just read The Sheltering Sky in class. Broseph is obsessed now. Maybe you can get him to pull over and put it in park." Brick and The Driver walked up to the passenger window and looked in to see a farmer-tanned white guy in long dreads sitting in the driver's seat staring intently through the windshield, hands at ten and two on the wheel.

"Hey Trenton. How you doing, buddy?"

"Good man, good. Gotta concentrate on the road, though. The French made them narrow as hell, that along with the shifting sands and the camels, you can't trust 'em. It's tough, man. I can't even make out the horizon, the dunes are playing tricks with my eyes. Maybe it will be better in the morning? They say the moon is a trickster that lights the desert false as if by day."

"Maybe, man. Why don't you pull over, take a break? I gotta piss." Brick opened the door, grinned at The Driver.

"We're really close, though. Took us all day to get through Algeria and check it out, I can just make out the shimmering blue, blue sea on the other side. That has to mean we are close."

"Think he is looking at the row of port-a potties over there." A few hundred feet across the gravel and abandoned solo cups stood a motley haphazard row with long despondent lines and the threat of hair-standing-on-end odors inside the spring-loaded doors.

"OK, man, OK. Get us inside the city walls. We're counting on you." Brick closed the door.

"Excelsior! Marrakesh by sunset, Trents! Pedal to the metal!" Renfro yelled through a fruit roll-up he had eaten holes out of and fashioned into a mask.

"We will be swimming in mint tea and belly dancers under the palms by dawn, my friends."

"Dig it the most," Brick placated as they wandered back to the side of the van and Renfro singing softly off-key, along with the next floaty jam in-between chomps of his raspberry face shield. "Well, this is it." Brick summed up the experience as he fired up a spliff. "The master plan is chill with the fungi tomorrow on the river, drop a couple of hits of Jesus Christ Sunday for the show. We'll have to see if we can score you a ticket or just trade Renfro for a marble or hell maybe Trenton will still be on the road."

"I'd trade you my pinkie toes for the right marble. We don't need them."

"I'm sure you would, Ren and hell who wouldn't? Hard as hell to cut the nails, anyway. Would be a blessing." Brick handed The Driver the joint. "I can't believe you found me and today of all days, crazy-ass kismet. How did you even know where I was?" The Driver produced the picture with Amber's digits as he took a monster drag.

"Ah, that minx. She thinks you hung the moon. All she talks about is the big man who is going to come sweep her away from the ice lands. What do you think? She is a tight little package, got those fit legs in those tights all the time, those big cartoon eyes and smart as hell, that is a 12 out of 10 up there, like a leprechaun sucking a unicorn's dick my man, very, very rare." Brick winked a couple of times. The Driver shrugged and took another drag.

"I figured as much."

"When did I show you that tattoo? You been peepin' on me during bath time, Brick? You are a cheeky simile-thieving bastard. Took the artist hours to get the angle right on the little Irishman's fellatio technique. I was a stickler for details." Renfro gave The Driver the side eye and reached his hand out for the joint. "Give me that thing, ya bogarting goon." Nearby, a drum circle gathered up steam through the sun-sparkled magic dust.

Eventually, after the toddler fought its tormentors until it lay as an exhausted pool of limbs on the floor, night fell heavy over the chaos. He stood just inside the lantern light tentatively reaching out from the van, watching the peppering of trash-barrel fires and spastic silhouettes dancing for the favor of the flames. The guys were passing around Vienna sausages and saltines, eating from the wheel of habit more than hunger. Trenton had made his way from captaining the mystery ship through the dunes to the roof where he lay back touching his tickly soul to the backside of the universe.

"Hey fellas?" he asked down not really knowing where anybody was.

"Yeah Trent? You want some wieners?" Brick flicked one up off his fork but it arched over the van into the void.

"I can see us from behind. Like from the other side of the cosmic loop. The back of us, right here, right now. The big dude, he is looking right at me. My perception has torn a peephole through the red-velvet-curtained fabric of reality." Brick and Renfro looked up at The Driver who did indeed have his back turned to the van, a totem pole daring any offended god to approach.

"Hey Bunyan, you see Trents out there sucking Sagan's dick in the cosmos? Looking down at us, gurgling grey hairy space nuts?" The Driver looked up, withholding comment. A shooting star streaked through the ink but there was no divinity he could perceive. He was a long way away from sharing his omnipotence.

"Bunyan once delivered twins with his feet while hang-gliding over the Himalayans." Brick snort-laughed after he said it. It warmed his soul to put some sort of identity on this silent reaper he had once befriended and who just happened to slide back into this slanted reality. It was electric to be in the company of an actual killer, pitching a tent next to a volcano.

"Bunyan once played strip Twister with Hitler's ghost in a linen closet at Caesar's Palace." Renfro was all over any game of word porn. The randomness suited his ruthless firing squad of synapses.

"Bunyan once sculpted a perfect replica of the Venus de Milo out of elephant dung for a blind kindergarten class on the deck of the Titanic." Brick took in a satisfied breath relishing the taste, Renfro acknowledged his admiration with a raising of his wiener fork. The Driver kept his back to them to keep the game afoot, smiling only to himself at their offerings to his ludicrous legend.

"Bunyan over there, he once brought a delightful baby tear and Ripple pear wine sangría to Malcolm X's summer mixer."

"Bunyan started a lucrative mail-order catalog selling crocheted underwear to left-handed nuns."

"Your friend Bunyan, he once painted Urkel's head poking out of a kangaroo's pouch in pig's blood on his mailman's garage door."

"Well Bunyan also crawled through 10 miles of raw sewage to deliver a picnic basket of pvc pipe fittings to Yogi Bear's drunk uncle."

"He also baked a placenta lasagna to serve to the Queen of England in bed after a night of furious heavy petting."

Trenton poked his head over the roof of the van, a T-shirt fashioned as an elaborate turban on his head.

"Paul Fabian Bunyan, Esquire, once took a cold shower with Dolly Parton and a camel with Down's syndrome."

They all were seized with laughter, even The Driver, who turned around to shrug in affirmation.

"Guilty."

The laugh was a genuine laugh, a strange sensation of joy

and easiness in his gut that spread as gentle mudflow through white light limbs smoldering with THC. It was his best night. A fresh spliff was sparked and the rich camaraderie of the night moseyed on.

At some point, he made his way back to the rig and his heavy eyes worked their way through the empty streets to a Wal-Mart parking lot. He could have gone on with his life when the morning jostled him from a rare dreamless death slumber deep in the sleeper cab, left on a high note, figuratively and literally. Out of one eye he watched a stray hound pad across the lot through a slight fog looking for breakfast. It was a lean hound but healthy with white teeth and an easy pant. It popped a squat outside the rig and looked up at him through the glass in anticipation. The dog network must have gotten the word out that he was a friend, a patron saint to strays everywhere traversing the lands free only to survive. Would he now be that guy, the one singled out by a subway beggar because of the mistake of making eye contact or carrying the illusion of a charitable soul? He dropped his head back below the window and stared at the ceiling, flexed the feeling back into his legs. He looked at his watch. He would wait seven minutes. If his patron held true at the hostess stand with its simple-minded patience, he would buy them both some grub and head back to the Dead lot. If the canine hobo was gone, so was he, heading due south on I-5 to the stove-top scrub of Sacramento and his next haul. The seven in heaven like a hundred, more a purgatory at the crossroads. He looked at his watch a couple of times, only a minute or 90 seconds had passed. Time was so relative; a train conductor must feel as if he has lived infinite lives by the time he retires his commanding baritone. A boxer feels his mortality and rebirth in the seconds between the whim of the bell, empires rise and fall as a bull rider rides the eight seconds of thunder and lightning. He was a slave to the tick-tocks and he knew it, timing the radio-friendly hits to the yard sticks as he raced hammer down through hairpin turns, eating and pissing at 80 plus just so he can unload boxes of silverware to another chain restaurant or a pallet of bathmats so a fat lady in a Best Western won't break her head open on the faucet while stepping out of the shower, the basin three inches deep with a backed-up stew of cheap soap, pubes and dead skin. Petty had somehow instilled a self-imposed obsession with time, only to serve the materialistic new gods. Every installation had flaws but programming was what kept the machine from getting gummed up or hacked by Russian teens drinking diluted chocolate milk sitting on a crate in a leaky warehouse. When the wait was over, he took a deep breath and lifted back up. As soon as the dog saw his face he barked and trotted a tight circle of delight. The bastard knew the plan all along. Guess he would be extending his stay in Eugene, to immerse his virginal consciousness again in a rickety carnival ride of strange brews.

After a half dozen donuts and a can of slippery liver-flavored chow for his ward, it was back to the dusty gypsy town of debauchery. This time, he felt he had a better lay of the land and found the van after only a couple of wrong turns and one solicitation to lick a witchy woman's hairy armpit. When he arrived, bearing the other half of the baker's dozen, the crew was awake but dazed, their nerves faulty as the glands were working an overtime shift to flush out a myriad of foreign secretions.

"Yo Bunyan is back! What you got there?" Renfro tried to yank the box away but The Driver raised the box above his head.

"Everybody."

"OK, Bunyan. Share and share alike. We are down with Marxism in this settlement. Can I at least see?" Renfro hopped up to try again at the box but it was well beyond his reach. Brick stretched a downward dog pose in a dying patch of grass he had found.

"Pink box, Ren, ya home-schooled runt. That is the universal symbol for donuts. We got some instant coffee and hot agua on the cook stove, big bud. Let's break sugar bread." Brick stood, shook out the blood and handed out a mismatched assortment of coffee mugs as the jackals tore into the downed wildebeest of donuts. "Keep track of your mugs, for these are now your keys to the magical land of 'shrooms here in a bitty bit, once the seas calm and we pull the anchors up." The Driver looked at his, it read, "Get your rocks off on Pike's Peak," with a donkey straddling a trail on its hind legs turning back to wink with a devious smile. An anatomically incorrect masturbating donkey would be his vessel to a strange new world of hallucinogens. Gradually, as the day stumbled toward a warm afternoon, the boys rediscovered their spunk from a rigorous regime starting with the heights of a sugar rush, a serious make-out session with Mary Jane, chased with a few lukewarm hefeweizens. Without any real regard for time or condition, other than a quick glance at the position of the sun in the cloudless sky, Brick deemed it time to fuel up the rockets. Renfro pulled from the depths of the van an ancient yet generous plastic bag stuffed with menacing white and brownish grey caps and stems, a woodman's pile of shrunken, twisted and gnarled evil fairy-tale trees. Trenton, back among the present and accounted for, offered up his gift of the Magi, a battle-scarred ceramic pot, and placed it gingerly on the cook stove burner. Once a half-gallon of water was dancing over itself in a rolling boil, Renfro tipped the sack and the contents tumbled into the water.

"I got these a while back from this dude Snatch, shit I guess about two years ago now, freshman year. Grade-A choice goods. Top of the top of the line. Aging in my sock drawer like a fine wine. Been holding them for an extra-special occasion and this one finally checks all the boxes. Remember Snatch, Trents?"

"Think so. I remember his sister. Too big an ass but could hang. Rose maybe? It was some flower."

"Yeah, they were twins. Just never came back after summer break. He was a cool-ass cat, too. Guess the drudgery of college life isn't for everyone." The Driver's heart skipped a beat at the sound of the names as a flood of vivid memories rich in blood and Shakespeare traveled fast behind that unwavering mask he showed outwardly. The only result was not any sense of guilt but his mouth watering from a powerful physical urge for a hunk of that dried ambrosia yum-yum and he cursed himself for not bringing a morsel or two along.

Brick stared down into his cauldron as if he might begin an incantation, calling forth a horde of mischievous minor demons. "Sure you can eat them, and that's totally cool, throw them on a pizza or chew them like a dumb cow, but you lose potency in digestion in my mind. Tea is the true way to travel. Pure, elucidated. It clarifies the fuzzy bubble. All the true shamans will pass you the cup, the elk horn of the universe to partake in the swirling cornucopian madness that is wonder." Trenton danced a soundless jig around the bubbling elixir. Renfro began elaborate calisthenics. The anticipatory galvanism was palpable in the saturated air. In the distance, a long, hungry howl traveled to them low over the camp. Perchance his morning furry liaison was signaling the opening of forbidden portals? The Driver's guts tightened into elaborate sailor's knots. Something far off the wingtips of the earthly plane was about to go down.

The tea rollicked in fervor as it boiled, the liquid reaching a chemical balance that offered knowledge of its grand purpose, gaining some metaphysical consciousness all its own. With a teasing maniacal laugh Brick doled out the servings, each cup to its brim. The Driver accepted his horny donkey and let the brew cool in his hands. He did not sip. Once the steam had stopped drifting up he threw it back as a medicine some other mother coaxed into her sick offspring to break a fever. Chunks of soggy fibers swam among the fantastic fluid, threatening to choke him, but he was able to open his throat against the impulse to gag and all went down, down to the very bottom of his sentient wellspring. Lowering the cup, he witnessed the others stepping through their doors, that peculiar face of knowing you have punched your ticket and the turnstile back out to Normalville has vanished back into the miasma of reality.

"Lettuce!" Brick announced and they popped to attention,

dropping their cups in the dust. The traveling vagabond gang fell into the blossoming fray of color and smells. The tea sloshed around in their bellies as they trounced through the crowds on a bearing south by southwest for the gentle shores of the Willamette river that sliced through the city and campus on its way north to the mighty Columbia.

"This scene lends itself to the bazaars of Jemaa el-Fnaa in the Medina quarter. The throes of humanity plying their wares, the senses assaulted, overcome with stimuli."

"Don't you slip back to Marrakesh, Trenton Sinclair – we need you in the here and now." Brick threw an arm over his bony, narrow shoulder and the bushy dreads, just in case he felt the desire to wander back into the desert.

"It's cool, just saying, if I were to see a saffron merchant astride his grouchy camel, I would not be the least bit surprised."

"Soon we should be ready and willing to see anything and yet hopefully retain the wisdom to know the difference between illusion and reality. Hence our dalliance to Mother Nature's bosom where, within her beauty, the reins can be more tightly held."

"Brickston on 'shrooms talk, why you so fancy?"

"Touché, Sir Renfro. I feel a need to entertain a certain chivalry in our quest today. Good trips come to those who respect the primordial powers that be." Brick jumped up unannounced on The Driver's back who again received him. "On Llamrei! The Holy Grail awaits!" They all began to trot Monty Python style, except for Brick who rode on The Driver straight backed in his imaginary saddle. As they reached the outskirts of the deadhead encampment and could see glimmers of the green flow, the enchantments began to reveal themselves.

Inevitably, they wandered down their own paths. The uptick of the psilocybin roller-coaster lends itself to introspective seclusion as each mind must roam its own maze and avoid the menacing Minotaur. It is innately a personal expansion, not one easily shared. Renfro found himself following a dragonfly down-river as Trenton sought out the high dunes through the swaths of droll pines away from the water. Brick and The Driver found themselves within eyeshot, both perched on logs in the shallows allowing them to soak their feet in the ripples. Brick felt the paternal impulse to watch over his virginal charge but at the same time knew it was a matter of reactions beyond his control at this point. He had led his steed out of the desert to this oasis of tranquility. The nymphs and fairies must now cradle them both. He was beginning to notice their presence, watching from the bark, the smooth river stones, just outside the periphery. The Driver watched the melting swirls of the water between his legs, melting among his toes. His head felt enormous yet light, a diri-gible at one with the air, the skies. He looked close at his finger-prints, the ridges the same as swaths of earth seen from space, the patterns obvious and purposeful. That purpose was what surrounded him, every molecule colliding and shared in a chore-ographed harmony left alone, a self-playing piano that would stay in tune long after humanity destroyed itself in fire and glut-tonous hubris. We were the outliers, our wicked self-serving demands upset the balance, our greed driving to procreate and consume. There was no innocence in our spirit, even infants suckled the nipple too earnestly, taking more than needed. We had secured the top link in the food chain and yet were no longer attached. Why and when did certain races decide to dominate their surroundings when others found harmony? Was destruction genetic? Was slavery the key? Civilizations were all built on the backs of the subjugated. He saw through the eyes of workers watching their peers dying among the pyramid blocks, being dragged out of the way so the supply line could continue unabated. Was that hell? Was that why the disenfranchised created heaven? There had to be a salvation. Did there? Or was luck in the shortest of supply? There were only four aces in the deck. The rest were mere shuffled creatures that manufactured their own misery. He closed his eyes, pulled out of the macro. He had drawn an ace, no need to wallow in guilt, take on the sorrows of the untold billions who lived in vain. Listened to the birds, the beat of the insect wings synchronized to the separated heart alive in his chest. There was beauty to behold, revel in as if all sights and sounds were performing for approval. A being endowed the center of the universe, all was relative to him right now. He felt that familiar omnipotence swarm back as simple as the thundering pollen so loud crashing to the soil. He looked out on to the river, how he could take a step and be on the other side. He was the modern-day Paul Bunyan, that origin of legend. His deeds would be passed down and exaggerated around campfires and fishing boats. He had long ago conquered his demons, they lay chained to the rocks far from his gleaming tower now-ness. He could squint and still see them, though, struggling weak under the surface, distorted by the bends of light through the water outside the sunken city full of bloated corpses of the banished, the truck-stop whores, the weak-minded fools, the inferior challengers of his might. Then She appeared, a liquid phoenix, vast and rising, larger than life, like a tormented storm cloud lassoed and tied to the earth. For so long, Her poison had kept him tamed, a shadow puppet of what he would become in the aftermath. She had no idea of his current power! She would be nothing more than a cornflake forgotten under the oven being fought over by ants if She were somehow to orchestrate some satanic resurrection. Whatever gods – or was it from his very loins that called up that biblical night – had written it to be as a transcendence, his deliverance to fulfill destiny. She must not gain foothold again on this earthly plane. He stepped off the log and pursued her languid shadow, pushed her down, back to the ninth circle of hell. She fought, at first with a savageness that impelled him to put on more steam. Soon She grew limp, slipping back down to her dark, dank lair, of worms and shit and rot. It was only then he realized this was not his tormenting mother he had kept from resurfacing but Brick, his only true friend in the world. He lifted the lifeless body up out of the maelstrom, waded to the log that Brick had been seated on and laid him out. How did they get here? He started the CPR he had learned in truck-driving school. Such training seemed less than trivial at the time, he was a destroyer of life, never would he need to fetch it back from the clutches of the reaper. He breathed hard into the mouth, compressed down on the chest plate. Again. Again. He felt untethered from his working limbs, his lips, his life-giving breaths. He willed himself to push harder, blow deeper, squeeze out that faint glow of life force, rekindle the fire. Was it there or had he stamped out yet another? Quite suddenly in between violent thrusts the eyes jerked back into some semblance of focus; water gurgled out of Brick's lungs. He took in a gasp, pushed against The Driver's close face. He was back among us, the damage for once undone. They sat there in soaked silence looking through one another in the river, Brick grasping through the hallucinations at this awful new reality, this brush with the infinite darkness.

"You killed me. You fucking killed me, man! Like that clown in the street! Do you remember that guy? Does he not haunt you? You made a hole where his face used to be for nothing! What are you? What are your inclinations? Oh shit... your eyes are crimson! I see the flames!" He stumbled back, out of the water, on to the bank. "Your name! You never say your name! I know your name! You are Lucifer!" He ran. Straight into the woods, forever gone. The Driver stood in the waist-deep water, his arms, muscles wrought with betrayal loose at his sides, looking to where his best friend had vanished, the faces on the trees holding judgmental sneers of disapproval.

"I'm sorry," he said to no one as Uncle John's Band was lifted up and carried over him on the breeze blowing south across the stadium. The day's concert had begun:

Come hear Uncle John's Band, by the riverside
Got some things to talk about, here beside the rising tide

8

GANGSTA'S PARADISE

I t was a time of self-imposed damnation. A trail of tears from Amarillo to Galveston and back. Over and over without respite. High desert, punishing traffic jams through DFW and Houston, then on to the marshlands littered with the man sewers of filthy refineries. He let all the ancient demons free and they were merciless as they roamed. Guilt, regret, frustration, help-lessness all took baseball bats to his temperament. They were the old guard that She had unleashed from her stables with such fervor in the time before. For no good reason he would replay the haunting memory of a recurring childhood nightmare when-ever he would pass Huntsville, that obnoxious statue of Sam Houston and the enclave of convicted murderers and rapists who were too stupid to not get caught and now sat in rows of concrete working the broken system to dodge the forever needle. It would start with him snug in his little bed, hugging his favorite Ronald McDonald doll. The irony of the early comfort he found in a clown was not lost on him. A conventional green glowing ghost would burst out from his closet and sweep him under its spectral arm. It would race with him out into the hall, past the darkened living room where his parents would be watching the archaic wood-accented floor-console TV, a flickering glow of sickish yellow-grey mucus illuminating featureless faces of nothing but skin. He would yell and scream to no avail. His captor would float with him through the back door beyond the kitchen without opening it, into the night. How that dream would strike him down with a nauseous fright every time he would wake up from it under the twisted saturated sheets. It still hit him in the soft undercarriage between the kidneys and low ribs and he wallowed in the metaphysical pain as one would take in a spoonful of medicine after faking a sickness. He craved a flogging, to be ridiculed in the public square, held fast in the pillory, spitting children taunting him with rotten cabbage or even a good surprise punch in the back of the head She would reward him with when he watched Three's Company too loud. She hated Suzanne Somers, said she stole her look and did nothing with it other than act like a nitwit. Suzanne was just one line item in a long list of people and things she hated, that triggered yelling at the TV, the radio, his dad, him. There was no joy to be found around her and, if you could carve some light out of your existence, you had to cradle it secretly or she would root it out and stomp on it till nothing was left. It necessitated his hours and hours sitting in the diner studying the veins of pavement and water that was the unique fingerprint of each state. He dreaded being trapped in that emotional cage with the banshee, having to take care of her needs, tightening the curtains to keep out any leak of daylight before flipping the vinyl of some sixties band. This current purgatory he found himself in, trapped in the ever-rolling cab he once took for a sanctuary, his bastion of solitude and source of power, had become a sensory-deprivation tank that delivered him directly back to the hellscape he endured as a child. He grimaced as he relived each verbal strike, cigarette burn, being cold-cocked by whatever was close enough to grab and throw. Lipstick-stained drinking glasses hurt the worst, especially tumblers. He always tried to turn his back when he saw it coming, catch it in the meat between his shoulder blades.

There was a perpetual bruise there he could still feel when he rolled his shoulders back and forth. Most kids of abuse could always segment out the good times, the day when Mommy or Daddy didn't drink and they had a good Christmas or a summer on the lake. His only fond memories were her absence, in the diner when his dad would bring him another tall cold glass of milk and a plate full of whatever had to get cooked before it turned. They would sit in silence usually, Dad folding his apron carefully like the flag on the table, bonded over their dread of the night, or occasionally Dad would ask him how to get through Vermont on an imaginary vision quest to Yosemite. On a good day, they would giggle about how Oklahoma was Texas's hat.

No. Shut it down. Fond memories are not for the wretched. Let Her darkness shine.

How he would be in the living room bored, watching an old tennis ball roll ever so slowly along the imperceptible slant of the mobile home floor toward the tattered screen door. She would kick his cup of cherry Kool-Aid he had next to him across the room, then make him clean it up with nothing but spit and a crusty rag. When her Big Brother and the Holding Company record skipped during a bender of wine coolers, she ripped it off the turntable and broke it over his head, then found the sharpest piece to see "how he would like to be scratched". Then made him sing as blood rolled down his leg. He rearranged his ass in his seat while stuck in bumper-to-bumper traffic south of Denton on I-35. The lack of motion allowed him to be pulled back under to feel the cuts across the meat of the cheeks, how she offered him a sip from her Bartles & Jaymes as he pulled his underwear up over the pain. It felt a lot like the sweat now, wet and sticky. There was no way to keep cool in a north-Texas summer, even with the A/C running max. His thoughts wandered to an imagined relief from the heat, a determined walk from a lonely cabin as he removes soiled layers, plunging into a jagged hole cut in a frozen lake, becoming disoriented and losing the will to search for the opening as the body numbed and the overcast sky becomes a blanket pulled over lifeless eyes. He wondered if he could strike that final match, how would he? Steer the rig into oncoming traffic after waiting for days for a school bus to approach from the opposite direction? Or find a pleasant rest stop, flip the switch and let the sweet-release exhaust float him downriver to Hades. He did know there would be no letter, no confessions. Those who had died by his hand would have no posthumous justice, no closure for an investigative TV show to end on a high note. Maybe he would die only to walk among them. Would they be afraid? Or would they seek vengeance? You can't hurt a ghost but if She lingered out there, and he was sure She did, She would know the way. He could see Her above the long line of cars, as wide as the windshield would allow, amongst the thirsty live oak, her fire-red rouged-up wolf jaws drooling for another crack at him.

The day came when he had filled the tank just outside of Wichita Falls, where there were no falls, by the way, climbed up, shifted into gear and forgot which way he was going. The route had become a blur, both legs a mirror image of a bare wall. He always stopped in the same places, tried to shit, got gas, neglected the mildewed shower stalls. How long had he tortured himself? Was it enough or should this become the entirety of his existence? A future local news story about the trucker who has run the same route for 50 years without stopping. His long white beard tucked into his overalls so it doesn't get caught in the steering wheel. The glory found in no longer remembering when you started, or why. Driving with blurred vision from the cataracts, arthritis forming your right hand into a claw where you have clutched the gear knob for decades. Outliving Casey Kasem twofold, the music becoming foreign and painful to hear with the tinnitus ringing incessant day and night. Wait, the music. His forgotten companion forced to sit in silence while he served his penance. The countdown that centered him, giving him 40 reasons for the season. He turned the knob, dialed in the station he inherently knew would spout forth a current hit. The tail-end of a tree-topping commercial (Let us go out on a limb so you don't have to!) led him back to number 19 for the week, falling from the top 10 the week before. He was about to hear a song for the first time when the rest of the western world had already had the inane chorus stuck in their heads as they tried to eat a frozen dinner and then hit the sack too early so they could be prepared for the quarterly-report meeting the next day. He spotted a crow take flight from the dumpsters over the truck stop and head south. He followed.

It shouldn't have taken so long to find the pink house of Petty's second family. He didn't expect a universal myriad pink houses, from faded almost white from the endless salt spray to the rich freshly coated pink of a baby's flesh and a dozen shades in between. Petty had never given him the actual address as they had never ventured together to this armpit coast, only to Lucinda to calm the perpetual storm brewing just below the sentinel yellow poplars towering over the cabin from that sheer ridge in Robbinsville. He had only mentioned that the other residence was one of many in a row running down the shoreline, sitting on top of tall stilts overlooking the vast brownness of the water where oil platforms dotted the horizon. His plan was to take the main drag out of Galveston slowly south out of town, searching for Petty's and maybe a way to get recentered, reclaim his power. The teacher had taught him how to hold ultimate sway over his dominion and somehow, after he simply downed a few mushrooms, it all went catawampus on him. "But hey I'm a... fungi!" He should have said as Brick sprinted away from the river, fleeing a devil incarnate. Hindsight. He passed a slew of small, rickety seafood shacks and open-air college bars blaring rap music. Rolling through a green light he had to slam the brakes as a kid with a popped collar, plaid shorts and a yard-long frozen fruity drink stepped out of an eighties raunchy comedy to cross the road oblivious to any semblance of caution like a true second-act villain. The kid looked up, laughed, flipped him the bird and went on his zig-zagging journey to the other sidewalk, 60 feet closer to the ocean and hopefully an accidental drowning. It felt good to fantasize about the kid, drunk by the moonlight, being pulled into deep water by the undertow, struggling in vain as the crabs licked their shells in anticipation of fresh eyeballs and tender face meat. He considered pulling over, luring the twerp behind a whitewashed wall and snapping a neck, clean and crunchy. A kite flying erratic above the sands somehow stayed aloft as he watched with purpose. An unspoken count, the kite prevailed. His disappointment as the coin landed; head on down the coast in the palm of continuance, so he obeyed. Bloodlust may have been an elixir for the soul at this low point but it was not to be quenched. Other plans had been written in his cave book.

Stalking through a neighborhood around Jamaica Beach, he finally hit pay dirt. The house fit the bill, pink and tall, a chubby flamingo that had skipped leg day at the gym. Landscaping consisted of sand, an old skiff, "the horny hooker" and a few sick palms scattered around a corner lot. Leaning against the trade winds was tough on homes and, though far from immaculate, it looked loved. The steep flight of stairs up to the porch and front door were swept clean and the turtle-shaped mailbox standing by the road was straight. He felt the steps groan as he made his way up. They shared his trepidation. He hadn't spoken to anyone in a very long time. Should he try to speak before he knocked? Make sure he still could?

"Test. One two three. This is Casey Kasem. Welcome to the American Top 40 countdown."

"Are you Casey Kasem or did you eat Casey Kasem?" He spun around to see a woman down below on ground level, sitting on a bike with a basket and banana seat. Sun-kissed short dirty blonde hair, a blue-sky simple cotton dress revealing just enough of a fit body to manage to keep the curves in the right places. She leaned the bike on a piling, lifted a bag of sundries out of the basket and made her way up the steps. When she got to the top, she took off her black-rimmed sunglasses and looked him up and down. It took a little while. She was not a tall woman but well-proportioned, from big eyes that matched her dress to a Roman sculpture nose and full lips that needed a great deal of attention. She would tell anyone who would listen that her true addiction was ChapStick. She placed the basket in his arms and he received it with without protest.

"C'mon. I'm sure you are one of Petty's strays." He followed her inside, too embarrassed to speak but mesmerized by her presence enough to follow her about anywhere. It was obvious to him immediately she was the sun to Lucinda's moon. He could sure use a deep drink of that, a beam of light piercing through the black clouds. The house was the quintessential beach crib, countless seashells bordered by bright colors and glass tabletops. They walked to the kitchen where he stood, not knowing what to do while she took the basket and unpacked the farmers-market wares.

"My name is Sonya, pleased to meet you and all that but I'll tell you straight off, Petty isn't here, hasn't been for months." Sonya. Lucinda. The sun and the moon. A coincidence he considered not likely as she smiled to herself and the world while putting fresh vegetables away, pulled out others. "It's par for the course, though. I can only take him in small doses, anyway. These days he'll roll in whenever it tickles his fancy, say hi to the kids if they are around, rub up against me till I give in, then he is back out on the road. If you came to see him you might as well get comfortable, could be later today, could be next year for all I know. I've learned to take care of this family just fine. He puts money in the bank and that's all a woman can ask, I reckon. Sit down, let's eat a bite of lunch. You can sleep in Harry's room tonight if you like. He is out living the college life. Sophomore at U of Houston, doing God knows what at a frat house, which I don't really approve of. Beer and chicks are what they major in.

He used to be such a sweet child. Of course, Petty is to blame. Never around to provide guidance, a boy needs that. Now he is close enough to get his laundry done but far enough that Mom doesn't see what he is up to. Hmmm, looking at what your umm, dimensions I may have to make you a pallet on the couch, think your legs would hang off at the knees in Harry's bed. Look at me talking up a storm, just haven't had anybody in my kitchen in a while. The lonely old hag up in her crow's nest."

"You, uh, don't look like a hag." He had retreated down into a seat in the breakfast nook, watching her grace as she bent and reached.

"Well, thank you, kind sir. So, did Petty teach you trucking? Or you just randomly appear at my door to sell me magazines?"

"He did. Everything I know."

"Well, that is one thing he can impart in spades. You got any family?"

"No."

"Where you from?"

"Nowhere, really."

"Aren't you a mystery. Want a beer?"

"Sure." She set down an unidentifiable can nestled in a koozie and a plate of cucumber slices and cream cheese on Triscuits. She sat down across from him with a beer of her own and studied his face.

"You don't look very old. How long have you been hauling?"

"Five years about." He took a cracker and put the whole thing in his mouth. Tasted like summer.

"A regular veteran, aren't ya! I think Petty had been driving about that long when we met. He had a lot of ghosts but he could sweet talk a bull wearing a red suit. I hadn't been out of Texas and he soon enough had us driving all over the country seeing things nobody bothered to find. This place was my folks' and when they died in a crash down on Padre, it just made sense to settle into it. Petty though, there is no settle in his DNA. He came around to knock me up, make a few birthdays but you sure couldn't set your watch to it. He stays away longer and longer now. Guess I could divorce him and find a man who was next to me snoring every night and peeing on the toilet seat but I consider it a blessing. I get to do whatever I want and I live on a beach. Could be a shit ton worse if you'll pardon my French."

She took a long gulp of her beer and demurely burped, followed by a giggle. "Why don't you grab that cooler in the corner and throw some ice and beers in it. We can go sit on the deck and enjoy the afternoon. Not many things finer than wasting the hours in the salty air with cheap beer and good company or good beer and cheap company. Add up about the same."

They set up shop on the expansive deck that held a multitude of forgotten beach toys, weather-beaten Adirondack chairs, a rusted fire pit and a wobbly table made from driftwood that needed all the varnish in the state. They lay next to each other in a couple of plastic lounge chairs and cracked fresh beers. The sound of the waves teased the ears only when the wind picked up, otherwise it was motorcycles and barking dogs. She rustled up a dented jam-box radio and he offered to find a good station. She requested anything but that tear-in-your-beer country that Petty preferred. As he fiddled with the antennae and dial, she skipped all the steps of forming trust in lieu of modesty and pulled off the sundress to reveal a pink-and-white polka-dot bikini that did her body a lot of favors it didn't even need. Once he was satisfied with his top 40 find. he looked up and unabashedly took in an eyeful. She countered his ogling with a wider grin and he was astounded at her lack of inhibition but then realized there was really no reason for it, they were practically sunbathing out here and she had the goods that a girl his age would run to the sign-up sheet for. Thus the afternoon sauntered on, more music than conversation, more beer than either. Eventually he even found the gall to take off his overalls and down to tired boxers let the sun reacquaint itself with his vampiric skin.

As drunken lazy afternoons often do, time was left to its own devices and went unnoticed as it ran wild over the hills to a sudden night. The beer was replaced with bourbon and bloody burgers with grilled onions and gouda cheese on rye toast were devoured in earnest. They sang terribly, even danced. He proposed going down to the beach to wade in the cool water under the stars. She told him you never know what you might step on at low tide in the dark around these parts, a needle, some trash from the rigs, a piece of dolphin, someone's severed arm. Padre was the place for true beachcombing. She missed it, going there as a child with her parents in their old Ford Bronco, driving down the beach for miles and miles without seeing a soul until her dad would slam on the brakes, jump out with their pirate flag and claim an unremarkable patch of dune as their camping spot. They would play in the surf and build towering bonfires as the days and nights melted together until the invading sand had penetrated their sleeping bags, their water, their food, their eyes and ears and her parents would finally have had enough. She always wanted to stay longer no matter what, to hold the magic of being the epicenter of their world with no other souls in sight. Then the bourbon spiraled her down and even her golden smile succumbed to the sadness of their deaths, how they had gone down without her as she was rolling through Montana with Petty. How a drunk redneck in a monster truck with a blown headlights fuse had hit them head-on in the vastness before they even got a chance to plant their trusty flag. They had gotten a late start and her dad was for whatever reason pushing farther down the coastline than ever before. Maybe he was looking for the end, the very tip of Padre where it dipped its skinny toe into Mexico. It had taken most of the next day for the powers that be to reach the wreckage and the seagulls had feasted on the broken bodies. It would be still another week before she returned home and learned of their fate. She had gotten the flag back. It was folded correctly on the shelf of her closet and held many of her tears. Showing a tenderness that was foreign and frightened him, he softly grasped her hand as she fought for her composure, to end the evening on a happy note. She could just see his eyes in the moonlight and they showed her that pain was not exclusive. That helped.

When lightning began to dance out above the gulf they decided to call it a night. Sonya made up the couch.

"Thank you, Lucinda." The Driver dove headfirst into sleep before any questions could arise. He dreamt of savage gulls pecking at his eyes as he lay chained to an outcropping of stone surrounded by frothing sepia waters. Petty floated above him on a throne of gold and jewels, Lucinda and Sonya each clutching a knee. He was Alpha and Omega, The Driver a modern Prometheus tortured for eternity. Some time later, he awoke, not knowing where he was. He reached out to find some recognizable piece of his sleeper cab but instead he found a glass table and sharp, brittle shells. He sat up and remembered, remembered the sun on his burnt skin, remembered the bourbon and felt the headache but most of all remembered Sonya's glowing skin in the afternoon heat they shared. Could he steal such heavenly knowledge? Be a thief in the night right under the nose of God? Why should Petty have such gifts? It was more than one man deserved. He stood up wobbly, realized without consequence he was naked and padded across the tile to stick his head under the kitchen sink faucet to drink deliciously as if returning from a failed desert quest. When he could drink no more, he walked on down the hall. Framed photos passed his periphery, the family holding fish, black-and-white ancestors long ago crumbled back to dust. The kid Harry's room door was open, typical boy from what he could ascertain. Sports, rap, oil-lathered supermodels in haphazard mood boards covered the walls. Typical childhood he never experienced. He never owned a poster and he would never dismantle his sacred atlas by pasting maps on his walls. He had missed so much.

The time for missing out was in the rearview now, though. It was the time for taking.

The door to the master bedroom was cracked open, the sound of a box fan muting the coming storm. He half-expected to see Petty, arms crossed, standing at the foot of the bed, barring entry to the paradise he was to now revel in, taste that glow on his rough tongue, feel the warmth against his body. But there was no Petty, only Sonya lying asleep on top of the sheets in nothing but a sheer oversized T-shirt. He climbed on to the bed, leaned over her, not knowing exactly how to approach a seduction, forced or otherwise. He yearned to be the Petty/Zeus of his fever dream, to take the virginal maiden in an overpowering passion to which she must succumb. As if hearing his inner longings to conquer, her legs spread to receive him. The thin shirt rode up, he was mesmerized by her soft mound, a first look at the gateway to all. He entered her and she gasped, wrapping legs around his back, receiving his burnt offerings. He kissed between breasts through the shirt, tentatively caressed her nipples with unknowing lips, leaving a dampness on the material that bridged the now raging storm to his mind. She moaned and he licked her salty cheek, her mouth found his and their tongues wrestled playfully. Suddenly she opened her eyes and a realization rose within her, one she surely knew but was able to fend off behind the ignorance of closed eyelids.

"Who is Lucinda?" she was able to muster as her breathing dripped heavy and he whispered the answer close to her ear. Her hips contradicted themselves by rising to meet his thrusts while also half-heartedly trying to dislodge him. He gripped her tighter and his own wave rose in fervor. Her hand pushed against his face, then slid around to the back of his head, gripping his hair as she began to cry out in ecstasy. For a man foreign to the ways of love, he had quickly mastered the mechanisms. He ripped her shirt open and her hungry body flashed supernova from the lightning strikes outside the windows. They both reached a limitless crescendo as thunder rattled the house, her pushing and pulling, crying and screaming with pleasure, he falling into a bottomless well of release as if tied by rope to a pitched-over stone. Or rather chained.

They lay intertwined, as one with the hard rain.

"I've always known, I suppose," she said, still gripping his hair fierce for an anchor. "Had the feeling I held half a husband but hell, it made me double the woman." He grunted in agreement as his fingers continued to explore this new map he had unfolded, the dips, the tight curves, the smooth folds. She was venturing back to arousal while dealing with a life-choice bombshell. She slapped his seeking hand away.

"You have to leave."

"No." He wanted more of this new drug. Much more. She stood up, a vivacious ink silhouette he needed to dip into and get lost writing for ever.

"Yes, and right now. Petty could very well drive up any second. That would just be that bastard's style. I need to think. A lot. Alone. This, what we did, was good and I needed it but it's over now. Mark it up to a fun night that we both shouldn't be too proud of. Please respect that. Jesus on a cracker, I don't even know your name!" He slid off the bed and gathered her tenseness in his arms. He whispered again, the smell sultry sweetness in her hair brushing his face. His name. The whites of her eyes grew wide in the darkness. Her shock swam in the heat coming off his sun burnt skin, it felt good, comforting. His manhood stiffened and she almost fell back into another helpless fervor of forgetfulness but held fast and backed away.

"Go." She pushed him out of the room and shut the door. He stood dizzy and naked in the middle of the hallway. Given a taste of delectable cookie but denied the rest. He could kick in the door, ravish her until dawn and beyond but he could hear her crying, cursing, a bubbling inferno of emotion. He would give up the fight, he had done enough damage, given fire to the mortals, stolen from his master. He would go, unhappy and unsatisfied but aware that he still held the power he had thought lost.

By the time he got dressed and back in the rig, the storm had passed and the moon revealed itself full and close, pulling back the tide. The streets were shiny from the deluge, standing water on the pavement still seeking a forever home. He didn't know where to go in this dead zone of early morning, maybe back up towards Houston and follow the easiest path from there, whether it be I-10 east to New Orleans or west to San Antonio, or even lonely highway 59 northeast towards the cypress swamps and the new influx of riverboat casinos around Shreveport. He felt like gambling, rolling the dice as Petty had taught him, a tester to see if he was truly back in Chance's good graces. Maybe pull some fat stacks then stampede across the flatlands to Lucinda and complete the set of conquering.

On the other side of the state park on the main drag of 3005, a red light beckoned the truck to stop, he laughed at the luck as he was the only vehicle in sight. Across the intersection he noticed a lone figure slightly weaving in his direction on the hot side of the curb. He couldn't quite tell through the pools of streetlights but might this be the very same asshole kid that had flipped him off earlier? Was the shirt the same color? The plaid shorts? Was the fickle lady throwing him the meatiest of bones to make up for his abbreviated first sexual encounter? He looked at the objective digital clock on his dash, it read 4:26. If it changed to :27 before the change to green outside, he would know what to do. The stumbling shape stopped for a second, reached down to tie a shoe or pick up a penny, nearly face planting. He watched the folly ahead, the clock, the stoplight all in a cosmic dance deciding fates.

Tick tock. No second hand making the mystery ever more exhilarating.

Pop. 4:27. Still red.

The almighty code had spoken so he killed the headlights, a prior lesson learned. Threw it into first and gunned it straight through the crossroads. Whoever it was never saw it coming, the truck clipped its target in third gear revving hot at 40 miles per hour, a hard shot in the right corner pocket, the snuffed-out bag of bones ricocheting up off the street, limbs angled all wrong still connected to a crushed torso flying high over the sidewalk to points unknown. The Driver never even glanced up at the rearview mirror. Instead, he accelerated, gripped the wheel tight with both hands and leaned forward, thoroughly focused on finding a coin-op car wash before dawn.

9

MACARENA

Mexico could have the state of California back for all he cared. Maybe trade it for the Yucatán and throw in Chiapas and a crate of mangoes to seal the deal. Cradles of ancient civilization are instant national treasures. As for Cali, any unspoiled beauty that would have been worth experiencing in a covered wagon had long ago been infested by the unstoppable procreation of pale protestants and their land-grab greed. Sure, he loved him some Hollywood and there were still pockets of quaint to discover around San Luis Obispo if you had more money than soul. All in all, it had become an abomination, at least virtually everything south of Monterey over to Fresno. What they hadn't put their blood-stained grubby fingerprints on was uninhabitable deserts left for the Natives, cults and Airstream outcasts. He did find some romance in the Joshua Tree, wouldn't mind curling up under one, eat a popsicle, thumb-wrestle a lizard and dream of the perfect road. He could also see sparing the time to stand on the shore of the eerie Salton Sea at daybreak, taking a step into the pages of Inferno, dance a last waltz on the edge of mother nature's sanity. Sooner or later, it would all shake into the ocean or burn up from the sparks of incessant drought, then Nevada could have its shot at being a coastal paradise. Vegas as the new Monaco, Reno by the bay. After dropping off a load of lemons, apparently just in time to leave him stuck in the middle of the Chula Vista Lemon Festival, his pessimistic desire for large scale cataclysmic destruction was reaching a fever pitch. He would have preferred the instant vaporization from the turned-key nuclear blast to crawling his way inch by inch, uninterested traffic cop by inept traffic cop, back to the expressway. There was so much yellow, so many fat babies stuffed in itchy lemon costumes, that were then stuffed in strollers who would not remember a second of this hellish celebration unless the rash they incurred left a scar. It was a miracle more people weren't victims of vehicular manslaughter; he would have severed and eaten his big toe to be able to drive roughshod over the lemonade-drinking sheep he watched parade mindlessly before him at every possible jaywalking point. The rhythmic thump from a litany of flesh fodder against the grill, the newly created soft speed bumps tossing him up from the driver's seat, the screams as if he were The Beatles stepping off a plane. Then the white-gloved officers would blow whistle songs with glee jumping up to give him a high five and a key to the city, motorcycles escorting him to a clear eight-lane bypass as he left a well-deserved massacre in his wake. Headlines the next day: Police force forever thankful for the day of the glorious big rig! Chief never again has to police this misguided worship, celebrating a fruit that isn't even sweet.

By the time he broke through the hours-deep perimeter and found near ecstasy in shifting out of second gear ramping up to the expressway, he was hungry, thirsty and in need of all relief. The first exit he saw was for the town of Lemon Grove and a cruel irony left a sour taste in his mouth as he veered off to search for the best asphalt oasis.

"That your rig?" A question he had heard repeatedly from amphetamine junkies, whores, chatty troopers, retired truckers in appreciation. This sounded different. He turned around to something he had not experienced often, another pair of eyes on his level. Not three feet away stood another large man, a red-braided-beard Viking pillager who, in millennia past, could easily have been recruiting a hearty bunch to sail back to England for more of that delicious ultraviolence. He even matched him overall for overall, although his looked pricey, more recently purchased at a posh outdoor-clothing outlet store.

"Yes." They sized each other up in the late-afternoon parking lot that baked dry in the heat, neither showing a glimmer of perspiration.

"Step into my office." The Viking walked toward a nondescript van that looked like it should have been parked outside of an Italian social club in Queens gathering evidence for a RICO case. Was this guy FBI? Was his past finally catching up with him? Why another van crossing into his life? Coincidence? Or were the reality threads becoming finite? He stood still and breathed deep, a purposeful hesitation to ponder all of this and his possible moves. The Viking noticed his reticence at seeing what looked like a government issued vehicle. "Don't worry, man, I'm a civilian. I'm on your side. Just want to make you a business offer. A damn good one, involving you hauling freight for me." He slid open the side door, displaying a mobile office, complete with desk, phones, a floor-to-ceiling filing cabinet. It did little to sway The Driver's trust. "C'mon. I'll leave the door open. I'm alone. You think the Feds would send one agent to detain the likes of you?" That made sense. He looked deeper into the van, there was no one behind the wheel. He looked back behind, didn't see any creeps in aviator shades looking on from the magazine stand inside the convenience store. The Viking eased into an office chair, grabbed a file folder. "Have a seat. This is somewhat time-sensitive." Going with his gut as he tended to do, The Driver had a seat in a metal folding chair next to The Viking. "My name is Gustav. I have a trailer in Calexico that needs to be delivered to an apple orchard outside of

Minneapolis in three days. Can you make Minneapolis in three days?"

The Driver was already doing the math as the locales left Gustav's lips.

"Sure. 1,800 miles and change. 600 a day. Joy ride."

"Good. Today is day one, though. I suggest driving through the night. You need to be parked at that orchard August 6 before midnight. Still good?"

"Yes." He would have it there a day early just to show off. "How much?"

"Ah, the brass tacks. Five large. Cash. Half right now, half in Minnesota upon arrival." He pulled an envelope out of one of the cabinets.

"Ten. I don't know you, I don't know what's in that trailer. I have a hook in Bakersfield waiting on me." The Driver folded his arms. Gustav smiled.

"I don't have it." He considered pulling the hidden cords out of the Scandinavian's thick neck, taking what cash he did have, closing the door and heading to Bakersfield as planned. Mark it up to a quick and profitable side gig.

"You don't have a lot of options or you wouldn't be approaching strangers in a parking lot the day you need that trailer heading north." It felt good to bargain, play hardball, hold all the cards and, most of all, voice it – he hadn't talked this much since Galveston. His heart fluttered at the thought of his sun goddess. Fingers tapped the desk. They appeared at an impasse unless Gustav relented.

"OK, 7,500 – 2,500 now and we make up the difference on the back end. I'll let them know you are worth the additional expense. A stranger, yes, but I have a warm fuzzy feeling you will not disappoint. Deal?" Gustav put out his freckled meat hook to seal the pact. It was still triple what he would have made on the Bakersfield run and, if they didn't pony up what was promised when he arrived, he would just take the trailer to one of those 10,000 lakes in Minnesota and dump it right in. He put

out his hand and they shook, each gripping tighter than necessary. More than a few drunk cowboys and wildcatters would
have wagered a week's paycheck watching the two arm-wrestle
for the favor of a busty stenographer and a pitcher of cheap beer
spilling out on to a sawdust floor. "OK, good. Good!" Gustav
laughed as it was easy to see a great weight had been lifted from
him. He handed over the cash and the folder. The Driver glanced
over two aerial maps, one with the location of the trailer in
Calexico, the other the location of the orchard. He had the exact
route in his head, perhaps the first in human history excited to
see the next dawn bloom while barreling through Kansas. He
quick twitched his way out of the van, it was a seamless transi-
tion into mission mode.

"One more thing." Gustav said while he still had his fleeting
attention. "The trailer locks from the inside, so however curious
you get or whatever you think you may hear, let it be."

He had the rig hooked and was heading east by five, away
from the low sun and the compromised coast, back to the flat
heart of the country where it was safe and easy and people
weren't crawling over each other to get the ocean view up in the
hills, the right dick to suck for a bit-part ten-day run on a soap, a
parallel parking spot within walking distance of Rodeo that the
poodle won't get skittish over. As for what the big ginger agent
said, if it was a trailer full of baby dinosaurs making paper
airplanes out of the Dead Sea scrolls, that was just groovy with
him. He found the bad boy just where the map said he would, a
half mile south of Calexico off the only real road, sitting all alone
in a dusty lot, the last kid to be picked for dodgeball. Looked
normal enough, industrial-grey and rust-free, maybe some kind
of exhaust pipe coming a few inches off the top, but it would
clear an overpass. It was unnerving seeing the tin sprawl of
Mexicali just over the border, hordes of enemy troops amassing
for a never assault. Border towns existed to show which country
got the best of it. When you see a city of a million-plus fluctuat-
ing, depending on which cartel was running the gambit, filled

with strife and murder like Juárez, just over the border from sleepy El Paso, half the size – you see who wants in and who wants out. Then he thought about Detroit and his theory blew up Daffy Duck with a spinning bill after a stick of dynamite style. Still, he was looking forward to getting up to that middle north, he figured that was where Gustav hailed from, Scandinavians were thicker than rats at a cheese party up in those parts where it's nine months cold and unforgiving and people fish in huts on ice with handsaws and handles of bottom-shelf scotch.

By the time he got to Phoenix, he was feeling off. Maybe it was the adrenaline and the thought that he would be driving through the night, maybe it was the new redundant Latin track that was dominating his beloved top 40. He could feel it drilling hot mercury straight into the top of his spine. Since its debut, he had been hoping beyond hope that it was a passing fad, a one-hit wonder that would hit the skids after the kids got tired of the playground melody. No such luck and now every time it came screeching from his speakers – and it came at least every half hour, it seemed – he had to twist the volume knob all the way to the left and wait four minutes, 12 seconds. A simple annoyance had grown into a real disruption of his flow, he was noticing the miles too much, it seemed the night would spread eternal before he could get across Arizona. If only it was the weekend and there was a countdown, he would be offered some clemency, the warden calling down to issue a stay of execution by 39 tracks. Twice as he wound through the destitute Indian reservations in the northeast part of the state, he could have sworn he still heard the song even after he had silenced it, a phantom haunting him through rogue radio waves, some update of an ancient Hopi curse. A half-moon began taunting him, stretching the road beyond an unreachable horizon. Was the other half hiding behind in shadow, plotting frozen antelopes and state troopers to slow him? A cold sweat formed in beads down the small of his back. He took a swig of water; it was metallic and thick on his tongue. He felt his forehead, it blazed. Something was amiss, he didn't get sick, never had a thermometer in his mouth or a spoonful of cough syrup while Mommy's chilly fingers applied vapor rub on his chest. Of course he must have been at some point growing up but his barricaded memories spared his fevered mind the actuality. She had just beaten the inconveniences out of him, really given him something to worry about with a well-placed cigarette burn or shaved-off eyebrow. Whatever this was rampaging his system, it was rattling the locks on the gates of his banished past and, if they didn't hold, Minnesota would be oceans away... he squirmed, couldn't get comfortable, muscles were cramping, a well-timed charley horse in his left leg almost took the whole operation into a dry gulch past the New Mexico border. More like Slightly Used Mexico, he laughed to himself in an attempt to recapture some mojo.

"Funny joke, mon ami! Want to head back to the Ship Rock? A slight detour for such beauty and the snakes! Oh, dear me, speaking of those majestic reptiles I neglected to introduce you to my petit ami, this is Jacques." A luminous grey Gaspard was sitting in the cab with him, his now rotting flesh almost touching his leg, intimately close as Europeans often do. The rattler was affixed to his neck and he stroked its long tubular body, grabbing the rattle violently and shaking it as a fussy baby in a cradle. "Hello, Mr Driver! Hello murderer! Long time no suck, no? I went back home to my beloved Mont St Michel in a cardboard box packed with dry ice. Never again to dance with the tides, witness the gay colored lights shine on the wet cobblestone as I stroll to the next glass of pastis." He leaned in close with a heavy breath of gas leaving the body, his yellow eyes loose in their sockets.

"Do you still have my Leica, thief with no name?" He grinned, showing off fangs dripping the venom of unrequited justice. The Driver screamed a new scream, a teeth-rattling sound from someone who had never succumbed to overwhelming fear. Against the very fiber of his being he slammed the brakes and gave all momentum over to sparkling clouds of white, glowing sand. The burst of cool air refreshed him even as his knees buckled a bit after stepping off. It was probably just something he ate. Maybe the Snatch jerky had turned or the unsettled spirit was embodying a minuscule bacterium, some vestige of revenge from beyond that was finding root. He was alone with this crimson devil moon and they somehow had to make amends. His dreams of Kansas by morning were fading fast. He considered crashing out for a few hours, sweating the sickness out in twisted sheets, a porous purge to get right. He could make up the miles lost if he was back in tip-top shape. But what if he overslept or it just got worse, advancing on him like a freight train as he slept tied to the rails? He should push through, wrestle the gorilla and hope for the best. At least he would be conscious, wielding his godly willpower. He felt as if skin had been peeled back and hot coals had been dumped into his lower back. The subterranean burn was finding routes of least resistance into his stomach, he dry-heaved bent over as a lizard flickered over his boot, racing for the drops of sweat interlaced with spit that landed on the thirsty earth. He staggered to the back of the trailer, it would be just his luck he was hauling pallets upon pallets of antibiotics or at least some plop-plop, fizz -fizz. That stout demon hustler Gustav who had led him down this dark path had not lied, there was no way to open the doors from the outside and he lacked the energy to figure out a way to force his way in.

Why did he still hear that infernal music? Get behind me, Satan!

He attempted a deep breath but the razor blades embedded in his lumbar cut it short. On the long arduous journey back to the cab, he promised himself he would allow a stop in Albuquerque, get some Dayquil to serve as his co-pilot and then be like fake nails and press on.

"You play your cards right bucko, you might just have time to punch the clown."

"Right on, Brick. Right the fuck on." But Brick was not there. He was alone in a giant vessel, sails up with unfavorable winds.

By the time he was left to rely basically on muscle memory, the blacktop arteries imprinted on the tissues of his hippocampus, having left the vastness of I-40 and veering north on the ghost highway 54 up to Texas, the Dayquil he had guzzled had done as much work as it could but it had just pushed the boulder up the hill. The fever had subsided, his chills less severe but the pain in his guts was now a gurgling volcano with a bad disposition. He had also lost an hour to the time-zone change, something he was faintly aware of but only to the point of cursing whoever thought the concept was a great idea. He felt behind, sinking in quicksand with no vine of convenience in reach to grab to pull his ass out. The sign for Dalhart was too bright, the morning was taunting him by arriving ahead of schedule. He didn't even think he could make it to Kansas, much less before first light.

Buck up! It's a stone's throw now, you little girl. Just a landing strip of Oklahoma and boom we're almost to Wichita Falls. No, that's Texas. Wichita. Kansas. No falls in either one! Which one? You can't spell Kansas without can! Can can can!

He made himself a deal, a fair deal, the new deal. Suffer through the wildfire raging through his core until the Sunflower state, then he would allow himself a breather, a respite from Loki's special torture show. He made a pledge then and there never to trust a Scandinavian again. They always had some trickery hiding under their wooly beards. Gods full of vanity and selfishness, Ragnarök could not come soon enough. He knew the first town over the Kansas state line was called Liberal. Perhaps they offered socialized healthcare. He could get an IV and some Percocets to go or they could just grant him mercy, put a bullet in him and bury him among the corn, a toppled scarecrow for the worms to feast on. While traversing the sliver of

Oklahoma the sun rose and found cruel humor in shining right into his eyes as he limped northeast. Petty had at last caught up to him, Apollo astride his golden chariot, punishing his attempt at progress. "I'd do it again, you glutton! Deceiver of love!" he shrieked at the sky. The mythologies melted into the mold of a devious overlord, retribution levied at him, the champion of mortals and righteousness. This was a war that was destined for many battles, god Petty was hell-bent on grinding him down over time, over years, decades if need be. Death by a thousand maladies. He would win eventually. Why not cancel the charade? Succumb, bend the knee and take the lashing. "Relent! The pain is too much, my insides are boiling…" Petty in glittering robes offered his benevolent hand, a kiss of white glowing rings surrounding pulsating jewels offered relief in exchange for humility, subjugation. This could end. Minutes passed without his even realizing he was driving. A fortuitous route on one of the straightest roads in the country during an early morning of no traffic kept the rig from swerving into a lane of disaster. He stared too hard, too long at the Petty/Sun. He asked forgiveness, confessed sins real and false. Gravity kept his foot on the pedal. His hands were locked on to the wheel at ten and two. Although he was not aware, Kansas was swiftly approaching.

Petty's radiant hand had spanned the heavens and now touched his forehead, the heat was immense, all-encompassing. Raptured away from the internal horror, following a blinding light. Next he knew he was sightless, buried in rubble. He could feel, knew of sheetrock, splintered lumber, insulation wet and itchy.

"Here you were born. Here. Where I granted you life." He heard Petty from above, away, everywhere. He could not move as he struggled, helplessly pinned. He opened his eyes, there, an inch away from his face…

The Driver's defeated body slumped over to rest on the bench seat and in due course the rig gently rolled to a stop on the highway, as if cradling its fallen general on the battlefield.

Just ahead, in the pleasant dewy morning, a pair of crows cawed their curiosity while perched on top of the "Welcome to Kansas" sign. An old farm pickup drove around the rig with nothing more than a couple of inconvenienced honks. For 10 minutes, all sat dormant surrounded by seas of swaying cornstalks until the song that had abetted The Driver's madness erupted out, spooking the crows into flight. The back of the trailer had opened.

Fast foreign tongues all around him. Fluorescent light attempted to break through his eyelids but he would not succumb to its harsh charm. He felt the uncomfortable push and gaps as if laying on a row of stiff passenger seats. Was he on a plane? In a bus station stranded and penniless? The pain that had overtaken him was now replaced with an other-worldly numbness. If he wasn't strewn over the musty-cushioned chair frames, he would feel as if he was floating over his body, attempting to gain a bearing on his current circumstance with a bird's-eye view. Something was leaking out of him, he felt a pulling, probing but abstract, akin to eating with a stuffed-up nose. He reached his hand up to explore the work site, what was entering or leaving him. Judge the severity of the remodel. Voices got louder; his arm was held down with a soft touch. He heard a woman calming him, "Sssshhhhh," as if he were causing a disruption, hell, he was barely moving! He had every right to know what they were doing to him and what the plan was – was this how the aliens lined up an anal probe? His limbs were dead but he had to give protest. A bandana, rank with someone's sweat but also a pungent chemical, was pressed over his face. Breathe deep. White diamonds marching through the rubber skulls. Goodnight, Sonya wake me up to the smell of biscuits and bacon frying in the Peter Pan.

Crusty sleep melded his eyelashes together. There was definite movement below him. Over a rough road, by the feel of it. Instinct drove him to persuade his right hand to feel his pocket for keys. His overalls had been rolled down and it took a while to find any coordination and dig around but no, not there. Without even opening his eyes, he could deduce two things – someone was driving his truck and he was not in the cab. Two blasphemous conditions that forced his eyes to open sudden but too wide, especially since they had been closed for more than a day and a half. Those bright lights assaulted him, white kung fu-chopping rows that left him blinded and even more pissed at such a brazen violation. Driving his rig! Hit the wrong button, flip a switch out of curiosity and guess what, friend... you die. This machine was James-Bonded-up and only he knew the intricacies. He lifted his head and shook out the cobwebs left by some silk-shitting big-ass spider. He was indeed in the trailer but it was anything but the typical vessel full of stereos or hanging meat. His assumptions hours earlier when he had floated through time and space were correct, he was lying in a row of four airline seats bolted to the floor. There were about ten rows, he figured, if numbers still held true. He could make out posters taped to the walls, old Spuds MacKenzie, the band Cinderella, Troy Aikman, Kathy Ireland covered in sand, some incarnation of Menudo. Low in a corner was a children's area with some battered cabbage-patch dolls, a fire truck, some drawings of pink unicorns on the metal. There were modern conveniences as well, a porta potty, a refrigerator, even a bungeed-up tower of box fans that must have had some tie to the exhaust he had seen sticking out of the top. Something to do with circulation, he figured but left the details to the back pages as his thoughts were plugged with cotton and there was a fire smoldering on the right side of his gut. A head poked over the seat from the row behind him. It was a cherub Mexican girl with mole-sauce-brown eyes as big as donuts. He got lost in them – they somehow made him forget the pain, his anger. He could taste their bittersweet chocolate on his swollen tongue. She giggled, was pulled away, that was when he noticed there were others sitting in the seats, women and men, young and old and they were all staring at him with a mix of fear, concern and awe. Then that infernal song started up on a radio somewhere hidden among these transient vagabonds of the highway fantastic.

"Please turn it off!" He managed to get out as the cold sweat he had swum in not long before reemerged from its icy depths. Even in this state, he would kill them all to find the source he linked to his suffering as the smell of a candle might bring a survivor back to a concentration camp. An old woman who now held the magic girl in her lap looked back with a subtle shake of her head and the song was silenced. A short man with a kind face framed by a long mustache brought him a Dixie cup full of cool water and a couple of white flaky pills.

"Buenos días." He motioned for him to take the pills. Before he obliged he noticed a large bandage covering his stomach, he immediately thought these gypsies had stolen his kidney but even the simplest of rudimentary knowledge confirmed that was not where they dwelled. He threw the pills into his mouth and the water, so very fine, washed them down past the sandpaper plastered to his throat. The man smiled and pointed to his own stomach. "Appendix." Pantomimed it being taken out and pointed back at The Driver. "Todo bien." He offered two thumbs up.

"Dios mío, Hector, quit acting like an ignorant peasant. You've been speaking English since you were five. Think we can skip the act-dumb stage of the operation," an exasperated man sitting in the last row called out as he finished rolling a joint. "You had an acute appendicitis, gringo. Luckily my abuela there behind you has always been handy with a scalpel. Midwife, dentist, tonsils, amputations, shit she even castrated a pedophile back home when he was passed out but that is a story for another 'tequila-around-the-campfire' time. Bottom line is she saved your life with an assist from the lot of us so before you go all Yankee and get your ass up in arms for getting hijacked, I suggest showing some gratitude to the multitude." He lit the joint and exhaled into the direction of the fans, the smoke blew back into his face and he inhaled it again. "Two puffs for the price of one."

Hector made his way back to the man, bracing himself with a hand against the sidewall as the trailer swayed around a sharp turn. "Pass it over Armando, be a good hermano. Helps with el mareo." Abuela put her leathery hand on The Driver's forehead then nodded. Motioned for him to lay back. The magic girl peeked soothingly between the seats at him as the brothers smoked and the little migrant pod pressed on north.

After some slow hours of drifting in and around sleep he was stirred awake by an absence of movement – the rig had stopped. The inhabitants of the trailer/cabin rose and began putting together belongings excitedly. The last-row man, Armando, casually walked up to the trailer door. "Make sure you don't forget your picking gloves, we have reached our final destination. Gracias for flying migrant worker airlines!" He unlocked and pushed open the double doors. Feathered early-autumn afternoon sunlight invaded the trailer, along with an Edenesque fragrance of ripe apples. The Driver turned his head and saw nothing but trees bathed in gold. "You hang tight, amigo. Let us get the women and kids back on solid ground and situated and we will then medivac you to an actual bed, if we can find a wheelbarrow big enough for your giant ass." After a greedy final drag Armando flicked a smoldering roach out the door and jumped down effortlessly on to green grass, stretching his wiry frame and bellowing out a long wolf call of relief.

He would later find out that the abuelo, his surgeon's capable husband, had commandeered the rig after his sudden indisposition and completed the journey without stopping or touching anything that did not directly affect moving the truck forward. They had made the deadline with hours to spare and he had been paid his bonus in crisp bills while still bedridden in one of the Orchard owner's guest bedrooms, as far as possible from his two highly inquisitive teenage daughters who occupied the top floor.

The man's name was Mr Johansen and you could not call him by his first name, Richard. One of those typical marble-cold third-generation Swedish-Americans, short on words and affability. A wispy blonde combover sat on top of a rail-thin frame as if the food he ate was not welcomed to hang around and do any nourishing. He would have been better suited as an undertaker in some rainy Victorian novel who tortures kittens before saving them in jars of formaldehyde he keeps on the mantle to put a chill into the recently widowed of the village. Contrarily, not only did the master allow the abuela to enter the sickroom to tend to the wound, but all the workers had carte-blanche access to the farmhouse, cooking and eating in the kitchen. Children ran and slid reckless through the halls in their socks when they were not jack-and-jilling buckets full of apples past his window. One or both of the Johansen daughters could also be caught peering through the double-paned portal of the injured prince, hoping to catch a glimpse of a sponge bath to ascertain if his belly button was an innie or an outie, as a significant wager of an NSYNC CD had been placed on it. All his peripheral would catch of their surveillance would be a flying blonde pigtail quickly bobbing down or the sound of embarrassed laughter. It was on one of those days as he stared helplessly at a large disturbing clown painting dominating the far wall, trying to decide if that was what one considered irony or cruel coincidence, that Armando sauntered in after the work day to check on the patient. He had crept to the edge of the window and jumped out as two sets of thick mascara eyes were straining to drink in The Driver's downy-haired taut midriff, a prone golden treasure so inviting only a few lazy sunbeams away. Girlish screams exploded into the room. Armando sighed, watching them scamper around the corner of the house.

"You are quite popular, mi amigo, I should sell tickets to all the farm girls in the county. Come witness the half-naked golden Adonis on his feather-bed throne! Fainting is not the fault of the proprietors!" Armando pulled up the single sheet and looked down, The Driver grabbed it back in a reflex of modesty. "It is an outie! Excellente! I got 4 to 1 odds on that little protruding button. I am going to clean the primos out tonight! I need to find a camera." Armando sat down at the foot of the bed, then lay back over The Driver's feet, staring at the ceiling. He looked over at the door then back at The Driver and half whispered: "Weird place, right? You got this creepy gangly albino mo fo running this place, who has no wife nor any trace of one living, with two budding blonde blue-eyed daughters who are hornier than three-balled tomcats itching to see what you are packing... and get this, they just appeared a couple of years ago out of nowhere. Did he buy them? Make them out of clay and breathe life into their butt holes? There aren't any family photos to be found. The head honcho, he sure isn't talking. It's like a bad romance novela la abuela reads to us on the trips back and forth since she can't watch the television but, ay papi, better you than me. I don't trust myself from making an Armando torta with those two and getting strung up on from the tallest apple tree for it. You know it's been cinco años we have been up here and it hasn't gotten any more normal. I get the goose bumps whenever I see this place. There is some evil you can't quite see, ¿ya sabes? I have also picked about a million apples and got paid straight cash under the table so don't rock the barco, right? Been paid high hog by Mexican standards. I go home, live like a king for nine months out of the year living on cold cervezas and the good sinsemilla. Maybe I will get into the music business. Produce a Tejano band, I've got an ear. Took accordion lessons when I was a niño. You heard that new song? Bump budda bump budda bump budda budda... The gringos can't get enough, might be time to capitalize on their lust for the Latin beats. What do you think? Get outta apples while the getting is good."

"You talk like a white guy." The Driver had an urge to see his wound. It itched.

"I should, I did most of high school in Fort Worth. Lived with mi tía. You could smell the stockyards when the wind blew wrong. Somehow it made one miss Mexico. I went back south after a couple of years, help take care of the familia and here I am, picking apples all day for the undertaker and lying on a bed way up in Minnesota with a dude who has never said his name."

"A long, strange trip."

"Sí, indeed. I'm starving, Marvin, you want me to bring you a plate? Think there are tamales to be had."

"Have the daughters bring it in, I'm in the mood to dish out some cheap thrills."

Armando stood up, shook his head, "Ha ha! You must be feeling good, señor! Be careful, though, there is a tree out there that's even tall enough for you!"

By peak season, as the leaves were giving in to their dying colors, he had recovered and thus felt obligated to hang around and join the effort, driving whatever had a motor, the tractor down the long rows, forklift in the dusty storehouse, lawn mower, old delivery truck with a sticky transmission to local grocers, bakeries or the farmers' market in Edina. It was payback for a life saved and the crew welcomed his strong, quiet presence. The orchard held about every variety of apple one could name and each grew heavy on the limb at different times, dictating where the workers concentrated their base of operations. The trees were strategically planted so the action drew closer and closer to the house as the days grew crisper and shorter. When the bushels piling into the crates shifted from Honeygold to Golden Delicious, everyone knew the end was nigh. He had had plenty of time to witness the subtle movements coming from the house while sitting in various driver seats, the futile subterfuge of Richard Johansen and the various nondescript packages he brought inside the house and down to the basement where a naked bulb would flicker on through a narrow window packed tight against the earth, the daughters flaunting nakedness and red-light district waves from their upstairs bedroom windows when they knew he was mowing the grass. The house was divided during harvest, each level segregated. Rarely did the factions mix that he could see. He slept in his nondescript room on the main level, being stared at by the too-white face that glowed in the night with a droopy frown that barely hid a devious glee. The background of the painting matched the color of the wall – it seemed the clown was just floating there in its billowy red jumper, watching him sleep. The frame was no fence for the creature's ability to bounce around the room through the darkest hours – it might sit about to pounce on top of the knotty-pine dresser or slide giggly under the bed. The last straw was the night he opened his eyes and it was lying silent next to him, gloved hands seeking his throat in revenge for its fallen brother. That episode disturbed him to the point that he resigned himself to sleep with the door open, finding comfort in the cicada-like rhythmic sounds of snoring from the crew in the living room, who slept on every piece of available furniture or on the floor in sleeping bags in an unspoken system dictated by seniority. He ate all his meals at the kitchen table with the rest of the workers, spent his nights outside around the fire, listening to what he could make out of their stories from home, laughing when others did and offering a solemn glance when the elders grew quiet. Other than the raised eyebrows from Armando when the daughters offered to wash a vehicle sans bras, there was never gossip of what went on inside the home up above or down below. Either everyone knew or no one cared to screw the golden goose, he couldn't quite decide.

During a crowded dinner of a family recipe of spicy green chile stew that originated from back when Spain still held the reins and fresh corn on the cob slathered in butter and cayenne pepper, he imagined how the atmosphere changed after the lively energy of the temporary tenants withdrew back south, leaving the pale trio to endure the brutal winter. If the Johansens repossessed the main floor and huddled with blankets and hot chocolate around the fire, counting the days when they could again go their separate ways or perhaps stare past the flames and tip over to thoughts of gothic horror during the too-long dark nights, wielding an ax and spraying the sitting room with the blood of their relations. Such fantasies played fancifully in his head during and after dinner, leading up to what was the last of the nightly bonfires as the harvest was ending and frost had begun to encroach on the fallen leaves. He had finally summoned the wherewithal to wrestle the bastard jester off the wall and sneak it out of the house under his arm to burn it to ash as it so well deserved. He doubted anyone in the house would notice. Whoever had painted it, bought it and hung it were all certainly in a particularly nasty circle of hell getting sodomized by John Wayne Gacy. Armando was particularly thrilled to watch the clown incinerate as he recounted a near miss with one of the rodeo variety who had tried to lure him into some holding pens with a handful of Bit-O-Honeys and a pint of mezcal when he was an undersized freshman in high school.

"Burn the witch!" Armando yelled, spitting spite into the fire. Everyone laughed and cheered on The Driver as he threw the painting in, crackles and pops mixed with a faint whine/cry as the canvas bubbled. At least one ghost was put to rest. Armando handed him tequila and he took a deep slug. The whole scene felt like a ritualistic ending of a chapter of his life, a brief respite from his life on the road, that he would miss and look back on fondly as he was driving alone through somewhere like Eastern Wyoming, spotting the occasional jackrabbit and not much else. No apple trees, no smell sweet in the cool morning, no loud table of rich food with competing voices teasing in fast Spanglish he couldn't understand but still appreciated. This momentous evening, everyone not named Johansen was out around the circle, the women, the children, even the matriarch abuela.

"Are you sad to leave? he asked no one in particular. He definitely was. The magic girl appeared between a couple of the cousins sitting on stumps. One put a gentle hand on her back, the other reached in the cooler behind and handed her a juice box. It was apple.

The bonfire reflected orange sincerity in her giant eyes. "We will be sad to lose you, gran hombre." Saying her piece, she busied herself with getting the straw in the box. If he had a heart, it would have melted. Even without the albatross of emotion, he wanted to scoop her up in his arms. If her gaze held such a calming effect, what would her touch elicit? He hit the tequila again. It would have to do.

He stood staring at the girl with a slight smile on his face as Armando grabbed back the bottle and looked at how much was gone, shook his head. "How is your scar?" The Driver lifted up his shirt and turned toward the burning glow. "Damn, that is nice work. Barely even there. I told you Abuela was the best semitrailer surgeon north of the Red River. She may or may not have put your appendix in a pot of pozole and served it to you back when you were laid up but that's all part of the healing process." Armando looked for shock or at least a retch but got nothing. He didn't know he was trying to gross out a casual cannibal. "Hey, remember when I told you she snipped the cojones off a pedophile?" The Driver nodded, reaching for the bottle. Armando kept it at arm's length. "It wasn't just some random dude. It was her nephew, my second primo Zorro, like the swordsman. He was a luchador, wore all black, rode in on a white caballo, played the hero in the ring. One match he got thrown over the top rope, was supposed to land on a trick table that was meant to break his fall but that table had been mixed up with a real table. He broke his back. While he was laid up, our girl over there, she was maybe three or so, she would come sit with him and he would read her stories, high as a kite on morphine. You know the effect she has, she made him feel better. She was his only light, a canary in a cave of pain. He got hooked on the drug, got hooked on her. His mind left for another plane, man. Loco. He started talking about how they were going to get married. One day he asked Abuela for her hand all naked and sweaty, holding her tight on the bed with him like a stuffed animal. The girl was crying, who knows what he had been up to. Abuela shot him up with a full dose and when he nodded off she got the girl out of there and fetched her tools." The others had listened to the tale, shook their heads as Abuela nodded hers.

"What happened then?" The Driver had fetched the bottle back.

"Zorro got the gay blade," Abuela answered with a sneer, spitting and crossing herself. A few stifled guffaws slipped out among the group and soon everyone was laughing. Even the magic girl, but the memory of Zorro was still in her, a weed with strong roots in her soul.

Once the dancing started and that singular evil song, which had become as physically repugnant to him as someone creasing paper with their fingernails, popped up on the play list, he said his reluctant goodbyes and headed back to the house. He hoped against all hope that it wasn't too late and the sonic tripe had already dug in deep with its claws to play non-stop all night in his head as he tried to fall asleep. There was the absence of the clown overlord watching him lie restless among the old quilts, one comfort he could hang his hat on if he ever wore one. Undressed, he scampered over the floorboards and third base slid under the icy covers ready to battle the unstopping gears of his brain. It was all for naught. Thanks to the tequila, the internal radio station H.E.L.L. was off the air and he drifted off into a dreamless sleep devoid of sound. Almost.

Some time in the deep curve of the night he awoke to the creak of a door and he knew immediately which one it was. He also felt a sense of wrongness at play, it took one who cooks in that kitchen to know the subtle gamey smells adrift. He got out of bed, slowly opened the bedroom door he had personally lubricated the hinges of so as not to awake his amigos when he needed to shuffle down the hall to urinate. He felt his way toward the living room, tiptoeing on the worn planks, the familiar sounds of sleep, young and old, helping to direct him. As he caught the ring of dim light around the crack of the basement doorframe his eyes adjusted to the rest of the room. Instinct led him to step closer and take stock to see if the manifest met the true count. He knew with a grave certainty it would be short one and he was right. The magic girl was missing. He met a pair of open eyes seeking him out from the far wall by a moon glow window, they were Abuela's as she sat in a recliner draped with a soft fur throw. She motioned with her steady hand for him to approach.

"¿Dónde está la chica?" he managed to question.

"No lo sé," she whispered back. They both looked back toward the basement door. He turned away to seek the girl out but Abuela grabbed him in a fierce grip. From under the blanket came a scalpel, catching the moon, a glimmer malicious. He took it, a strand of hope from some uncharted place that he could make her proud. His mission was not one of the hero, though, it was purely selfish, to again feel the calm the girl brought to the tormenting sea. With his size, it was near impossible to take the stairs down soundlessly. It was an equation of urgency versus cautiousness. It helped that Billy Joel was down there singing about not starting the fire to cover the creaks of his descent. He never liked the song, one he remembered hammered the top 40 charts as he was just starting out on the road. A world in miniature unfolded before him as he reached the bottom step. The entire orchard recreated to scale on an enormous table that dominated an unfinished room. Every tree, farm hand, vehicle was represented. Little pennant signs rose up among the broccoli-sized plastic clusters, denominating each apple variety. On the other side of the table, Richard was a grey thin smear, shirtless in a glistening sweat as he held the magic girl in his arms. She was helping him place the tiny workers around a cold fire next to the dollhouse/farmhouse. The Driver felt the scalpel lithe and ready in his fist.

"Come play with us, gran hombre!" They both looked up at him, a colossus in boxers towering over the little world, a vengeful god given to selfish dalliances when left unguided. Each held a smile on their face, too wide to be natural. Her eyes were beyond enormous under the harsh light of the hanging bulb.

"You are not allowed down here, this is my domain. Please rectify your trespass." Each word came out of Richard's mouth as if they were their own sentence. Long pauses from licking his lips. A Cheshire cat with a lizard tongue. "She helps me place the workers. She knows where all of you are. Helps me keep track." He reinforced his grip on her, a possession play. The girl picked up a larger figure and put him inside the house.

"¡Eres tú!"

"Very good! Now where should he be?'

"Bed… room."

"Bueno!" Richard squeezed her, swam in her eyes. She put the figure in the guest bedroom of the scaled-down home. The Driver could even make out the clown painting, a postage stamp of condensed haunt in the detailed recreation. Billy Joel restarted his song.

"Come. Abuela wants you." The Driver made his way around the shrunken orchard. Richard sensed the impending danger to his bliss. The blonde behemoth he had welcomed into his home was threatening to wrestle away the central cog to his perfect little world. His seasonal empire surrounded the drug-fueled sanctuary, all to rule with the child queen. Soon enough, The Driver was close enough to touch, to trace the metal flesh ridges of rippling muscle. Richard was enthralled, frozen, not knowing which dessert to cherish most. A great hand possessing both violence and benevolence reached down from the heavens for the girl, Richard was helpless to stop him. A last shudder of ecstasy through his fingers and she was gone. Pain and panic rose from the dead to gnaw again at their unfinished meals. The Driver looked down at this pathetic reptile. The code was not needed here. Leaving him to this lifeless world to stare at as snowdrifts rose slowly to cover the basement windows would be punishment enough.

"Yo, can we get a break from this old dude song, Dick? We

need some beatsssss. Beats. Beats. Beeeeeeeatssss." A voice purred nasty from somewhere in the void behind Richard. The Driver peered toward the source past Richard's bony shoulder and a smile the smile of a mischievous boy who has been caught with his fat hand in the cookie jar but is too greedy to let go. There was a teasing movement of shapes leaning to-and-fro, stripes, triangles, stars. Bending lines of an unnatural rainbow, they cut behind darkness only to reappear melded with some previously unforeseen form inches to the left or right as transforming luminous creatures. They flowed and pulsed inside a narrow room containing nothing but a squeezed-in bare queen-sized mattress that bowed up in the middle. The walls were covered with the same glow-in-the-dark paint as what twisted about on the bed, smiley faces and puffy hearts intermixed with archaic symbols that would cause a revival preacher specializing in sermons thick with the meteoric rise of satanic cults to pound his fist on the leg of his circulation snuffing high-waisted polyester Sunday best. Almost lost in a corner under some amateur graffiti and a precise sigil of Baphomet lived an innocent purple unicorn, alone in the savage wilderness, naïve to the evils that surrounded it. Surely this inanimate creature was the magic girl's talisman, both at a loss for their deserved innocence. The kinetic shapes that had been separated from the walls and given demonic life floated cloudlike off the bed out the edge of the incandescent 60-watt light to welcome the intruder, a man for whom they had been baiting the hook for a fortnight. The animated patterns were revealed to be intricate symbols brushed all over the "daughters", loose-limbed and nude except for the paint clinging to their hot skin. They both stepped closer to drink in the scene at the model table with synchronized wide starving eyes, especially for The Driver who would make the meatiest of sandwiches.

"Now it's a party!" One spoke and her doppelganger meowed, motioning for him to join their pile with a crooked finger and pink tongue as another hand reached down for the nether regions of her companion.

Richard moaned at the sight, not wanting to share his treasure but seeing an opportunity. "You can have them, devour them, just give me back the girl." The Driver kept her high in his arms, overloaded from the assault on his senses, the succubus luring cries, Billy fast-talking his way through the pop culture decades. He noticed now the paint pockmarked on Richard, too, who sat there on a common metal stool in nothing but his underwear, a gaudy-looking gold-and-silver-striped thong, precious debauchery. "Take them! Break them! Fill their voracious holes! Return my grail fiend, my young chalice... I must drink..."

The situation had mutated from leaving this walking cadaver of Liberace be to deciding the fate of an orgy in the illicitness extreme. There had been far more complex palavers with Chance than this loaded dice roll. He examined the magic girl, who stared through him, grinding her teeth with that tragic smile derived from fierce chemical means. Simple enough, yes, if the pack of she-wolves had their way with her back there, if the paint was on her... their sparkling mark of the beast... He reached up with his free hand and punched out the bulb. Richard yelped like a dog hearing thunder.

The Driver's ward looked down at her arms, legs, grinned as she whispered in his ear: "I... shine!"

He threw some kindling over the soft glowing coals, built the furnace back up to a respectable heat. Abuela and Armando stood there with him, watching the flickering flames bouncing off each other, theirs a triad of unwanted knowledge, the unfathomable truths. The motions that led them were free but felt guided by some forgotten text. He handed the scalpel back, Abuela hiding it within the folds of the blankets draped over her in an efficient move honed to perfection over time. Armando met his eyes, as if nodding to the prison guard to flip the switch on the electric chair from behind the viewing glass. "Throw them in." He spat, unwilling to offer any signs to Jesus for blessings or humble pleas for forgiveness.

The Driver held a severed pair of testicles, the sticky blood caked dry between his fingers. He held the globes up to the burning light for a last kiss of the night air... then Richard's manhood was a for ever part of the fickle flames. The gallery stood under the low moon and listened to them sizzle.

The smell made his stomach growl, he wondered if they could hear.

CANDLE IN THE WIND 1997

A ll he had left of her was a single photograph he kept on the glass of his dash. The magic was dim but, if he focused on it and emptied his mind, the pink-sky morning winds scattered enough to get through the day. He often asked her image why he had been a witness to such darkness? Not many men could say they have encountered cannibals, nympho hookers, road-raged clowns, ecstasy-fueled satanic pedophiles – all while just trying to transport goods through the good ole morally superior US of A. He wasn't a homicide detective in Brooklyn, a fictional cop where every week the extreme depravity of humanity is exposed to TV-dinner-eating dimwits. Was it his own goodness-sucking void that attracted it? A karma magnet? Did Chance lead him as a defining hand because he was so willing to deliver cold justice or able to simply kill on the whim of a butterfly wing? Thinking back even farther to those ever-so-light-sleeping monsters he held at bay, his destiny had always been tied to carnage, a reaper to sweep clean the spiders in the corner of the ceiling that fed on wayward souls. Do not ask why the fates continued to chatter, play your part and, at the end of the show, the unseen audience, the archangels and demons eating popcorn souls, will stand with fervor and applaud your dedication to the craft.

It was crisp, he had his window down pining for a waft of apple trees but there was a football game about to be played in Knoxville. He settled the rig smooth and firm in the right lane through the throngs of Neyland Stadium-bound out-of-state cars invading from all sides on to I-40. When he hit Strawberry Plains, it became a stop-and-go battle to the drop downtown that just sat on the horizon teasing him. Yet another day where his timing could have been better, when there weren't more than 100,000 fans congregating into a few city blocks to drink whiskey and watery beer, sloppily eating whatever mystery meat they threw on one of those black bubble-shaped grills that would taste strongly of the half a squeeze bottle of lighter fluid it took to get the coals hot. Throwing weak-armed duck passes to each other's ankles in the parking lot while wearing jerseys that hugged tight at the gut. The distant sound of the band calling them to stagger into the cement coliseum with a noticeable stiff leg that the flask is strapped to, singing along to the fight song, talking trash to the visiting fans who are all doing the same. He saw a lot of red as he fought through the yelling pedestrian traffic. It was the third Saturday of October and that meant an invasion from Alabama, his home state. This particular contest was a tradition mechanism fueled by the family money-boosters, old, broken, pickled-liver men, cheering on a revolving door of forever youth from the skybox, cursing them if they were a step too slow at getting a good shot on the QB, if the ball was not stretched far enough to move the chains. He never understood cheering for a team based on a state boundary. Having pride in those 18-year-olds that were bought under the table from different states to come play for yours. There wasn't much to be proud about being from Alabama that he could think of. Probably why football was a religion, same reason why slaves embraced Christianity, cling to the intangible that promises something beyond your putrid existence. These days, there are no chains, no snarling dogs chasing you through the bayous. Ignorance was now the slave owner, what kept people from just moving to someplace better, chasing the waking dreams.

He was chasing his, even when they were disguised as nightmares.

He spotted the Sunsphere as the game got under way. He could hear the deep swelling roar of the crowd rolling over the suddenly deserted streets. The gold mirrors from the top reflecting the promise of a cloudless sky meant he was close to the Old City and the warehouse that awaited his trailer full of coffee beans, as he determined from the overwhelming smell. He didn't understand the science, psychosomatic maybe, but it kept him awake and alert, his feet tapping along to the top 40 non-stop all the way from the port of Philadelphia. A clarity of purpose was the rule of the day as he had succumbed to what was an inevitable mission. He wasn't hitching up a new load in any physical sense. The pull he had first felt that sultry late night in Texas had gathered strength out in the gulf of circumstance. He was on that beeline south to Robbinsville and Lucinda, to see if he could also lasso the moon as he had the sun. Still alive, that unexplainable hunger ravaging his sense of closure to cheat the cheater, shake a trembling fist at his personal mentor/god. That fist was at the rail, the tipsy crowd gathered at the table and cheered for his success. He was prepared if the dice tumbled out to rest on a hard eight, if he was instead to pull up the gravel drive and face Petty, the surrogate Laius, he would push it all on the pass line and blow.

The house was quiet and dark when the rig crunched to a stop in front of the cabin, not late enough to turn on lights, even though the sun had sunk below the sentinel ridgeline hours earlier. Before he could even step down, he heard a vehicle behind him, it was Petty and the kids rolling to a soft stop in a khaki brown Jeep wrangler with the top off. His heart dropped and raced at the same time, a rabbit dropped into the chute chased by love and hate, both fighting to break through the numb membrane of his stony consciousness.

"Hey, kid." Petty offered from the driver's seat as his son and daughter crawled out, each giving the Driver a side hug before moving on to the continuation of their own personal endeavors, oblivious to the unannounced visit and the tenuous energies throwing sparks around them. The Driver nodded a hello in return. Petty made no effort to get out, rather sat and sized up the intent of the interloper, the return of the prodigal almost-son. The Driver was ready for anything, to be run over or kissed on the mouth. What did he know? He had to assume everything. He always did.

"Been a while. Years. How's business?" Petty pulled out his trusty pipe, loaded it while keeping his eyes up.

"Good. You?" He could pierce the brain through the earhole with that pipe, it would be just long enough.

"Semi-retired." He chuckled while he lit the tobacco. Stifled a cough. Were his lungs as black as his heart?

"Nice one. How's Lucinda?" He wished he had something to do with his hands like Petty did, keep the anxieties wrapped in servitude.

"Still mean as a bobcat with an itchy ass. She is up in Asheville with her friends, gawking at the Biltmore again. Makes this place look even worse when she gets back, makes her even meaner. It's a vicious cycle. She'll be sad she missed you, though – always had a soft spot for strays." Petty opened the door of the Jeep suddenly, as if testing the response of a surprise movement. The Driver held still, pondering his next move on the chessboard. Petty grabbed a bottle wrapped in a paper sack and climbed out. He strode past The Driver close enough to brush his arm. The smell of the leaf tobacco was pleasant, ominous. At the door Petty stopped and yelled over his shoulder. "C'mon in, let's get this over with."

Deer steaks cooked in a cast-iron skillet served with fry daddy tater tots and tomato slices. They sat around the reclaimed barn-wood dining-room table, as a family would have a century and a half past, eating unaware a band of Iroquois were squatting in a switchback from above on the mountain, sharpening steel while drawing out a raid in the pine needles under the gathering dusk waiting for the full moon to trigger spilled blood. Rocky and Lilac felt tension the way a pet senses cancer in its owner. It wasn't enough to damper Rocky's appetite as a growing boy entering manhood on the bullet train as he had quickly foregone the use of a steak knife and was just tearing at the meat from all sides around a raised fork. Manners were not enforced while mom was away as Lilac was pocketing most of her steak for whatever dogs she had sequestered in her room that week. No one was saying much except for Marvin Gaye who was simply asking what was going on from the turntable in the high-ceilinged living room, the timber walls adding to the richness of the sound.

"You came at an opportune time. A watershed moment. Rocky reports to boot camp tomorrow, don't ya, son?" Petty asked flatly as he sloshed the ice cubes of his triple bourbon around, The Driver felt it impossible to discern whether he was happy, mad or indifferent about it.

"Yeah. Fort Benning." Rocky talked through a mouthful of meat. "Catching the bus in Asheville. Gonna be a sniper, I can already hit red from 300 meters, can't I dad?"

"Dead on balls, son. Gonna be knocking them Arabs right off their camels."

"Just don't shoot any camels Rocky. They're sweet. They have three sets of eyelids and two sets of eyelashes to keep out the sand. I'd kill for those eyelashes."

"OK, Li, no camels. You gonna eat your tater tots?" Lilac counted out what she had on her plate and gave Rocky half. He winked and started shoveling.

"Nothing fun about war, Rocky. It's death incarnate. Hell on earth. Limbs and cooked entrails surrounding you, your eardrums shredded from mortar shells. You see toddlers explode in the middle of a dirt road and you are helpless, all thanks to faceless white-haired devils sending you out to kill so they can reupholster the sundeck furniture on their auxiliary yacht." The Driver looked at the blood from the rare steak on his plate. Would Rocky see that same color seeping from shrapnel that had cut through his stomach? Failing to hold his insides in, alone on a rooftop next to the worthless sniper rifle that's notched its last taken soul? "It's all for nothing, man. You aren't protecting anything when they ship you thousands of miles away. Just dumping you in to wreak havoc in someone else's home when you should be at yours finding what little joy there is to find in a fleeting existence. Homemade bombs are there to tell you a mistake has been made. They throw them under the Humvees every day like the morning newspaper, blow your legs into pink mush. Keep your legs, your sanity, your life. Yours." The Driver levied a heavy finger at Rocky who stopped chewing. The words hung heavy, a gas cloud of truth.

"Shut the fuck up. No greater honor than serving your country, son, if the need arises. Heroes are not born, they are made. This may be your time."

"What will you say when you see him come off the plane in a box and they hand you a flag and a handshake as they move down the line? Heroes don't die for nothing."

"Rocky, you better go make sure you are packed up. Lilac, you go feed your horde you got back there in your room. Just remember if they shit on the floor and your mom sees it she will lay waste to everything in sight. Make a little desert skirmish look like hopscotch." Rocky had turned green in the gills as he got up unsteadily. Lilac actually had to help him from the table.

"Thanks a lot. Kid is gonna go puke up everything he just ate. What a waste of good food."

"Someone has to tell him. I bet there were plenty of your buddies back in Vietnam that would have been well-served to have heard it."

"Suppose so. Part of being an American man, though – get a

gun, go somewhere, kill or be killed, come home or don't. It's our rite of passage like any other primitive tribe. You skip that, you are missing part of what makes a man a man." Petty reached under the table and pulled up the bottle. The Driver drained his Ball jar of iced tea and pushed it over to be filled. "Serious drinking man now, are ya?" Petty filled both glasses, passed one back and held up his. "Here is to those who wish us well, everybody else can go to hell." They clinked glasses and The Driver drank, hidden fingers crossed in his lap. He was pretty sure he hadn't missed a damn thing not being a pawn for the masters of war. He had been called to a higher duty.

Later, The Driver found himself in front of another fire, this one in an intricate stone ring set among the last frog songs of summer past. Petty sat brooding across the cauldron from him, bottle in one hand, glass in the other. He was hitting the sauce harder than he remembered, either topping off the tank with liquid courage or drowning an overwhelming sadness. Or both. There was no need to try and match him drink for drink, so The Driver took to sipping here and there, watching the flames lick the rocks and contemplating his next bet. He would glance up for a different perspective now and then, waiting for his eyes to adjust to the absence of light and reveal the big oaks below clusters of stars, planets, ancient gods lost to the winds.

"How's the big girl running?" Petty threw his glass into the black and took a slug straight from the bottle.

"Good. No complaints." The Driver looked through the heat at Petty's face glowing orange, seemed to be increasing in size, a supernova blooming.

"All the mods still in working order? You used them lately? They been tested?"

"Everything is as you designed it."

"Don't forget it. I put near a million miles on that tough bitch. All the little traps and springs and fuck buttons wired up in her were my idea. Safest ride ever built, you could take her through

Baghdad with the windows down blaring Lee Greenwood drinking a cup full of Sanka and come out not spilling a drop."

"Not going to argue with you about that."

"You been down in Galveston lately?" Petty leaned forward following the hard slider he threw.

"Lately? No."

"Well by lately I mean in the last couple of years, not in the last couple of weeks."

"I go a lot of places, Petty, you know that better than anyone."

"Sure, big man. Just that a couple of years ago, my Sonya, you remember me mentioning her?" The Driver nodded, remembered her quite well. His loins twitched. "Well, out of the blue she changed the locks on the house down there. Screamed at me through the door, that I was the devil's incubus who had brought hell down upon us, yadda yadda. I tried to talk her down till she topped it off informing me our son had been killed in a hit-and-run and that it was my fault, my unforgivable sins had caused it, my double life. She knew everything. Lucinda's name, this place, the whole chimichanga, bud. Now, how do you think she came by all that information?" Petty scooted to the very edge of the black metal chair he was in, his ass tight, throwing sparks. He was ready to pounce, draw blood, tear open gaping holes and climb in. Time slowed to a stop. The Driver was sort of amazed to hear about the boy, those were long odds but made sense in a cosmic-cruelty way. He felt no fear of the old man, even drunken anger would fall at his feet. He had absorbed about all of Petty's power. He had his rig, had had his wife, had slain a son. The question was whether or not to admit to it all. To confess to the man who had given him so much willingly and unwillingly. Was he in his debt? No. Lions do not show mercy to the former Alpha, they push them out on to the thirsty plains to die. Let him suspect, the uncertainty would devour him, making death more welcome. There was still more meat to pick off the bone anyway.

"Sorry to hear that. You had to know you were playing with fire, though. Tough to keep two fishing lines from getting tangled when they are cast off the same boat." He leaned back as Petty perched, letting the night air expand between them. Not finding a tell in The Driver's poker face, Petty let out a defeated sigh and brought the bottle back to his lips.

"I told Lucinda just enough to piss her off but not enough to cut my dick off with a butter knife. Told her I had a bastard before we met. She let me go to the funeral. All I got for it was a mortuary bill and a spit in the face from Sonya. Since I got back from that, Lucinda been the one gone most of the time. Went from two beautiful wives to damn near zero. She wouldn't even come home to see Rocky off, said she will say goodbye at the bus station. Always up in Asheville getting who knows what from who while I sit here raising these kids, trying to find out how the fuck it all went wrong at the bottom of the bottle." At the mention, he pitched it up again, finished it off and threw it out into the woods. It did not break. Even that satisfaction eluded him.

"I'll get you another." The Driver stood up, high over the dying fire. Petty's face was a mixed-up jigsaw puzzle of resignation, guilt that he did not push harder for the hidden truth he suspected and relief that he had not had to wrestle the bear towering over him.

"Cabinet above the sink."

Plates, bowls and pans piled up three feet high littered every ounce of counter space in the kitchen, caked with meals of days, even weeks past. He reached over the carnage and found a bottle of peppermint schnapps that was almost full and figured that would do the trick. He turned around to find a little ninja below him, Lilac in her pink pajamas, accompanied by a horde of dogs of various shapes and condition behind her in panting anticipation, all sitting at attention as if trained in a circus.

"I know it ain't pretty but I've got the dishes, Uncle, don't you worry your pretty giant head." She grabbed a pile and spread them out on the floor. Tongues went dancing over the earthenware. The clean-up crew had arrived with bells on.

On the way back outside to the evening festivities of watching Petty drown his sadness with the schnapps and a chaser of humble pie, he grabbed a greasy pillow from the couch. It looked like Petty had spent most of his recent nights bunked there. He didn't even consider why he grabbed it but as he came out he hid the pillow behind him. Petty was trying to stoke the fire or the two that swayed in front of him.

"Here's that nightcap, I'll trade you for the poker." They made the exchange and Petty fell back on to his chair, unscrewing the cap.

"Never trust a woman with a scorpion tattoo." He drank long, his Adam's apple hopped. "Minty." If The Driver carved out that cartilage with a paring knife would it look like an actual apple? Crabapple maybe. A last gasp of reanimated flames shot up as he rotated the charred logs and leaned back with the pillow behind him.

"My daddy was born without nipples, did I ever tell you that? He was terrified that I wouldn't have any either. First thing he looked for when I squirted out my mom. Don't know why he gave a shit, what's the point of nipples on a man? He was the one more highly evolved! Probably didn't have any wisdom teeth, either. He was always an efficient man. No wasted movements. You got nipples? Show me them." The Driver did not move, just sat silent, looking through him. "They oughta cut 'em off when they slice the cap off your pecker. Jews missed the boat on that one. Missed the boat. Nice half-ass work Moses, ya goat fucker. I bet the burning bush was just him having crabs."

The Driver thought back – he had never seen Petty drunk. Drinking, sure, but never drunk. He was a broken man. From a larger-than-life figure who could save a boy and give him direction and meaning to one who sat trapped in the corner of a freshly painted room brush in hand wondering how he got there. A king in tattered robes, a kingdom lost. The pillow was there for mercy, blow out the faded light rather than have it flicker out slowly. He could remove Petty's pain, snuff out all the life here in this house, prevent Rocky from killing a family in Tikrit because of faulty intel, Lilac metamorphosing from a governess of strays to drowning her twins in a bathtub after another fight with her cheating third-shift factory-worker husband. Find Lucinda, tell her there is nothing to go back to, make rough love to her in puddles of tears. Chance may be giving him the opportunity to save much more than would be lost. Take the tree out now by the roots. It would be the ultimate payback for all Petty had given him, all the knowledge, wisdom, even his rig. And wife. And son. He wondered where exactly the horizon tipped as he sat there watching Petty snore. When did he step through the curtain from revering the man to wanting to take all he treasured? From taking a bullet for him to firing it point blank at his drained face. Was this the reason or was it hidden somewhere in the dirty Texas sand? Had Petty known all along that things would go south eventually? Petty was well aware what was inside of him – they shared a cold heart with a long fuse. He was Petty's self-destruct button. When the time came, he was to scorch the earth with the turning of the key.

"Is that it? Are you calling in the marker, old man? Is that why you saved me?"

Petty's eyes remained shut, the bottle an infant content cradled in his arm. "I saved your life! This is how you repay me. My son. I always, you. Like a son." Petty fumbled with his pipe, pulling it from his breast pocket, it took a suicide leap into the hungry coals of the dying fire. His empty eyes flipped open and he stared at it over a long soul-bearing sigh, a metaphor for his life, what once held the power of smoldering destruction now melting to ashes. Just past his gaze out in the gathering gloom the vigorous force he had nurtured unto manhood squeezed a pillow, the moon hiding its big white eye behind the clouds as the night bird sang.

"Rocky, wake up, grab your duffle – we gotta hit it." The

Driver flipped on the egregious overhead light and stood in the doorway.

"What are you talking about? My bus doesn't leave till three – we got hours still."

"Get up. Your dad told me to get you to the bus station ASAP and we are leaving in three. Three goddamn minutes."

Rocky peered around the blinds of his window. "Jesus, it's still dark out."

"You wanted to join the Army. Get used to it."

Rocky was chaperoned from his room to Lilac's room, where he had to maneuver around the floor full of dog tails to say goodbye to his sister. In her cotton-filled child's mind time was for ever, she wasn't cognizant of the weight of his departure from their home, which would become a watershed moment she would look back on with regret as the lonely days without her only human running buddy stacked up.

"Bye, Rocks. Have fun." He kissed her forehead. It was hot with that sweet child's-sleep sweat.

"Bye sis. I love you." She giggled with embarrassment and dug her head under the sheets.

Back out in the hallway Rocky asked "Where's Dad? Isn't he coming?"

"I talked to him. He's not feeling good. Said he would see you once you get settled in."

"Settled in? I'm going to boot camp, man, I don't even know when we get a weekend pass, let me at least say goodbye real quick."

"He said no. He's sick. Let's go. We can stop and get some breakfast once we get on 74."

"He said no? He doesn't even want to say goodbye?" Rocky's emotions started to rumble as it all was becoming real. He was leaving. The Driver shrugged his shoulders in response.

"Ain't that some shit. Whatever, Dad." Rocky yelled out into the dormant house, then dragged his bag behind him down the hall to the front door. Abandoned by his father as he made good the bargain to perform the ultimate sacrifice for God and country, no tight bear hug, no pocketknife that once belonged to a battle-tested fighting ancestor. At least his mom would see him off at the bus, unless she too shunned her duties to her progeny. Neither had been present the last year, really present where you could count on their advice, their unconditional love. Now, at the witching hour, they avoided yet another chance to impart their wisdom. He was to forge the rapids alone, he finally had to accept it. Manhood was quicksilver and here was the forming drip. By the time he had climbed up into the rig, his shoulders were straight, his eyes, while red-rimmed, were dry and resolute as they took in their last glance of his home, that black mountain above that framed his existence till this final chilly instant. The sun was still below the lip of the bowl just starting to warm the foggy rim. "Let's go then."

They sat in a nondescript roadside diner, but a local one that cooked unfrozen food and used brown eggs in their omelets. It was comfortable there with Dolly Parton sounding far away and close at the same time, reminding him of his childhood and self-imposed study sessions of county lines and time-zone boundaries. Morning had taken hold right at the point where the coffee tastes best. Both nursed a cup, Rocky pouring in sugar and cream like they were soon to be forbidden to those with buzzcuts and no rank. The Driver sat somewhat mesmerized; he had never seen a kid (other than himself) ushered hurriedly down the aisle to adulthood before his eyes. Instead of finding guidance from a wise father or empathetic mother as he made his way in the world, it was to come from a drill sergeant whose job was to simply foster death, not from the driven winds of chance but the flag on your sleeve. In this abandonment they shared a kinship. It was his turn to make an impact beyond hopeful persuasive dinner talk, a positive one to rectify any future damage done by another gun-toting ignorant pawn caught up in an unwinnable war. Yang was pulling harder than Yin, at least so far this morning.

"There was a reason why we left early, told you your dad was sick." Rocky slammed down the sugar at hearing yet another adult confessing a white lie.

"You mean he isn't? Why would you do that? I needed to see him!"

"Because I needed your undivided attention, it had to be just mano a mano." Rocky sipped his coffee loud with eyes suspicious over the chipped lip as The Driver began his pitch. "You remember what I said last night?"

"About me going in the army?"

"Or not."

"I have to, Unc. I signed the papers. I can't go AWOL. They put you in jail for that." The thick-ass waitress brought their food and Rocky was sure she was going to call 911 right after she topped off the coffee to turn him in for even listening.

"If they catch you."

"I cried leaving the house this morning and now you want me to go on the run? All alone, with the feds tracking me day and night? How would that work? Hopping trains, poking through Red Lobster dumpsters in the dark?" The fugitive talk wasn't affecting his appetite as he poured syrup over pancakes and bacon during the rebuttal then commenced shoveling. "The plan is to go to boot camp like I'm supposed to. Become a sniper so I'm perched on a roof, not a grunt going door to door searching for the enemy. I'll be safe, it won't be like you said."

The Driver grabbed his feeding arm tight. "Who do you think the enemy looks to take out first? When their brothers are lying in front of them? The sniper! The sniper gets the mortar shell, the rocket launcher, their sniper! You will draw all the hell, kid! You will die with a bullet in your eye, right through your scope. That will be it. No more Rocky. No wife, no kids. No parade, no medal pinned to your chest by a sexy senator's daughter. Your bloodline will spill, pool and dry out in the sun. No more trout fishing in the morning mist. No cold beer in the shower after you cut a half a cord of wood. No feel of a good woman's mound grinding on your leg as she whispers butter in your ear. You will die in the sand in a town you can't pronounce and no one will care, it will not matter. Do you get that? It will not matter. The only thing different about the world is there will one less dipshit kid who thought he was gonna be a hero." He let the arm go, the diatribe more than he wanted to say, more than he maybe had ever said in a breath. The kid sat at the crossroads with his pancakes and sweet brown coffee. As lead prosecutor, The Driver had delivered his closing argument but a decision had been made at some point there at the table. Either naïve Rocky followed the fork The Driver laid out or he would feel death close around his windpipe before Asheville. The chances of this kid reporting for duty were far more none than slim.

The waitress walked by on a separate mission. It wasn't hard to get her eyes and signal for the check. She smiled, picked up half full bowl of cereal from the booth beside them and swung her best stuff around to their table.

"It's been picked up, sugar."

"Who?" he and Rocky both asked. The waitress leaned in between them, her top button straining as pendulous breasts threatened to invade their plates. She smelt of baby powder, bubble gum and fried meat.

"Willy." She waved at the window. "Right there." They followed her smile outside to a rugged man in his fifties wearing a Vietnam veteran ball cap, complete with his division patch, sporting enormous arms and shoulders under a plain white T-shirt, a guy you would bet on to win a pull-up competition. Him missing both his legs at the hips wouldn't hurt his chances. They watched him maneuver his wheelchair into a van and climb up into the driver's seat. He saluted Rocky, who stared back with syrup on his chin.

"That is Willy. He saw your duffel bag, put two and two together with my help. Used to be known as Freight Train Willy McCormick. All-state running back, still got records, I reckon, homecoming, prom, hell everything king every year. Got drafted to 'Nam after he turned down a full ride to Clemson to help take care of his sick mama and his baby sister. Killed a bushel of gooks but he won't never brag about it. That is a bona fide man right there. If he still had working tackle, I'd marry that son of a bitch in a heartbeat." She sighed and thought of what could have been as she walked her untapped wonderland back to the kitchen with the cereal bowl. The Driver raised his eyebrows at Rocky.

"See that patch? On his hat?"

"Yeah, I see it."

"Sniper."

The plan was explained as they left the mountains and rolled into Asheville. Rocky would take a bus, in fact multiple buses, all the way to Anchorage. Once he got there he would find Marny's apartment over the garage on C Street. Ask for the whereabouts of Amber, maybe even Brick, if he had been reabsorbed after his stint in Eugene. An obese roll of hundreds, 10 grand worth, would be his to help get him settled, no payback needed. The Driver explained as they pulled into the bus station parking lot that Alaska was where you went when you wanted to disappear, start over fresh. The army would just mark him down AWOL, they wouldn't be sending out search parties or alerting the FBI. If he kept his head down, got a job that paid cash, in a few years no one would even care. He knew his way around a gun, knew how to hunt, fish. Get on with a guide company during the summer months, lay low in the winters with a meaty girl who would keep him warm. He could be his own man, living his life free as the forefathers intended. There were hundreds and thousands of dead kids watching from beyond right now wishing they had had this opportunity, this option to circumvent the reaper. After a while he could even call home, tell Lilac tall tales of sled dog runs over the tundra, tell his mom he was getting plenty of fish in his diet.

This was it. His chance to really live, avoid the machine. Was he down?

Rocky sat in the passenger seat, thinking hard, shoving unwanted tears off his face. His window was down and maybe it was the diesel fumes from the arrivals and departures that made him lightheaded. He slowly nodded in assent. Immediately, The Driver threw the softball of cash in his lap. Promised he would come check on him some day soon. They climbed out together, headed into the station, The Driver shouldering the duffel. He bought Rocky a stack of tickets linking him up to the great white north, eight days of seeing two countries through a saliva-covered window, sitting on thin seats and eating gas-station hot dogs. Not quite the harrowing adventure of a tour of duty in the Arabian Desert but plenty for an 18-year-old who had never been past Atlanta. The relief at Rocky complying was so great that The Driver even stuffed a small bag of his precious ever-dwindling supply of jerky into Rocky's clammy hand.

He put one of his big mitts on the kid's tussled black bedhead, tilted it up. "You take it easy on that jerky, it's addictive." Ten minutes later, Rocky climbed on board the first of his chariots, this one bound for Kansas City.

"You'll come see me up there?" Rocky asked at the top of the steps as the bus driver inspected his coupon book of tickets.

"Guaranteed, kid." He watched Rocky disappear into the bowels of the bus. As it wrenched into gear, the sight of this doe-eyed youngster in the last window made his guts glow warm – he had done a good thing. Picked the lead domino off the table before it could start all the tumbles. He didn't know if he had set things back in balance or upset them. Either way, it was time to catch a snooze in the rig and wait for the arrival of Lucinda, a mother expecting to see her son off to military service. Only then would he see which ways the scales tipped.

· · ·

Twenty till three, she flashed into being, a dark star inside a prism absorbing the rainbow of life shuffling around her. He kept at a distance, observing her quiet frustration rise to an internal boil as Rocky failed to show. She gave it an hour, standing thin in an even thinner snug black long-sleeved shirt and low-riding jeans hugging strong hips cut to fit stout cowboy boots with a heel she could manage. She was an unbending silver needle in a haystack of inferiority, lithe and tall, never relinquishing perfect posture. Her long curls played in the breeze created from the buses coming and going, diesel heat giving a subtle blush to her high cheekbones and a slight steam to her thick ebony-rimmed glasses. The derelicts gave her a wide berth as untouchables would treat Indian royalty somehow standing in their midst. She was a queen without a prince or king, alone and stoic with nothing to do with her hands but clasp them at her waist, checking her watch every so often in between gazing through the stinking crowds. His breath was steady but heavy with a soundless moan as he drank her image in. He wanted to caress her, confess all his sins, plead to her timeless stained-glass profile that his recent good deeds would make the world a better place. Over afternoon tea betwixt the baby elephants, he would describe how he saved her progeny, put the wayward son on the right path to a long, happy life. For this she owed him her secret, her crystal body, the drinkable essence she held. Without any wasted movement, she walked to a pay phone but no one answered on the other end. She showed no panic, other than the forceful slam of the receiver back in its sticky cradle. She did not retrieve her quarter but simply strode away back to the golden fields of her chosen existence. He walked to the pay phone as she departed the station, pulled out the quarter hot in his hand. He resisted the temptation to smell it, put it in his mouth, gain any sense of her he could. Instead he flipped it, glanced at the result then placed it in his pocket and followed Lucinda's fragrant path outside. She stepped into an old Chevy pickup, fat and wide. He followed loosely, feeling he knew her destination. She would retreat to her solace born from the Gilded Age, fantasize of innocent times in an American castle where everything was new and ready to be experienced each morning, a return to adolescence frolicking among the spires. The Biltmore.

It was quite late afternoon when the ticket clerk offered to sell him a ticket for the next day, motioning to the fold-out map and explaining that he might not have enough time to see everything before the estate closed. He just handed over the cash and shook his head, noticing the security camera without looking at it directly. Cars were trickling through the exit as he maneuvered the rig onward. He parked next to her truck in the nearly empty lot, as if the two vehicles were huddled together for safety from Serengeti night predators. The approaching golden hour bathed the mansion in a gentle caress from behind, creating a mere silhouette of grandeur. The front plaza, manicured to perfection, dozed as dragonflies zigzagged across the green snapping up a dinner of mosquitoes bloated and slow from feasting on tourist blood. Overhead, a grey heron loped its way to the Broad River flapping loud its heavy wings. As he traced the bird through the pink sky, he observed the immediate world had grown large, partaken of Alice's cake and was banging its head against the heavens. This place was fit for a giant and he was the demi-god beneficiary worthy of its magnitude. The trivial lands beyond were a marble in the hand of the macroverse vessel now towering in front of him. The architect Richard Morris Hunt was given the task of creating a chateau on steroids as only a brazen American trust-fund blue-blood like George Vanderbilt would request. Travel through France as they snicker behind new-money backs, come home and outdo the bastards at their own pretentious games. The Driver stood transfixed, going over every detail, the stonework, the verdigris-covered bronze, the gargoyles taunting him, knowing his intentions. He read it housed 250 rooms, a plethora of tight corners to trap his Lucinda, his night bird. Where might she hide? She would seek a place to lick the wounds inflicted on her pride. Her chosen room would be one that offered the clearest lens into the past glory where Edith would recline among Persian pillows and peacock feathers, sneaking an opium pipe or the novelty of a soft drink as the sun sank and the day was lost below the countless windows.

Lucinda saw him below beyond the fountain, a goon in canvas overalls taking in the majesty like a true country hick. She was in the observatory on the fourth floor, a sentry awaiting his presence, the same one she noticed at the bus station and far back behind her on the two-lane roads that led them to the estate. Should she flee? She knew countless ways to get out unseen. Why had he not approached her? She knew exactly who he was from that big black truck, Petty's charity case, Lennie to Petty's George. They were thick as thieves there for a while – he was likely to be found snoozing on the couch off and on for a year or two when he probably should have been in high school. It was easy to see he had definitely become beyond a man in a physical sense but mentally, how could one know? Was he there as Petty's lackey to steal her back home? And where in the hell was her son and why did he miss his bus? Scant comfort was found knowing he was on her turf now, this fort of forts was her play land, he was nothing but a barbaric invader on a foreign shore tentatively surveying a strange terrain.

He digested the brochure map and put it in his back pocket. Still had the childhood gift and the psychic memory muscles flexed Venice Beach-style in front of the rest of his consciousness. He entered through the vestibule and decided to start searching through the main hall and work corner to corner. The voice of the last tour guide of the day echoed from the banquet hall so he turned left into the gallery where framed art eyes followed him along the polished floor. It would be a hoot to Risky Business his way across these slick halls in tight white underwear. He giggled to himself as the hunt was making him giddy. Did ole Georgie V ever have some fun and take advantage of his immense wealth, his immunity to the consequences of moral depravity? Did he chase the maids around, wearing nothing but Egyptian cotton tube socks and a silk top hat holding in his flopping twig and berries? Sheathes of light leaned into the room from the sunset-bathed tiled loggia but he was not to be bothered searching in that direction, his tight pale mistress would be away from the warmth, nestled inside some unseen nook wrapped in darkness. A hidden unblinking doll waiting to be played with.

She floated down the spiral staircase to the third floor where there were a myriad guest rooms to stow away in if she felt so inclined. The Vanderbilts had dedicated an entire floor to entertaining guests by sandwiching in a hotel made of a hearty, if not particularly thick, slab of meat. She could shimmy under an antique feather bed or squeeze into a closet of one of the narrow cubes. Surely a security guard sweep would spot Lurch before he ever reached up there. But as she traveled the halls she became resolute. She was not made to hide. She would outmaneuver him and make a break for the pick-up. By the time he was cuffed or lost in the basement, she would be well on her way back to Robbinsville to find out why the puzzle she had been working on was missing a corner piece.

He made his way up from the main floor – it only made sense she would find refuge in a more personal, intimate setting, as opposed to the male-centric cock-strutting to be found below among the billiards room, gun room or the cathedral-like banquet hall where any strange commoner might find himself watching a corny ventriloquist over a rich dessert if they knew the right debutante. He was searching for a bedroom, an inner sanctum where Lucinda could channel Edith, become her confidante, share in the extravagance of French lace and silks. He made his way through the living hall and George's chamber (what a tiny bed for a man) and through their shared sitting room to Edith's.

She had detected the second floor reeked of more importance than the third from her many hours among the velvet walls and intricate rugs. She considered racing to Edith's, the mistress's sanctum was by far her favorite place, the subtle rounded wall, the gilded mirrors in front of sultry upholstered chairs and daybeds, imagining Edith, reclined in her stockings and unzipped evening dress waiting for the divine beyond the door. Better than a queen as she had an American power, freedoms that came from money, as opposed to blood. No unwritten generational rulebook heavy with responsibilities and ritual that could drown a privileged spirit. Would he expect her, though? Would she mind if he took her there, ravished among the musty bedcovers as Edith watched suspended from the tray ceiling? A willing sacrifice to her goddess, a release that would transport her tired soul back to that gilded golden age.

As he soft-shoed back into the bedroom after peeking into Edith's bathtub for his prey, a lovely gift happened to appear in the doorway, none other than the luscious object of his quest. Lucinda looked a little flustered. Her hair was wild but he was sure he detected a small smile in the corner of her mouth.

Fight or flight? He took a step toward her. Was there actual malice in his eyes? He didn't speak, no soothing words, no leopard purr before the pounce. She was scared, excited as a virgin bride on her wedding night. "Where is Rocky? I know you know," she whisper-screamed at him. He came closer, she could smell his thick musk, it made her dizzy. "Did that weasel-dick Petty send you? Are you supposed to deliver me back? You can tell him to suck my lady nuts." She stayed pat in the doorway as she knew entering the room would leave her cornered.

He could taste her essence, it made him thirsty. He needed to consume her, possess her flesh as the lord of the manor would, violently without threat of repercussion. They were at a stalemate as he did not want to spook her by taking another step, even if that step would place her within snatching distance. Neither knew the other's intentions and communication was nothing but a series of subtle gestures open to interpretation.

The room was succumbing to the fast-approaching evening. Shadows grew bold. She watched his hands as an indication of motive. The fingers flexed. There was no tenderness in those illicit digits, only pain, possibly death. With the dusk also came the dawning of a sudden realization that he was nothing but a monster, created in Petty's mobile laboratory. She ran.

His fantasy of sinking into her ivory skin inside the mansion dissolved as Alka-Seltzer in the water glass, was replaced by a searing anger. He wanted to punch through something, ransack the dollhouse room in frustration. He took a calming breath as he heard her clicking footfalls diminish.

She knew if she broke for the truck now he would be on her before she reached it. She hoped he figured she would take that chance. Where were the guards? The place was supposed to be closed up by now. She took the stairs as fast as she dared, knowing a tumble and broken neck would rob him of some fun but still serve his interests just dandy. Breaking through the now ink-black vestibule she broke right toward the immense gardens, hoping the night green would afford cover and a chance to gain some separation.

He was back on the main floor bloodhound sniffing as the night had fully invaded the rooms. He surmised the Vandys forgot to pay the electric bill. She was gone. He stalked quickly outside listening for the crunch of gravel or a pickup truck starting. He heard neither. He rolled his cosmic dice again. They came up singing that she hadn't gone that way, the obvious way. She was still playing baby games. He turned for the gardens, quickening his steps.

She ran through the walled garden among tulips and poppies, their sweet fragrance enhancing the danger she felt. She tried the doors of the conservatory but they were locked. Good thing the guards had their priorities in order.

He ran through the garden stopped and picked a yellow tulip that he thought would go perfectly behind her ear among those tumultuous curls.

She shuffled close around the other corner of the conservatory. Perhaps a different angle to the parking lot would afford a great escape. All senses worked overtime in the blackness as the Indian maiden carefully backtracked to the mansion, knowing full well the shark was circling somewhere in the bloody waters ...

He lifted her up in a one-armed bear hug as she backed right into him, placed the flower just right with his free hand then covered her struggling mouth tight. The waxing moon was young and low but promised a long walk across the heavens. They would have just enough light for the evening he had planned.

TOO CLOSE

"Helluva deal, bud. Hell of a deal. I mean, there is the threat of a major hurricane but, strictly financially speaking, you got some damn good timing." Rupert managed to sip on the watery coffee and powdered creamer mix while keeping a tooth-pick in the corner of his mouth. "Whaddya say? Pot or get off the shit. Ya takin' her?" The Driver popped his fingers through the cheap blinds and took a look at the trailer. It checked all his boxes. Basically it was a gigantic cooler of beer. A refrigerated trailer filled to the brim or what they called in the biz a "reefer." Not the worst forethought that a bar owner in Key West wanted plenty of cold ones in case the wrath of approaching Hurricane Georges included knocking out the power. If he would brave the dangers of a category-four hammer coming down upon him, his hazard pay would be fat on arrival with a bonus piled on top for every gallon of diesel he had left to keep the rig running and in turn the condenser on the reefer. He liked beer, was honored to be its captain and the idea of bowing up to Mother Nature and racing the wind appealed to him. He had felt the oily wave of malaise rising again as of late and this would be just the jolt he needed to pump back up the balloon of vigor that had been slowly deflating inside him with a slow leak. Ever since Lucinda, that high of highs he felt when she struggled taut against his barrel chest, he had been empty, nothing out on the horizon to look forward to. No universe-bequeathed act of random violence would deliver him back to the crest of the wave. Oh, how he had tried. A smarmy overnight hotel clerk in South Dakota could attest, at least the parts of him stuffed in-between a couple of boulders within eyeshot of the presidents on Mount Rushmore. Maybe what he needed was to wrestle an omnipotent force. Georges off the top rope with a razor blade hidden in his wristband. Square off against a worthy adversary where the thrill of mortality could feel real.

He turned back to Rupert. "Hook her up." Rupert clapped his hands and got the paperwork together. A tiny TV on the desk filled itself out with a snowy weather radar of Georges's spin. It looked like a ghost floating in the blue, an apparition that took on a physical form when it delivered its true evil.

"Don't you dilly-dally gettin' down there, son." Rupert looked down at the screen. "Beat that storm and hunker down. Them keys are not something you want to be driving on when them waves come in, hell the main drag is skinnier than an anorexic Ethiopian and they're about under sea level with zero surge as it is. I don't know if you got some custom job parked out there but last I checked, Mack trucks don't float."

Pulling away from Rupert and his stern yet goofy-ass warnings and on to a collision course with Georges the water demon, he felt like one of those bighorn rams he watched on the Sunday afternoon nature show, about to lower his head and push off into obliteration until only one of them would be left standing.

He needed to break into a case of the cold beer by the time he hit Orlando. The drudgery of billboards and roadside trash had slowly worn thin on him like the fabric in the crotch of his overalls. He wasn't even getting much enjoyment from the trusty top 40. The music was changing, losing those killer hooks for what empty-headed choreographed dance could be developed for it. Do the dance, buy the stuffed animal, the video game and the cereal! If he had a lawn he would have yelled for the kids to get the hell off. The rift between hip teen and jaded adult had widened to a chasm he could no longer straddle. The list of things he could identify with was shrinking by the day. He turned off the radio as a menacing wind slapped at the windows, licking to get into the cab to torment a truly lost soul, ignored for his heroic deeds as he was still free from his horrendous ones. If he strode into a police station and slapped his wrists on the desk, they would laugh in his face, consider him a simpleton truck driver with an outlandish imagination. That is until he offered explicit details, firmed up a timeline of bloodletting that would cause nightmares and counseling to the uniformed cops on duty. A fresh beer cracked as he switched lanes to pass a station wagon with Mickey Mouse ears affixed to the roof, on its week of vacation Mecca to the magical kingdom of consumerism. A back seat filled with rejected jawbreakers, boogers and wide eyes scanning the horizon for fake castles. Hope you don't puke on the rides, kiddos. You have a lifetime to feel sick.

The Florida Turnpike, two skid marks across the ass of endless swamp. At least traffic was light heading south – seemed some people had heeded the warning that a big wet hammer was coming down. He wondered how many cars he would pass going the other way until he ran out of land. Thousands. Thousands of families nailing plywood over windows, overfilling the cat's dinner bowl, locking the door and saying adios house. Good luck and God speed. Hoping not to come back to a madman teepee pile of insulation and drywall where the discovery of a loose frying pan would send one over the edge of desolation row. Maybe he would buy a house one day. It sure as shit wouldn't be where a natural disaster will inevitably come and wash it off the map. How did you get your mail after that? Did the mailman still come by and just drop it in the mud where the box used to be? He found it hard to have sympathy for people that choose to live where there is an obvious pattern of death and destruction. There is resolute and there is stupid. Living in a flood plain is stupid. Building a log cabin on a fault line... stupid. Dropping a mobile home down in Tornado Alley is stupid. He could attest to that one. After a final tip and sip he crushed the can between his palm and thigh and threw it out the window. Give the baggy-orange-jumpsuit prisoners something to do, if they survived. Oh, but they would. Prisons were conveniently built to withstand about anything Mama Nature had in her handbag. High, thick concrete walls and lots of metal bars about... reverse fortresses built to keep what was in, in, not to keep what was out, out. You never heard of a prison damaged by anything other than angry prisoners. His mind rewound like an insolent yoyo against his will from burning rolls of toilet paper and broken-jawed guards back to...

Tornado. Why did he have to have that thought?

Flashes of terror chained to chaos assaulted him. Unconscious motions cracked another beer, lubing up the barbs on the snakes of trauma that were slithering among his limbs, looking to launch their first real attack in over a decade.

"They are feisty slippery serpents today, Cinda! Flicking around for the mouse dropped in the cage. Here's to liquid courage!" He yelled into the rearview mirror at her, the world, himself. Stared at his reflection coming off the dead screen of the TV. "Turn off that TV right now – I cannot stand that weather girl! I would rip her vocal cords out and strangle her with them if I ever got the chance. So shrill. Shrrrrriiiillllll! Nails on a chalkboard, that elf bitch."

"It's off. Just wanted to see the radar, supposed to be bad tonight." He sat crisscross applesauce in front of the dead TV, wishing he was inside the box.

His mom walked heavy-footed into the room. The trailer never felt level or properly anchored, so her walking made everything rattle, the porcelain clown figurines, the myriad stained wineglasses forgotten on every available flat surface. She wore nothing but a pair of her husband's old boxer shorts loose under a pink robe too thick for the season that stank of menthol. She had been beautiful once but her vanity had been discarded to the winds long ago. Big blue stormy eyes ringed by whatever mascara managed to still cling to dry skin from a drunken application in the middle of the night earlier in the week. Smoke wrinkles had set up shop around her violent mouth, her nose leaked continually from a cold five years ago she was never able to shake. Her hair was a rat's nest of blonde and grey waging a trench war of attrition among the roots. He body had just started to droop from inactivity as an ice sculpture at the end of a gala would, once sharp and hard, now a mere shadow linking it to the talent of its creator. She kicked him in the ribs with one of her slippers, spilling some box wine on to his shoulder.

"You in love with her? My boy got a little hard on for that catch-you-next-Tuesday? You watch her every damn night, all googly-eyed. Well mister man, I've had it, I just can't. The very next time I hear that voice I'm putting your head through that screen. Glasgow kiss that little turnip face. You just watch." He got up to escape her onslaught by slinking over to the sole window in the room, slid it up. It smelt like impending rain outside but he could also feel a low current of pressure and electricity. Gave him the goose bumps up to his neck hair. He considered walking over to the diner, warning his dad about the fast-approaching front. The broken man would be sitting behind the counter reading an Auto Trader magazine, holding out hope a few customers would show up he could sling the rest of the liver and onions special to, nothing crazy, a few bucks to justify being open and to help pass the time in his own private purgatory.

"Close that window, snothead, it's freezing out there!" He wanted to tell her it was in the low eighties but bit his tongue. The starburst lights of the diner cut through the grime of the glass as he lowered the protesting thin pane back into its seat. It could have been on another planet as far as he felt from away from that bright cool place of something akin to joy, time spent studying his maps as Dad brought him milk and the last slice of apple pie. A grain of feeling buried a mile deep under layers and layers of psychic sediment would regret not going to see his dad that night, even if it was some god's cruel joke, it was only his all-encompassing hate for liver that kept him away. He turned back into the room to see she was at her station on one side of the couch, the arm about worn down to the wooden framework. The boob tube was back on and Judge Wapner was holding court over people you watched on TV to make you feel better about yourself. "Why don't you get your sweet mother a refill? She jabbed her travel mug out into the space in front of her, never making eye contact with anything other than the court case in progress. He knew the routine, was resigned to fulfill his role as servant. A full cup was shoved back into her hand while a lit lighter was offered to her other. She leaned in to meet her lips to the filter and take a deep drag, her breast falling out of the robe as she inhaled. He sighed in disgust, quickly looking the other way at the Wapner ruling, the boa constrictor was indeed the responsibility of the defendant and all unrealized profits from the plaintiff's litter of hairless kittens would be paid in full. She tapped him on the back with a bony finger and when he turned spat a mouthful of wine in his face.

"What? You don't think your mom has nice tits? I caused a fatal wreck in downtown Birmingham with these bubbly ta-tas once. Fella was wrapped around a telephone pole but left this world with a smile on his face. They may not be as perky as your little weather wench but they can still slow down a school bus, I promise you." She smacked him hard on the back of the head for good measure, making no effort towards modesty, wiping wine off her hand on to his already-sticky wet shirt. "Go clean yourself up, mongrel, and try to keep your hands out of your pants thinking about your TV girlfriend or your mom's bodacious tits." Down the dark hallway, he fumed, dripping pinot behind him, the birth of a new voracious anger crowning inside. As he stalked, he closed his eyes, fingertips dragging the walls, he could feel his way to the bathroom. Eyes shut. Tight. Standing small with clinched fists in front of the volcano in his chest. Feeling the lava building, turning over itself, liquid hate fire. Eyes shut tight. A blaring horn forced them open – he had about run a UPS van off the road into Lake Okeechobee. He laughed, reaching for another beer. Sorry pal. That little brown uniform won't show the brown you made in your britches, another victim chalked up to his steamroller presence on this ball flying through the vastness.

"Look at all those long Cadillacs pushing north! Gonna be a run on hard candies and adult diapers at the Georgia line! Right?" He looked back as if Lucinda was there, sharing his joyride rocket ship shooting into the eye of Georges. He had had the sun and moon and now he would conquer Poseidon's swirling demon. The outskirts of the sprawl of Miami looked apocalyptic. No cars other than the abandoned ones lined up as Aztec sacrifices at the dealerships. Plywood over everything. No signs of life. No beaten-down dads leading families to the overcrowded beach to sit among all the other unfulfilled dreams. The moms who slayed it as the lead in their high-school play never acting again as they learned how to clean teeth next to a grabby dentist. The dads who sketched mini masterpieces in their chemistry notebooks, thinking up complex superhero universes until the ideas were tossed in the bin on the last day of school, pussy and the kegger taking priority. They were all instead back in landlocked states at home in the fetal position on an itchy couch, watching Oprah as the dog vomits on the carpet, wondering if the shower rod could bear their weight. It was easy enough to take down for sure, just a twist and he could walk right back out there and spear it right through her chestplate, a flagpole through a frozen pond. Be way more fun than finding a cleaner below the sink to kill her softly with, also a helluva lot easier as household cleaners were a rare mineral in their little corner of the world. He was one time forced to use one of those little colorful jugs of bubble solution with the plastic wand and a dirty sock to scrub the toilet after he had gotten sick from a can of potted meat and had missed the bowl in haste in the middle of the night. The half-hour sitcoms were followed by more tumblers of wine and then the record player as the chemical mint smoke accumulated heavy over the room. Over Joplin's Pearl he could hear their home-made wind chime clanging in the violence gathering outside. He and his dad had made the wind chime out of old forks and spoons from the diner, drilling tiny holes in them and hanging them with picture frame wire from chipped coffee-mug saucers. It didn't sound all that sweet but was a trusted harbinger all the same. When the heavy metals tumbled together, it meant serious weather was on the wing. She stood wide-legged in the middle of the room, swaying to Janis complaining about her boyfriend Bobby. He hated the song, it went on forever, felt it was masturbatory vocalization at its best and scratchy whining at its worst. He wished he could flip the TV back on and see the radar, find out if the squall line had crossed into their county. Wished his dad would call it and close up, come back to the trailer, protect him from the storms brewing outside and inside. The box of wine had gotten light and that meant that, unless she passed out, the gin would be the next potion added to the cauldron.

"Damn, she could sing. Freedom's just another way to lose! Taken too soon! Listen. Listen. You stay away from the needles you little prick… hahahha… Don't you ever go chasin' the drag-on." He could see an oily sweat shining on her face and chest as the robe had been shed under a harsh ceiling light. He tried not to look at her nakedness, her vulgarity, but it was a perpetual car wreck in the other lane. "Booze'll kill ya but it takes for ever. Slow ride! Take it easy! Put on Stevie Nicks for mommy. We gots tonic?" She laughed as she lit the wrong end of a cigarette. The trailer started rocking but it wasn't from the classic rock. He went to the window; sheets of rain rendered the view of the diner to smears of color. It was darker than night outside but he could see the blankets of clouds moving fast over the pancake terrain. The lights flickered in the diner then went out, along with the electricity in the trailer.

"Son of a bitch. Go tell your daddy to get his greasy ass in here and fix the lights!" Should he make a run for it? The wind chime was about sideways, it sounded like a thousand minotaurs were thumping at the door. He squinted through the glass as she cussed but the bullets of water fired a constant barrage so damn hard he had to turn the wipers up to fuckin' 11, man. There was Key Largo – he was officially in them, the Keys. He was the key master. One of those big-ass keys to haunted mansions that were as big as your forearm, black and intricate.

"Lucy, you the gate keeper? Baby girl? We made the Keys! Beer me – it's time to celebrate!" Lightning flashed over the water; he felt the thunder through the sloshing roar of the engine. He had to reach deep into the cardboard to find a fresh beer, he had done some damage, the casualties were piled up in the floorboard. "Clean up on aisle five!" He chugged. The rig was utterly alone on the straight road that was beset on both sides by the building storm surge. He was drunk and feeling nasty, ready for a fight. Like mama like son. "Like son like mama needs a candle or something, move your ass!" She had fallen back, splayed out on the couch. A fresh smoke was dangling from her mouth as she held out a lighter, her torch in the dungeon. A window in one of the back bedrooms had broken and the sounds of swirling madness was whipping through. What were they supposed to do? He couldn't remember. Hide in a closet? Under a bed? Did it matter in a box sitting precarious on cracked cinder blocks? Closet made the most sense, the one in his parent's bedroom. Mysterious and always off limits to him, full of guns and sex toys and drugs and all other salacious contraband a teenage boy was scared of and yet involuntarily drawn to. He reached down over the couch to grab her arm.

"What in the hells you doin'? You tryin' to get fresh? Told you, not when you smells like that kitchen go take a shower, then go take another shower." She was an immovable slug of lead. Even as a high-pitched snore escaped her, she was able to pinch his arm hard, making him recoil in pain. She giggled in her half sleep. What was the point of trying to save such a horror show? Humanity would be far better off without her. He would get away with a murder committed by an act of God. Leave her on her precious couch to rot in the rubble. The walls were breathing. Air was rushing out of the room then twice as much forced back in. Mayhem was taking the throne. Chairs were busting against tables, glass shard pinballs gutted cushions. He ran for it, hands over his head cutting his feet on unseen hazard lights on, not like anybody was gonna see 'em. He was dialed into a marathon drinking sesh and it seemed only fitting to stop and grab another case from his mobile supply closet in Marathon. He was all about getting high on his own supply. No reason to find a place to pull over when you are the only one on the road so he just rolled to a stop, put her in neutral and threw on the brake. He sat there tapping the last empty beer can, gathering his gumption to step out into the deluge. He messed with the radio dial a bit but couldn't find any countdowns, just robot voice man reciting emergency procedures. When the door to the cab swung open, the storm nearly claimed it. "Damn Georges! Chill. I'm on your side!" He jumped down into a good foot of water. "Glad we got our boots on, Lucy Lou! Dress for the occasion!" He waded against the wind and sheets of stinging rain to the back of the trailer, swung the door up and scampered inside, closing it behind him as fast as his buzzed mind would allow. It was dark and so very cold, didn't help he was drenched. The torrent outside lashed against the metal, it was deafening. "Lucinda! Where are you? I can't see you."

"Over here, Daddy." He climbed back to her voice. So sultry it warmed his bones. He unzipped a black plastic bag against the back wall. Lucinda was inside. Her body was stiff and well preserved in the rolling cooler. He traced his finger over her blue lips, caught what little scent was left in her hair. He poked his tongue out, licked her frozen nose.

"Careful hon, you are gonna get stuck on me like licking a flagpole in winter."

"You're right. I'm a goof. What would I do without you?"

"You'd be lost. A boat lost at sea but no matter. I'm here. And you know what?"

"What?"

"I forgive you."

He smiled and winked at her faded blue eyes. "I don't want forgiveness."

He got them rearranged with her body pulled in front of him like they were about to watch a summer concert on the grass. "Baby, this Bud's for you." He placed a cracked open can of beer on her head as the waters outside rose, tickling the bottom of the reefer. The wind howled its threat to unmoor them. He huddled down and hugged her tight, their faces almost touching, as if they were flying through the air. Everything was in the air. Everything taking its own direction. He never made the closet. He saw her in the corner of his eye as the inside and outside morphed into one. There were no longer thoughts – he surrendered to the forces. Two-by-fours, sheetrock, aluminum insulation, shoes, a soap dish, a remote control his dad had lost last year, fruit bowl, a can of peaches, a bird nest. He closed his eyes. A butterfly was now in the cocoon. He would awake to a reality washed clean. Aloft, pushed, pulled, punctured, he felt physical pain but regarded it as insignificant, burns on the feet after walking across coals. A true transcendence had occurred. He was no longer a rag doll; the dryer had stopped. Was he alive? He dared open his eyes. He wanted more than anything to take stock of his battered body. He struggled. He was completely pinned down, could not even move his head enough to see his limbs. The only thing he could see, as if invisible hands had framed it, was her lifeless stare not inches in front of him, that shower curtain rod he had considered earlier that evening had impaled her ragged through the neck. Even in death she mocked him with an evil grin, eyes slanted away in disregard. For reasons that would always be unknown to him, he stretched his tongue out and licked her nose.

"Hey kid! You alive? Don't move."

"Can't."

Hands probed, pulled. "Jesus. Don't... Keep your eyes closed. Hang in there."

He tried to nod, couldn't.

"Be right back. Gonna grab a crowbar. We'll get your ass out toot-sweet, OK? And by the way, today's rescue is brought to you by Petty."

1 2

BELIEVE

Needless to say, the payload did not beat the hurricane's landfall to Key West. The rig did survive, sitting right smack dab in the middle of highway one in Marathon, but barely. The floorboard of the cab had flooded and all those empty beer cans had their own private flotilla until the last band of Georges passed on its way to the gulf for a refuel. He woke up a few hours after that, with a blacksmith pounding in his head and a bladder burning tight with untold ounces of used beer. Lucinda's head had settled into the crook of his armpit as he had slept as if patiently waiting to be burped. Her hair didn't smell as nice as earlier, nothing smelt very nice. He had run out of gas at some point and the reefer's AC unit was dead, turning the trailer into more of a wet sauna than a cooler. He didn't know what was sweat, what was melted ice, what was condensation, what were bodily fluids. He just knew he had to get out.

The sun was a blast furnace dipped in the steam of the devil's taint rising from the asphalt. Clear cloudless skies immediately after a hurricane ensured the mortals could witness all the glorious damage wrought upon them as soon as they crawled out from their hidey-holes. A forceful stream of urine from the edge of the trailer splashed down on to the road that was already showing dry patches after being submerged mere hours before. A mosquito attempted a meal from his penis as he evacuated.

"Cocky bastard," The Driver muttered as he flicked it away. He chuckled to himself at the pun. "Did you hear that one, Lucy? Cocky. He landed right on my pecker." Silence from inside, other than a few water drips from the depths. "Fine, be that way. I got shit to do, anyway. Somebody has to get us back up and running and I don't see you lifting a finger." He jumped down and grabbed the rope to bring the door down. Before he closed it he swiped another case of beer. The smell of rot continued to billow out and hang in the still air.

"Enjoy the ride. You know one time I rode for hours in a trailer after major surgery? I'll tell you that one sometime. See ya later, alligator." The door slammed. As he walked back to the cab he actually saw an alligator, belly up, being torn into by a horde of vultures, for whatever reason the gods had decided with a laugh and a round of sweet-nectar-shots serendipity was Mother Nature's major play that day. Right before he grabbed the handle of the door he heard a faint squeaking. It was high pitched and sentient, not some screen door swaying in the breeze. It rattled the pain receptors in his temples. Morbid curiosity led him to the sound as one rolls the tongue repeatedly over a sore in one's mouth. It took him over the edge of the highway where the waves were crashing lamented over the rocks of the levee that the road was built on. Between himself and the water was a beached dolphin, young, not yet full grown but still five feet long and a few hundred pounds. He didn't know much about how big a typical dolphin got but looking at the innocence of its face it had to be a kiddo. A damn baby dolphin stranded on the rocks, crying weakly to the pod he could see circling out in the swirls. No way he could leave it to the buzzards still snacking away on the bloated alligator. Carefully, he stepped down 20 feet over the mossy rocks, dodging all manner of plastic flotsam pulled free from the grasp of ignorant humanity during the raging tempest. He cursed people for the millionth time as he almost lost his balance kicking a Styrofoam take-out container out of the way. A few feet from the top of the foamy sea, he reached the creature, felt its fear. The dolphin's eyes took him in full, reminded him of another stray dog, infinitely sad and resigned to the worst of fate. He felt a wave of rare emotion and almost shed a tear at the sight. Funny how the absence of humanity brought out the pure intentions of a hero in his countenance. "Not today, little buddy," he said soothingly, putting his rough palm on the gray, slick skin. It bayed pathetic in response, not knowing intent. He squatted as low as he could and, asking for a hernia, he lifted the animal up in his arms. No way a mere mortal man could have lifted the dead weight and even The Driver uttered a low-core grunt. The family breached and spouted, swimming as close as they dared to the shelf. They hoped for the best, expected the worst from just another of the two-legged fiends. From his position, he crouched catcher-style and shimmied on his butt down the last few crags to the surface and leaned forward, lowering the beast as gently as he could into the water. Mom and Dad raced to encircle the child as it floundered and cried out for Poseidon's benevolence. He sat there, hands submerged, watching the struggle for life. His boots got soaked but he never noticed. Long snouts held the patient up as they slowly made their way away back to the open sea. The rest of the pod enveloped the trio. "God speed and all that," he muttered. Just before he turned to start the ascent, he swore he saw the baby breach and squeak out a thanks to the gentle giant who allowed it to see another day. But that only happened in Disney movies. It was, however, a triumphant start to following a new code, one decided by him, not for him. He laughed at the coincidental cheese-dick cliché of the scene but by the time he had two feet back on the pavement, his dark reality again held sway. Any wave of warmth reaching his cold heart was snuffed out as a breeze through a window eats the candlelight. It might as well have been just another tale Casey related from a long-time listener on a lazy Saturday between number 20 and 19.

When he opened up the cab door, the floor was still spongy but other than that everything seemed to be in order. He switched over to the spare tank and turned the engine over. It sputtered slow, then nothing. "C'mon baby, dip your beak and let's ride." He pumped the gas, tried again. The engine choked, boiling off the remnants of the Atlantic. He eased the pedal, feeling her fighting for life. "That's it, talk to me, big mama..." Whether it was priming a purge of saltwater or a clan of soft-shell crabs, the lifeblood of diesel eventually found its way to the engine where, inside, the air compressed and the fuel ignited. He sat back and let the familiar purr under the hood soothe him like nothing else could. He could detect a tiny hitch in her giddy-up, one instrument in the orchestra was hitting the wrong note. Just something knocked off kilter from the storm or maybe the diesel in the spare tank took in some salt water. It would clear out, she would be dandy once the highway wind started whipping through. The AC unit back behind bolted to the reefer roared back to life, another win. The beer would get cold and Lucinda could get comfortable – the heat did not agree with her one iota.

He fingered the dial with finesse until he lucked upon a countdown still in the mid-thirties. Even if the songs were being made for 11-year-old daffy girls practising kissing on their old cabbage-patch dolls, things were coming up rosy-ass roses. It was now decision time. Continue on to Key West? Would he even get paid now if he showed up? Sure as shit wouldn't get a bonus. He could see the owner now, a fat gay guy in a banana hammock and a bad toupee, weird tan lines that didn't add up, wrapped in a feather boa drinking warm margaritas wondering when he should call the keystone cops about his lost/stolen property. His clientele, stuck tourists and a social club from New Orleans operating an initiation weekend complete with assigned blow-up dolls outfitted with duct-taped-on dildos to be treated as the baby egg in Home Ec class would be irate about the lack of ice and the electricity necessary to watch the Saints game. Petty would say see if that horse fly can make its way out of the cracked window, if it does, you continue on. Or will that turtle cross the cracked yellow line on the road? Or hell, flip a coin, he was sure to have a quarter in his pocket. Let the randomness of the world guide your hand, always. Chance was where divinity dwelt. "Screw all that, Petty," he said with finality to the retreating waves past the windshield. It was high time to choose a third path while standing at the dusty crossroads. He had never missed a delivery in his life, hell had never been late one second but acts of God were even beyond the control of masters of the universe like him. If a hurricane was going to dictate defeat, what was the point of throwing the dice any more, now that his perfect record had been scratched? He had enough beer to fill an Olympic sized pool, his girl was in the back chilling. Why not shake the reins, take a break, go on a little road trip? Sure, it was like a chef going out to eat but hey, drivers gonna drive. Boom. With his immediate future settled, he reached back into one of the many compartments and pulled out a stack of license plates. Found a New York one. New York. New York City. Gotham. Gomorrah. He had never navigated the boroughs, the intricate grid of no-horizon Manhattan with a wilderness in the middle full of rollerbladers, vagrants and flashers, stolen from what was once a vibrant Negro settlement. Might be a real pickle tickle. He jumped back out and switched the plates on the trailer. He couldn't switch the VIN number but it was at least one line of defense. He performed a three-point turn as Casey came out of number 29 hot by relaying a story about a lost dog traveling 3,000 miles by train to reunite with its owners and soon he was headed north, back to the meat of America. The dog story almost made him cry a little again. What was it about hangovers that made you emotional? He shook it off, didn't want to be a big pussy. Damn lost dog. What he needed was the hair of the dog. Was it beer thirty? His headache said yes, please.

· · ·

"You like numbers, kid?" Petty was fiddling with his pipe as he perpetually did, The Kid leaning over, steering the rig with a big, steady left hand, staying perfectly between the lines as they flew down I-80 hours east of Reno. They had been driving non-stop for a week since the moment they left his dead mother neck-deep in a pile of mobile-home wreckage. Careening through a dozen states, Petty the instant mentor, teaching how to hook and unhook a trailer, how to use your mirrors, how to drive a stick, since The Kid could already easily reach the pedals. The days, the lessons were all a blur, even though he always knew precisely where they were, moving away but never be far enough from Nowhere, Alabama. Like Lot fleeing Sodom, he had been scared to look back to see if the diner and his father had fared any better that night, so he didn't. Out of sight, out of mind for ever.

"Earth to Kid! Numbers… do you like them? Like 1, 45, 666, 3,297? Like in a general sense, not one in particular?" He nodded. Petty spun the dial on the radio until he hit the American Top 40. "Then you'll dig this the most, little man Tate. Made for long-haul truck drivers like you and me. It kills hours, you get to follow it week to week, hear which songs drop, which songs rise. Most of them are pure shit but there is always a few that'll stick in your head for days, the chorus on repeat drilling right into the center of your brain about drive you bonkers, they call 'em ear worms." Petty stuck his pinky in his mouth and then poked it into The Kid's ear until he squirmed away. Still the rig held true to the road. "That is until the next week and then you hear it again and that night, when you lay your head down, it's gone. Ain't that an ostrich feather?" The pipe finally got lit after an inordinate amount of dicking around, which was more Petty seeing how well The Kid could steer around curves and buses than uncooperative tobacco. He took the wheel back as the kid bobbed his head offbeat to something new from Prince that had climbed to number 12.

· · ·

Well shit, he thought, now it is almost 1999. Guess it was indeed high time to party. It felt very freeing to drive away from his responsibility with a trailer full of contraband. He was always wired to be an outlaw but pride and Petty's stupid-ass code always kept him in check. What would unchecked power mean to him now? A steamroller in gear left to its own devices. He could kill an entire sorority over a labor-day weekend or save a dozen unwanted animals from a raging inferno at the county pound then raise them as his own in a dog-hair-ridden Vermont chalet. He was giddy to find out how the cookie would crumble in the kitchen of good and evil now that he was the chef, the recipe in the trash, just throwing things in the pot and making it up as he went along. He noticed that hitch in the engine again, if he could run an EKG, the residing doc would notice that the irregularity was popping up with more frequency. He hoped it was just the Florida air. Maybe running over so many drowned nutria and coconuts had unseated the bolts. He may break another code and take a look under the hood. "Let the pros handle the fixin'," Petty always preached. He didn't tell nobody how to change a fan belt, just as nobody sure as hell better tell him how to drive. The Driver always followed that advice to the letter, too. He didn't even know how to change the oil or fill up the windshield-wiper fluid. Petty said if you keep the maintenance up and bring the big girl in to the mechanics you trust, then you'll never need to know a damn thing about how it works. Astronauts don't know how they get to the moon, he would proclaim. Another rule looking to get broken or his ass may wind up stranded somewhere on 95 wondering how in the hell he got started down this proverbial road. Never mind, he knew.

She was a cocktail waitress in the loosest form. More of a well-seasoned steak of a lady who brought you drinks until you bought her a drink and then the buying escalated as the real menu appeared. Although vastly underage, The Kid was bellied up at a slot machine with a bucket of quarters, courtesy of Petty, when she rubbed her breasts on his back and blew softly on the nape of his neck. "Hey, tiger, you feeling lucky?" she purred into his ear. When he turned around, he found Petty behind her, stifling a laugh. Petty pinched her ass and she jumped a foot in the air.

"You getting fresh with my boy here, Jackie?"

Jackie giggled and caressed The Kid's face with a sincere tenderness Petty failed to witness.

She was all sequins and pantyhose, flesh pushed and squeezed into the right areas to give her an hourglass figure. Her Ann-Margret fire-engine-red hair could have been a wig but framed her face as a sexy lioness. Makeup hid her true age but the eyes did not. She had seen a lot and wished she hadn't. Separating galoots like Petty from his money had become her eventual profession. Find out what you do well and do it had been her mama's motto and was the only thing other than a gene for breast cancer she had inherited from the cold bitch. "You winning, sugar?" The Kid looked through her. She got a visible chill, turned back to Petty. "Seems quiet, kinda spooky, is he retarded?"

"He talks when he has something worth saying. Shame more people don't subscribe to the notion."

"Ah ha, the strong and silent type. He'll be a lady killer one day."

"Sooner rather than later." Petty raised his eyebrows knowingly at The Kid, who turned back to the machine. He pulled the handle and a flurry of coins dropped. "Kid has the touch!" Petty hip-bumped Jackie out of the way and leaned down as The Kid raked the winnings into the bucket. Petty picked up a quarter, flipped it and caught it on the back of his hand. He looked at it secretly. "Jackie, looks like we are hitting the craps table." She winked over a tall glass of Malibu and coke that had materialized out of magic casino dust. He crouched down even lower to meet The Kid's eye, even though he felt a twinge in his lower back. "You hang tight here a while, kiddo, a girl will come by and give you a free soda. If they ask you how old you are, just say 21. They need all the business they can get. My friend Jackie here has some dice to blow on. I'll be back. I always come back. Don't ever forget that." The Kid nodded while digging his fingertips under coins trapped in the corners of the bin. Petty put his hand under The Kid's chin, lifted his head to gain his undivided attention. "Don't ever forget it. Got it?" The Kid nodded again, wanting desperately to collect every bit of his treasure.

By the time Petty came around to collect him he had multiplied his bankroll into three buckets of quarters. He was also starving, not having any idea what time it was or how many meals he had missed. It could have been days or two hours. Another pre-teen in his situation could have gotten worried but where was he going to go? He also had to pee really bad from all the free sodas the waitresses brought him, the rough girls huddling up at the bar coming to the consensus he was the cutest 21-year-old degenerate gambler they had ever laid eyes on.

"Let's scram, King Midas." Petty tugged at The Kid's ear, holding his right arm against his chest as if it were in a sling. The Kid picked up two of his topped-off buckets, motioning to Petty to grab the third. They headed straight to the exit and out to the vastness of the parking lot where the rig sat beyond the lights horizontal, taking up eight spots far away from any other vehicles. Petty climbed up and waited for The Kid to get his winnings situated and take a leak. As soon as they both were in the truck Petty got her moving toward the main drag and then soon enough north on 445 toward Pyramid Lake and the reservation. The Kid rustled around for something to eat. He turned to look in the back of the cab as he had seen Petty pull snacks from there in the days prior, usually jerky or long plastic sleeves of peanuts. "Don't poke around back there. Eyes front." Petty tugged him back with his right arm. Blood was dripping from the cuff of his sleeve, The Kid stared at it dripping down into the darkness of the floorboard. Drip. Drip. "Don't worry about that. Just got nicked. A band-aid and I'll be right as rain. I got a job for you. OK? I want you to look out your window and hunt for a shooting star. As soon as you see one, you let me know." Petty raised his arm above his head to slow the bleeding as if he had a question for the teacher but wasn't getting noticed. The Kid did what he was told – it sounded simple enough. He looked up at the blanket of stars as they rolled through the desert. A couple of times, he thought he heard a soft moaning coming from somewhere inside but figured it was probably his tummy growling. He would have killed a kitten for a plate of his dad's liver and onions at that point.

About half an hour passed and a shooting star had so far eluded him. He tied witnessing the phenomenon to finally getting to eat so, as the minutes dragged on, he became frustrated with the heavens. He fantasized about seeing that celestial streak low and bright outside the window of his dad's diner, the smell of a juicy burger below him with a side of piping-hot crinkle fries and a tall strawberry shake. Petty was a nice enough fella, hell he had saved his life, but he did not prioritize the most basic of needs like eating, sleeping, evacuating or, unfortunately, having to co-habit a tight space, bathing. It was all about the miles, the destination. Whatever you could accomplish as you moved forward was gravy. Reno was the first time they had been out of the cab for more than an hour. He guessed that Petty afforded himself a break only when his libido demanded it. Maybe Jackie was an old friend he stopped by to visit on the way to California? He didn't believe that. From his limited observation Petty didn't seem like the kind of guy to have old friends. Truck drivers were solitary creatures. Not much time to write letters to that autistic pen pal in Switzerland they had corresponded with since the sixth grade. Truck drivers swam in the deep end of the social lake, out past the rope, doing laps while everyone else had chicken fights and bounced around a beach ball in the shallows. It was a calling that suited The Kid well, he was realizing quickly. Living on the road, away from the nagging and constant demands of others. Take this here, take something else somewhere else. Get 'n' go, got 'n' went. Repeat for ever. There was a romance in its no-hassle simplicity. He was thinking that hooking up a trailer of Little Debbie's would be just the ticket when he saw the meteor, it bounded across in a long, beautiful arc, dying in a ball of operatic flame. He turned back to Petty who was fiddling with the pipe, his hands a little shaky. A tug at the bad arm, careful not to be too forceful was followed with a point at the sky.

"All right, little buddy! Nice work!" Petty took the first turn off the road he saw, albeit way too fast, fishtailing on to a dirt track trailing into nothingness as he tried to downshift with his injured arm. The bleeding picked up its pace and splattered sideways on to the seat and The Kid's pant leg. "Sorry, we will get that out. Or, hell, you need some new threads anyway. Me and you gonna hit JC Penney tomorrow and spend those quarters, pinky swear." He held out his finger and the Kid didn't know what to do, he had never done a pinky swear. Petty lunged a little further and hooked their fingers. "Pinky swear." The crimson faucet knob was turned more to the right, dripping faster than the beat of a second hand. The Kid watched it flow. Dripdripdripdripdrip. He felt a chill as they drove through the ink. Petty was going to kill him out here, bury him under the moonlight deep enough to dissuade the coyotes. Was this fate, a quick death by the hands of a virtual stranger better than the slow methodical drip drip drip of Her lukewarm water on to his block of ice day by day until there was nothing but a rancid pool where he used to be? He had been liberated from a tyrant's rule only to be executed by his intrepid savior on a foreign shore. He would run. As soon as they stopped and the dust was still thick, he would run his ass off. Zigzag his way back to the main road and some semblance of a life. He had seen news stories about runaways living under bridges in the city, selling their bodies for heroin or a sleeve of crackers. He would take the vagabonds over and unite them into an army, become the terror of the streets, stealing from the rich and giving to no one but themselves. Marching on city hall with chamber pots for helmets and welcome mats tied around their taut malnourished bellies with duct tape for armor, they would overthrow the patriarchy!

The truck had been still for a couple of minutes as he had been laying out his new governmental platform. His strategy of running was already gone with the midnight wind. "Get out, kid, I don't like it too much but I'm gonna need your assistance." Petty dug around in the cab cursing, then reappeared in the staticky headlight beams holding a shovel. He motioned for The Kid to get his ass in gear and join him. They walked together through the brush for 50 yards in silence, The Kid judging Petty's malice through peripheral vision. Petty stopped and as if signaling the Kid's fears that future scavenging coyote picking at his corpse howled in the distance, hungry, not as hungry as The Kid, he ventured, but hungry still. "Time to hold up your end of the bargain. Start digging a hole. The quicker you get it done, the quicker we are sitting in a booth eating breakfast." Petty handed over the shovel and raised his arm back up, flopping it over to rest on his head. The Kid was weak, sleepy, He was worried that the hole he was digging was his own. What had he done wrong? Did Batman just decide that he didn't need Robin any more? Wouldn't it be more humane to drop him off at a bus station than this diabolical act? He didn't know what else to do but dig. Petty may have been losing blood for the last hour, maybe longer but there was no way to overpower him. The Kid was very tall for his age and already burly as all get out but never underestimate old-man strength. The few times he grappled with his dad taught him that much. Strength wasn't always apparent by a man's appearance. The coyote called out again, probably telling his coyote buddies that dinner was being prepped in the kitchen. It was a small blessing that the sand gave easy. Shovelfuls flew into the air to settle into tiny foothills around the deepening chasm. Just as he started to break out in that stubborn adolescent sweat, he was four feet down in the hole and dawn was whispering of its eventual approach. "That'll do." Petty got up from his seat on an ill-shaped rock and stretched. He reached out his hand for the shovel. This was it, The Kid thought. A good whack and it was infinite night-nights. Instead, he dropped the shovel and offered his hand again, lifting The Kid out of the hole. "Stay here, back in a jiff." Petty walked back toward the rig. He watched the man's brisk walk back, knowing he wasn't out of the woods/desert yet. If he was still planning to bolt, it was go time. He hesitated. Then hesitated some more. Looked over the rim into the hole. Guessed at its dimensions, lauded his handiwork. Put the tip of his finger on a cactus needle. Watched a lizard scamper in front of the fat moon. Petty reappeared carrying a large bag over his shoulder. Without a word he threw it into the hole. It landed with a thud followed by that moan he had heard in the cab. It hadn't been his stomach after all – it was Jackie.

Pancakes had never tasted so good. He didn't even mind that the bacon was touching the maple syrup.

"You gonna drink that milk? Had me spring for the large and you haven't touched it." Petty was sitting there watching The Kid gorge himself, toothpick swaying back and forth after a frugal meal of a cup of chili and two packages of saltines. The Kid took a white gulp, fork still in hand then got back to the stack. Petty's voice was extra gravelly as if it were idling rough, reluctantly gearing up for a long haul up a mountain.

He looked around the diner, they were all alone at that ungodly hour save for the waitress reading a nursing textbook behind the register, then dove on in. "After the events of the previous evening, even with it being a cliché doing all that unfortunate business in the desert at night… You know what a cliché is? A cliché is just another way of saying that something falls into a pattern of convenience. Lazy-ass French word like all of them. I'm sure you seen it done in a hundred movies but I doubt you couldn't spit out there in any direction without it landing over a pile of bones. Anyways, to get us back between the lines, I would like to thank you for your assistance in putting a bow on. I feel it is necessary to teach you the code by which I live and prosper in this evil world. You ready for me to hit you broadside with some knowledge?" He got a nod and a swallow; it would have to do. "All right then. Back in Vietnam, I was taught this way to survive. At first, I thought it was silly or just superstitious bull but after I watched a guy flip out, fall in love with his rifle and try to have sex with it, blowing up his insides in the process, I gave it a try and quickly understood the calming, focused power behind it. I made it through my tour and I have abided by it ever since. It's the theory of embracing chance. There is no good, there is no evil in the natural world, out there beyond the lights and people and TV dinners and misdemeanors and tax lawyers and all that manufactured shit. In the natural world, chance is everything. Life and death is decided by the fickleness of fate, whether a snake sees a mouse that don't see him. Whether he has the angle or where the sun is bending the shadows. We can embrace that truth. We can leave our lives up to chance. Let chance decide what happens next. Wasn't it something that I just happened to ride out a tornado across the interstate from your house? That I just happened to see the rubble and pick out your blond head sticking out among all that? Odds were against it but I did. Therefore I had to act, had to pull you out and take you under my wing. So far so good, right?" The Kid had stopped eating, mesmerized by Petty's philosophy of life being laid out in front of him so earnestly, without a shred of doubt. "So last night this woman, Jackie you met, she just so happened to approach me as I was warming up at the roulette table. I said to myself, if it lands on red and I win, I'll see where things go with her. If it lands on black and I lose, she can bugger off. Well you know how it bounced." Petty reached in his shirt pocket, pulled out his pipe and a bag of tobacco. "Next thing you know we partake of a couple of drinks and she is meeting my 'son'. Again I put it to chance by flipping that quarter you won. If it had landed heads, me and you would have been on our way to California. It landed tails, so off to the craps table. You go with the flow, follow the forks, whether you want to or not. That's important..." He held a match over the pipe and puffed till it caught nice, The Kid loved the smell and smiled involuntarily. "Yes, very important. You have to give yourself up to it completely. Remove any and all emotion. You may not want to do what chance decides, you do it anyway. You decide the terms but chance decides the outcome. That is the deal you make. Anyway, one thing led to another, we do good at the table – devotees of chance always do – and we find ourselves back in the cab of the rig. We do what we do, then she says she wants a cut of the cash I won and by cut I mean all and by cut I mean she pulls a cute knife with a curved three-inch blade and an ivory handle. I'll show it to you, fine craftsmanship. I tell her to look out the window. If the drunk fella with the tie around his head and stained wife beater makes it to his Nissan without falling down, I'd split the winnings with her. She seemed satisfied with the wager, we shook on it. The drunk was looking good till he misjudged or just didn't see a speed bump and down he went, face first. I told her fair was fair, she proceeded to put the knife in my arm." The Kid could still see some flakes under the cuff of Petty's fresh shirt. That mystery was solved. "Defending myself, I had to knock her unconscious. She was a danger to me and, by extension, you. Speaking of you, chance decreed that if you had won money, left by yourself for hours at a janky slot machine, then we would drive out to the desert. Sure enough, out we went. You know the rest. You didn't run, even when I left you by yourself by the hole you dug. Those forks led us to burying the crazy bitch. I's crossed and t's dotted. The natural world doesn't care about her, she had divorced herself from it as all these flesh-bags have. If anything, it just sets things a bit more right. You let nothing but the purity of chance lead you, you come up roses every time. End of lesson."

The Kid was hooked. It made sense. He never had any direction other than what the atlas showed and any way that was away from Her. This was an intangible map and he memorized it, held the simplicity dear. Over his formative years with Petty stretching to adulthood, he was molded into a true devotee. Petty offered numerous examples as they traveled and, regardless of the outcome, causing death or life, they felt invincible, protected by the gods that lay hidden to the rest of society. They played in the shadows while basking in the sun. Since he himself had taken over the wheel, it had never steered him wrong, no matter the carnage he left in his wake.

Crossing the Florida-Georgia line, he had now officially forsaken the path, while doing vital harm to his sensei in the process. Every student must eventually kill his master. He must forge anew. Chance could kiss his ass.

The empty cans were amassing up from the floorboard to the level of the bench seat. A bum's dream shaped in sticky aluminum cylinders. The stink of stale beer and unbathed skin clung to the walls of the cab, even with the windows down. The radio was off – he and Casey were on a break, this time a permanent one. He didn't need a countdown of audible cancer any more; time had lost relevance since he had no deadlines to meet. Lost and free at the same time, he barreled down Interstate 95, wishing for a brick wall to drive through or one of those wooden gates at the entrance of a parking garage. Splinters flying in his wake, an attendant shaking his fist in anger but envious inside. He felt desperate to get north, as if his demons dwelt in the humid flats of the south. New England would cleanse him, the cold crisp savageness of bus fumes and garbage blowing through the rape park no one wants to expend the energy to pick up. He could park the rig at a storage lot and charge into the Bronx head down, hands deep in his pockets, evading zero unlucky pedestrians in his path. Embrace a sedentary life. Days at a time never leaving his eight-story walk-up, forgetting to feed the cat as he watches snow fall through the one tiny window, huddled under three blankets because the radiator is far past its prime and the landlord can't fix it now since his head is in the freezer from the argument about the radiator not working. That may be the cops banging on the door but they are going to need a battering ram and the place is wired up with so much C-4 and ammonium nitrate the whole city block will be nothing but cinder-block dust and kitty litter the second they break through and trip the wire.

Good thing he wasn't doing any graded inclines on his way up the coast, the engine was revving higher and more erratic than it should, even though he was rolling flat and sticking to the speed limit. There was definitely something wrong. Next time he had to fill up, probably around Savannah, as he had no desire to stop and revisit any part of his South Carolina tour, he would take a gander and hope through some magical osmosis he had picked up enough mechanical knowledge to diagnose the issue. While he reached out in his mind to gather all he knew of truck engines in one place, he started aching for a change in the scenery. It seemed like he would drive down a straight road bordered by sand pine for ever, it had become his infinite purgatory, never running out of gas or reaching a curve. Heaven might have been so close, he glimpsed the wild rivers that tumbled through the dense wilds of southern Georgia into the Atlantic as he crossed over the wide bridges. To row up into the glass-surfaced water arteries of the tribes, footholds of the Spanish and French at their mouths wiped out under new moons as the ships sailed back to the Caribbean for more guns and slaves to reinforce nothing but their dead, tomahawked in the mud. He had to have some Indian in him, he felt, that resolve to eliminate waves of invaders, knowing their ill intentions, even when they spoke a foreign tongue. They held their own and might have successfully repelled the white devils for decades, centuries, even if the royal patrons had decided funding such folly was pointless. That first tribe to trade with the white man, feeling pity or seduced by a missionary's promise of everlasting life through Christ, offered their daughters and agricultural secrets for blankets laced with smallpox to seal the fate of all. Kindness led to elimination. Kindness was weakness. Wolves would always find a way to eat.

When he released his bladder for the first time since he had reversed the course of the rig and his life, it took over a minute and felt as if an angel had softly blown immaculate on his nuts. He had to brace himself with a hand against the wall above the urinal, it was either one of those kinds of pisses or he was thoroughly buzzed again. Maybe both. Walking back through the store from the bathroom he realized he needed to eat, give the beer some padding. He grabbed three pre-packaged egg salad sandwiches and a bag of Fun-Yuns and dropped them in a careless heap on the counter. A chubby girl wearing headgear from crooked-ass teeth rang him up without making eye contact. Her low self-esteem was hidden under a gigantic Madonna T-shirt. Big enough that Madonna herself could have been under the cotton tent, flexed legs wrapped around the girl's soft waist. She was scared to death and didn't know why.

"You know if there is a diesel mechanic around here?"

The alcohol from his breath made her eyes water, even from her subjugated posture far below. Even though she didn't want to, she nodded her head. Spoke while studying the expired dates on the plastic of the sandwich wrappers.

"My brother is a mechanic. He works on big trucks."

"And where might I find this brother?"

"He works up there at Yamasee Garage. Take a right at the light, about a mile down on the left next to the barbershop. You'll see the pole." She threw everything in a bag and took his cash, realizing she never told him how much it was but receiving exact change.

"What kind of pole?"

"A barbershop pole. You know, like a candy cane but it has some blue in it and it swirls."

"Never been to a barber shop so no, I wouldn't know."

Despite her fear, the proclamation sparked her curiosity enough for her to look up and see what must have been a drunken sasquatch but he was gone, the bell on the door settling back into silence from its violent ring.

For some reason he felt bad for lying to the girl. While it was true, he had never set foot in a barbershop, he did know what a pole was and even knew its origin stemmed from medieval barbers who were in the bloodletting with leeches or tooth-extraction business. Funny how an indicator from centuries past still held its relevance while others couldn't make it a generation. Barbers were their own breed, sweeping up hair all day (where did it all go?), cutting around what lived in people's ears or the fungus that took root on their scalps. No thanks. Shame it didn't pay as well as dentistry as it was about as foul a practice to deal in.

The well-worn garage wasn't doing much business, unless you called a guy in a frayed lawn chair knuckle deep up his nose while reading the TV Guide business. The Driver pulled the rig inside the single high bay without asking and killed it, despairingly taking note of a few clunks and clatters he had never heard come out of her before.

"New Simon & Simon on tonight, love that show. Can I help ya?" The nose picker had rolled up the guide and shoved it in the back pocket of his low-hanging jeans. He was portly but with too much head for his body. His KISS shirt had a multitude of holes and oil stains, making Gene Simmons look like he had fallen on a grenade. This must have been the brother and there must be a helluva good deal on band T-shirts at the local Wal-Mart.

"Need you to take a look at the engine. You know your way around a diesel?" The mechanic laughed, bent the visor of his giant ball cap, which was already tamed into an upside-down U.

"Shit, bud, I was fingering a piston since before I knew girls had holes." He jumped up on the front tire in one surprisingly agile leap. The Driver was not fond of how he haphazardly gripped the side mirror for support. "Pop the hood let's see what's crack-a-lackin'." He rubbed his hands together as The Driver remembered where the latch was, lifted up the hood and set the kickstand. The mechanic climbed in and crouched by the engine, pulling and wiping, smelling his fingers. "Can you start her up for me?" The Driver got behind the wheel and obliged. The engine struggled to turn over but did, hitting a few sour notes in the process that he hoped the mechanic had an ear for. "Give her a little gas." He yelled while he leaned over the engine. The Driver push the pedal down, just a bit, gentle. The RPMs raced up as if falling over each other, not a row of perfectly placed dominoes but rather a falling house of cards. He could hear the mechanic banging at something, he must have had a wrench in his pocket. It was bad etiquette to be hammering away at personal property without consent. He wouldn't cup the guy's moobs without asking. "All right partner, you can kill it."

"Damn right I can." The Driver thought. The engine coughed itself into silence. He got out and found the mechanic about ready to perform open-heart surgery.

"All right, man, good news and bad news. Good news is I know what the problem is. You got water in your fuel. Probably got into your tank and got all mixed up. That is pure hell for a diesel engine. Will do all kinda damage. That's the bad news. Now I can fix it but we gonna need to get all up in there and clean everything out. Reestablish the ecosystem, if you will, and I will." He looked up from the engine at The Driver and wiped his hands on the bottom of his shirt. The Driver could see the dollar signs in the hick's eyes. Time and money were two things he didn't particularly feel like parting with at this juncture of his new lease on life.

"How long and how much?" Seemed only fair to ask.

"Well…" The mechanic climbed out and rested his heels back on the tire, leaving oily fingerprints on the exterior frame above the wheel well. Sloppy disregard. He would not have that. "I can't be certain but I'd say I could have her back up to snuff in about five days. Now, due to my religious beliefs, I don't work on Sunday so..." He counted on those grimy fingers. "I'd say next Wednesday, worst case scenario. As for cost, hell, can't say until I get in there but if we gotta replace some parts and I figure we will, probably gonna run a few gees." The mechanic looked away as he couldn't hold eye contact with The Driver's icy stare after delivering such a negative message. "Shoot, man, you starting a recycling center?" He snickered and pointed his thumb at the windshield and the pile of beer cans in the cab.

"Can you show me where the fuel line goes in?" The Driver asked with a naïve flair. The mechanic ducked back under and poked around. The Driver braced the hood with his left and released the kickstand smoothly without noise. Then he took hold of the hood with both hands and threw it down as hard as he could muster. It caught the mechanic right under the base of his skull and by the time he got a scream out it was muffled under the sheet of heavy metal and the power of two cannon barrel arms. The body jerked, the work boots slid off the tire and he hung there as if attached to a gallows, the crowds starting to dissipate back to their dull, hard lives in some outpost town. The Driver kept his weight on the hood until any and all struggle ceased. When he lifted up, the body slid off on to the oily floor. The mechanic's head was still attached but only by some throaty flesh, the spine was severed. How about that? he thought, didn't have to see if a chicken would make it across the road or if the wind would blow a burger wrapper past a fire hydrant. New code felt pretty damn great. Act on a whim, however he deemed fit. He felt unfettered now, free to unleash his will on a submissive world. "Lucy!" He yelled as he reached down to grab two handfuls of scuffed ostrich-skin boots. "You got a guest coming for dinner!"

· · ·

States blurred as the hours passed but he failed to notice much, the effort needed to hug the right north bound lane of I-95 was the extent of his involvement with reality. The rhythm inside the cab became a steady gulp of beer for every three breaths. Every once in a while he would shovel down whatever processed food-stuffs he had randomly corralled at his last refueling stop. If it weren't for the signs, he wouldn't have realized he was driving past the nation's capital. There was no desire to sightsee, even if only to urinate on Washington's Monument or yell obscenities at Honest Abe sitting there all smug larger than whatever life had become. The world had become a shrink-wrapped microcosm of what existed between the two blank doors. He was doing time, trapped in a cell until he could reach the five boroughs where he had a frantic hope that the next stage would present itself as ordained in a book being read as it was being written. Past Balti-more, he purchased a few crab cakes for two dollars from an elderly lady selling them out of a rolling cooler in between the pumps. They were warmed from sitting on top of the dash by the time he got around to stuffing one down his throat and chasing it down with the remnants of another can. Not too bad, he thought – he thought he could taste the ocean in there some-where, grabbing the next one in the lineup as an anteater might mow down a row on a rotten log. He was nearing New Jersey and that meant he was getting close. The radio had been silent for hours and his ears felt numb and weak, not being inundated by the countdown melodies. All he had heard was the laboring engine, himself breathing, eating, drinking, crushing cans and popping tops. Voices inside the gas station snack shops were violent and pressing stimuli that made him wince. Grunts from the bathroom stalls left him wanting to punch through a wall. He had to get acclimated to the cacophony of the masses or he would kill as soon as he stepped on to a bustling sidewalk. He decided he should get ready for the audible chaos of the big city by tuning the radio to some jazz. The heroin-fueled tumbling notes would ease him into the sonic assault of car alarms, harsh accents yelling over bagels or prayer, beams clanging 60 stories above him as another skyscraper reaches up to kiss the sky and steal away the horizon, street performers beating hubcaps with taped-together chopsticks, ambulances fighting through the unmoving cars to deliver another soul to death's door. He fine-tuned the dial when he heard a trumpet and alto sax frolic along a starlit path. He felt a rush in his guts, an anticipation of ruling over such a vast kingdom, the dark lord of NYC. What would history books refer to him as? The Son of Sam was catchy but minimizing. He was the son of no one, not any more. He wasn't about any trinket left at a back-alley massacre, a cat's-eye marble or a coded note written in goat blood, pinned to a torso. He would act completely randomly and uncaring of notoriety. It would seek him out like a woman scorned, a society insecure and needing his approval and love so badly that people would make an event out of watching the news or grabbing the Post to see if he had struck terror again so they could try to connect at some level with his absolute disregard for the decency in presenting a profile to the FBI. His stomach rolled over again and he clinched his butt cheeks involuntarily. That wasn't antici-pation. The rig seemed to mirror his gastrointestinal protests and through a psychic connection sputtered itself, almost stalling out, even though it was rolling four ticks above the speed limit. He downshifted as a cold sweat formed on the back of his neck. He was prepared to go down with the ship but not until they reached the golden shore, Lady Liberty offering to drop the torch and service his every need. He placed a clammy hand on the hard, dusty plastic of the dash, settling her down, refocusing their energies into one. He felt nauseous but got the rig evened back out, although the laboring was even more evident. His tongue felt thick, his soul was being chipped away by an indus-trious Tlingit fashioning a dug-out. At least he knew it wasn't his appendix unless Abuela had left a chunk in to flare up at another inopportune time. He rolled down the window in time to vomit a torrent of beer and rancid crab meat, lumps of breadcrumbs stuck to his chin. His trusty gal had been mortally wounded by the hurricane forcing itself into the spare fuel tank, he had just been poisoned by some very spoiled crab cakes as, together with Lucinda and the mechanic, they rode on into the industrial wasteland of east Jersey.

"One hundred cans of beer in my gut, one hundred cans of beer! Kill the clown, pass her around, one hundred cans of beer!" He was just sober enough to do the math but the building fever didn't help. The way he was having to hold back evacuating his bowels, it was if his celebratory century-mark can was nothing but ipecac syrup mixed with pain. He was in a hard state of denial that the engine was in its death throes. The RPMs were all over the place, the needle behind the plastic having an epileptic fit. His triumphal entrance into the unguarded city gates was more the sad limp of a leper, vainly trying to keep step with a Thelonious Monk solo seeping from the speakers of the cab. He needed a bathroom, a bucket and a bed. "Don't think I don't know what you two are up to back there Lucy Lou!" He screamed out as his intestines spasmed around in the thrashing mosh pit of his stomach. Those two were up to shenanigans back there, he'd bet a batch of Snatch on it. He couldn't trust them to support him as he tried to break through to a new life. They were just along for the ride, chilling out, making the most of things, probably overtly flirting during some leg wrestling. Chilling out, yeah. Giving him the cold shoulder. Freezing him out… He was alone on this quest for the grail. A minor miracle allowed him to direct the rig rolling slow and easy into a long stagnant line of traffic lurching down the Helix, lining up to enter the Lincoln Tunnel but it served only to prolong his agony and delay any escape from it. "Lucinda! You vile succubus! What have you done to me? Your Duke, your green knight alone on the path of the elusive grail? I hope he is worth it, that flat-footed big-headed fuck! Oh, is that it? Is he good with his hands? Do you go for the grease under long, chipped nails?" The loud jazz brewed an assault down below again, the pressure was too much he succumbed to a second of weakness sharting into his already rank-smelling overalls stiff with all order of human secretions. "You think that's funny? Laugh at the sick man, Lucy goosey, laugh now because soon enough I will regain my strength and I will pop skulls like bubble wrap!" He bent over to quell the cramps, trying to drink out of the beer can with dog-like slurps of his dry tongue dipping into the hole. So thirsty, so tired, so damn sick. Were Petty's vengeful mistresses of fate exacting their revenge for his forsaking of their ways? Bitches all, bitches all his life seeking to tear down the golden tower he perpetually had to build back up. His very own Tower of Babel cursed by these women who act as if they were the almighty GOD to confound him. HE IS THE GOD! They have all fallen under his thumb. "You too, Lucinda!" They always will. He grabbed a deep breath, sat up, killed the rest of the thin skunky water inside can 100. "I AM GOD!" He crushed the can and hurled it out the open window. It clanged off metal...

"Four dollars. And the normal tube into the city is down for construction so you gotta take the center, ain't supposed to be trucks in the center it goes both ways so don't mess around in there, in and out. And watch what yo litterin' out yo window G.O.D." A large black lady sat in her booth neither amused nor impressed by his boast as she had done seen all the weirds the NYC arteries of filth leading to the diseased still-pumping heart had to offer. She held out a hand extended inches further by ornate impractical nails adorned with fake jewels and painted swirls. He looked at her as if in a dream, how could this woman be right next to him here, now? His fanned-out essence reformed itself. He was at the entrance to the tunnel; this lady was in a toll booth. He was about to enter the kingdom.

"Hey boy, four dollars. Let's get it." She looked at the line behind him, barely raised her eyebrows. She didn't really give a shit but this dude was stanky as hell, drunk six ways to Sunday and the engine sounded like a pig drowning in a pool of peanut butter. She needed him gone and out the other side. He reached in his pocket pulled out a crumpled pile of ones. He didn't even count them as he handed them across their clouds. "Have a day. Remember, center tube," she muttered as she rolled up the extra cash and stuck it in her bra, careful of her manicure.

He shifted and the truck stuttered into motion with a Bird alto sax progression on the radio taking its death march order with condemned pride into the blackness of the gaping hole that led down under the Hudson. The Driver was to be Orpheus upon a dying steed and Hades lay waiting.

The tunnel was a mile and a half long, burrowed in 1937 under the river almost 100 feet deep into the earth. The rig, his big black dutiful daily companion for a decade, one that had carried him coast to coast like a yo-yo all over the great land, in dire sickness and boundless health, finally gave out about half a mile in. He was fighting to stay conscious when the engine stalled out, anxiety over being trapped under the earth were stoking the memory snakes of being trapped facing Her, the lifeless sadistic matriarch, the raging fever wasn't having it, triggering his body and mind to shut down. The absence of that reassuring sound of engine noise roused him enough to try to restart the engine, employ all his tricks, but it was to no avail. Right as the truck slowed to a halt he cut the wheel to the left for no apparent reason other than to take everyone in the tunnel down with him. He almost clipped a minivan carrying a very frightened soccer mom heading out of the city who was already on edge after an illicit coupling with her broad-shouldered female aerobics instructor at the Waldorf-Astoria. The truck and reefer came to their terminal rest across both lanes, blocking all traffic. A symphony of horn blasts soon started bouncing off the cement walls. The Driver had to pull himself up by his bootstraps and get the hell out of there posthaste. Claustrophobia mined a hidden store of energy hidden deep inside his very own Lincoln Tunnel and, as the autopilot switch was flipped, he reached behind the seat to locate a single duffle bag from the row of boxes that housed his life. That particular bag was super-sized on the bag menu, and heavy. It contained the sum of all his efforts over the years, all the hard-trodden miles and deadlines beaten. He shook off all emotion trying to penetrate his tear ducts through weakened defenses. Took a last look about the cab, felt the ridges in the keys still dangling from the starter between his fingers, flicked the hoop on the rearview mirror for one last jab, made sure to gather up his security blanket of maps and then used his stony heart's rough edge to cut off the line to his traveling home like that hellhole trailer years ago. There would be no looking back. He staggered down and dragged the bag out leaving the door wide open, slinging the dead weight over his shoulder like a fireman about to head up flights of stairs at the academy and started to trek right back out the way he came in. NYC was not to be on the cards and he came to a sudden peace with that. It was for the best, really. What he needed was space and lots of it. No more lying about his true nature, he needed air and to exist with the wild beast, the flowering fields. After all, murder and destruction were not all that could drive his happiness; he would seek a deeper peace in retreat, to build back that tower one last time, stronger than ever. On the way past the reefer and the yells of other drivers shouting obscenities in all languages and variation in his direction, he placed a gentle hand on the back door leaving a print in the dirt above someone's plead of WASH ME. "Bye, Lu." In a simple pledge he promised to process a never-before-felt heavy guilt and yet cherish their short time together. The Driver then walked on, along the burgeoning cataclysm of trapped vehicles and stranded drivers, back to the beckoning light.

EPILOGUE

HOW YOU REMIND ME

R ocky should have been gearing up to fight in the impending war with the Arabs right about now. Running the urban desert obstacle course yelling through a gas mask holding an assault rifle sweaty and slick in his grip. Instead, the kid went AWOL and flat disappeared from the face of the earth. Other fathers would have felt shame for their son's cowardice but Petty could only hold out hope he was still alive. The chances were somewhere closer to none than slim. He knew damn well what he had created in his rogue apprentice. He had felt helpless for days trying to keep his daughter calm with Xanax milkshakes when he saw the all-too-familiar abandoned rig and the miles and miles of gridlock on the national news. Panic attacks, fisticuffs and an attempted rape or two didn't hold a candle to what they found inside that reefer. Two decomposed corpses in an intimate embrace. One of those his dark-swan wife Lucinda, the beautiful summer-afternoon thunderstorm, loud and vicious but always bringing cool relief and a sweet smell. The Kid had broken from the code Petty had so carefully imprinted onto him, that was evident. The one thing that could stem the blood tide had been pulled from the crack in the dam. He kept telling himself that Rocky hadn't been stuffed behind the cases of hot beer so there was a chance. Swinging at pebbles with a stick. Rocky would do that as a young boy for hours, never making contact. Maybe this one was that swing that finally cracked the rock and sent it racing toward the mountain in a cloud of dust. The rig had been the only clue and he seized on to it. There were prints taken but nothing matched, of course. The Kid never said his name, there was no record of him ever existing that any authority would possess. Petty had traced paths to a dozen states, a body found in South Carolina, a dead Frenchman who succumbed to a snake bite in New Mexico, one in east Arkansas, another assault at an apple orchard in Minnesota. They were all in a deck of calling cards that stretched back a decade and manifested into a sprawling conspiracy theory taped on the wall with news clippings and The Kid's precious maps, all leading to literal dead ends. His monster was off the chain and free.

Now here he was three years later, at the end of the earth, not even sure what led him to this lawless frontier, following the last strand he could grasp, the road-rage killing of a birthday clown years ago, how there was a girl who may have known the assailant. Fighting through the dense brush of the Alaskan wild, he felt desperate, tired, half-crazed even to be in the situation. He should have let it go or hired a PI but what would that have accomplished? He needed to wield the rag that wiped his mistake off the face of the Earth, not call some local cop with a tip. There wasn't a spot on the most-wanted list, nor any open investigations. No one knew how many people had been killed and there were never any leads on the score of random missing-person reports. The NYPD shut the book on it before the Mets highlights were finished. It was solely up to him and he was determined to exact all the revenge he could muster if the fates allowed it. There was a gravel road leading up to the cabin but he had decided that stealth would be a valuable tool, regardless of discovery. He had army-crawled to the crest of a wooded hill deep in the Matanuska Valley and a modest homestead spread out below him. There was a pond beside the home and a lush vegetable garden taking up half an acre on the other side. Gargantuan squash, cabbage a savage green the size of beach balls. He didn't see any vehicles around other than a four-wheeler covered with a blue tarp stationed by a side door. It would be fun to ride away up toward the mountain goat and glaciers, Petty thought as he gnawed on his cold unlit pipe. The evening was long under the midnight sun, ensuring his reconnaissance would be well lit but unconcealed. Vulnerable to anyone who happened to be on the lookout for an old man seeking answers in the form of blind desperation.

The hours passed, his legs cramped and his lower back became tight and uncomfortable, holding a rigid pose. He chewed a few aspirin and downed it with metallic water from an old army canteen. He watched a content moose family slog their way through the pond, eating everything they could fit into their faces on the way. He checked the scope on his rifle, he could have downed the animals from the 350 yards, no problem. His trigger finger was itchy but steady. His nemesis had no qualms about mowing down families, burning the bridges of blood they built. Maybe it was his greed, his cavalier attitude of balancing two lovers, two households that turned The Kid into an instrument of destruction. He should have kept it behind the walls instead of hoisting the kid on his shoulders to witness his triumphs, his women caged in ignorant captivity. At the time, it felt necessary as part of the training, of presenting the rewards that could be afforded if one dedicated oneself wholeheartedly to the code. Instead, the fates had punished his hubris with a reaper in overalls devoid of humanity. It was on him, the things, the acts he exposed to The Kid. Give the powerful stray dog a taste of human blood and meat then one cannot stand confounded when it rips out the throat of your family. He studied the pink clouds and found shapes that tied back to the grislier events of his career, before and after pulling out The Kid from the wreckage of white trash. As those affronts that, to others, would be unforgivable mortal sins floated toxic just below the heavens, grey smoke from the cabin chimney rose up to mix with them in the clean objective sky.

His heart skipped a necessary beat as he trained the rifle-scope down the train of smoke to the cabin, seeking life through the windows. He worked on controlling his breathing, but it was wrapped up too tight in the possible culmination of the long hunt. A figure appeared in front of a sink in the kitchen, filling up a kettle. A woman, young with cropped pink hair. A round face, pretty, content, glowing, in fact, as if with child. Should he take the shot at the chance that this was The Kid's woman? Attack the sheer gall at starting a family after erasing his own? If she looked out, up at him, he would put one between the eyes. Snuff out an evil lineage before it had chance to take root. If not, he would wait, observe. See if this was even the right place, if The Kid was even a presence here or out in the ether somewhere, starting families as he himself did those many years ago. He waited, settled his nerves, crosshairs trained on her forehead. "Look at me," he whispered. Throwing his will across the space. She kept her head down, appeared to be whistling with pursed full lips. In the distance he heard the roar of a pickup approaching. He waited, held true to his target held, held, until his curiosity pulled him away and she left with the kettle away from the window. He swung the scope over to the truck as it came to a stop by the front door. A cloud of dust settled around a full-grown husky jumping out of the back and sniffing the air with purpose. His heart skipped again and ran fast as if tumbling down a sidewalk in a desperate effort to avoid a fall. Pulling his sight up, the scope bouncing with the beats inside him, he caught the image of a man stepping out of the cab. A bit taller, more filled-out but he knew immediately. It was Rocky. His son. The urge to cry out or to just simply cry was near impossible to control. The woman came out of the front door, Rocky reached into the bed and grabbed grocery bags. She went to assist but he shook his head, laughed. She was indeed with child and far along. They did not caress, however, nor offer one another a peck on a cheek. Were they lovers at all? He watched his son travel back and forth from the truck to the cabin, carrying all matter of supplies, the woman did not pay Rocky any mind but rather showed attention to the dog, who seemed more and more interested in what was watching them from the top of the hill. Petty was confused, torn, emotionally dizzy with the ramifications of every possible scenario that laid out before him, multiple ongoing chess matches with the clock ticking that left him frozen and indecisive. There was no clear question to ask the fates at that moment, they had abandoned him in an aloof silence. He went from scanning the windows in a last-ditch attempt to ascertain the situation to watching a mosquito the size of a dime hover above the hand that still applied pressure to the trigger. If it landed, he would know what to do. The forces of chance would return to him surely. The insect, as if sensing its power, remained static in the air, teasing Petty and the latest crossroads of his tragic life. He held true, watched and waited, even as the husky broke away, barking and speeding up the hill, afraid to move or even exhale as it would sully the result. A man confused, beaten, belly itching from the moss, left wholly focused to the code, the mantra feeding the beat of tiny wings.

He never even noticed the hulking shadow of a titan with rather nefarious intentions grow over him, eclipsing the seemingly endless summer sun for ever.

Dear reader,

We hope you enjoyed reading *The Alternator*. Please take a moment to leave a review, even if it's a short one. Your opinion is important to us.

Discover more books by B.H. Newton at https://www.nextchapter.pub/authors/bh-newton

Want to know when one of our books is free or discounted? Join the newsletter at http://eepurl.com/bqqB3H

Best regards,

B.H. Newton and the Next Chapter Team

You might also like:
Chameleon by B.H. Newton

To read the first chapter for free, please head to:
https://www.nextchapter.pub/books/chameleon

The Alternator
ISBN: 978-4-86747-869-1

Published by
Next Chapter
1-60-20 Minami-Otsuka
170-0005 Toshima-Ku, Tokyo
+818035793528

28th May 2021